SHADOWS
ON THE
MOON

PETER FREEMAN VANTU

◆ FriesenPress

One Printers Way
Altona, MB R0G 0B0
Canada

www.friesenpress.com

Copyright © 2025 by Peter Freeman Vantu
First Edition — 2025

All rights reserved.

No part of this publication may be reproduced in any form, or by any means, electronic or mechanical, including photocopying, recording, or any information browsing, storage, or retrieval system, without permission in writing from FriesenPress.

ISBN
978-1-03-833125-0 (Hardcover)
978-1-03-833124-3 (Paperback)
978-1-03-833126-7 (eBook)

1. *Fiction, Multiple Timelines*

Distributed to the trade by The Ingram Book Company

To Dianna from Peter.
What is this life, then a dream inside another dream?

I dedicate this book to my wife, who has always been by my side and without whom I would have been lost in my anxieties and searches.

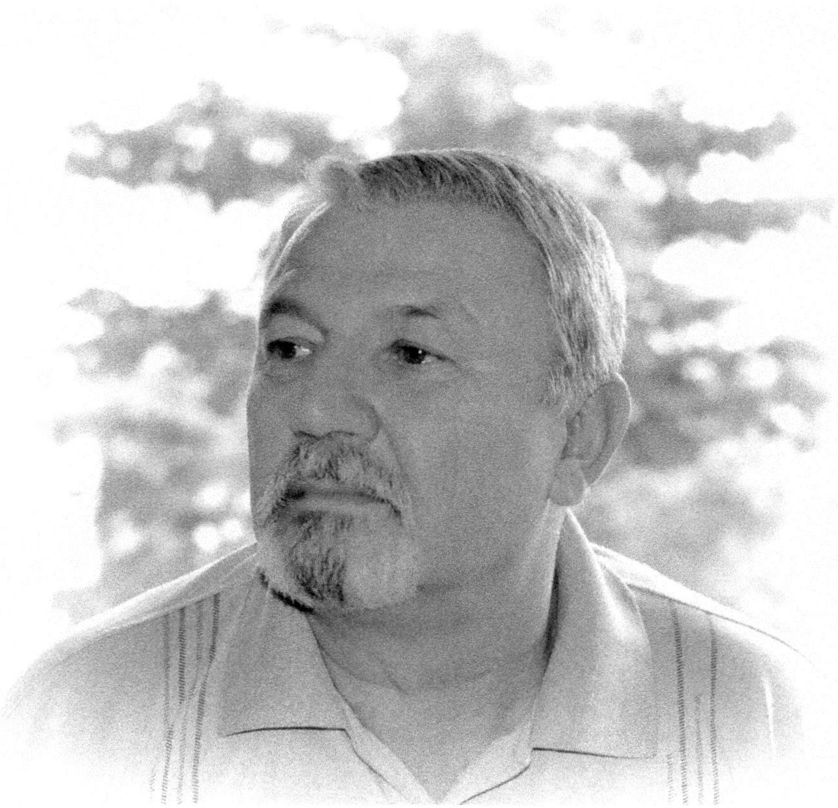

He gave an inaudible sigh.

The noise was infernal. In the crowded hall, the shouts were flowing in waves, rushing from above, from the ceiling, towards the white oval. The white light reflected by the ice sent light arrows hitting players' eyes like needles stuck in their retinas. Everything was wrapped up in the tumult of the hall, heated up to madness. The enthusiastic crowds moved in all directions, like the waves of the sea before they crashed against rocks. The game was played with a passion beyond description. On the ice, the game was tough and fierce. Hockey players fought as desperately as gladiators—for the game, for the public, for victory, for honor, for vampires, for the Buddha, for God. It was emotional, not rational.

Bent between the goal posts, his eyes sparkling and gritting his teeth, he swayed his skates back and forth, scratching the ice with a squeak of a violin string. He waited for the next attack. Sweat trickled down under his mask, his face covered with the scars of old wounds that now stung him, especially the one above his left eye, which was hurting terribly now. Blinking often, he tried to wipe away the drops of sweat that were dripping from his eyelashes. His face, his T-shirt, everything was wet, musty, with the pungent smell of sweat, which accompanied him on the ice and did not leave him even in the locker room.

The blow came suddenly, shot over the stick he held in front of him. Crack! He raised his elbow, leaned to his left, then onto his knees, trying to shield the net. Crack! Sliding on his knees, he desperately looked for the puck between his skates and the players' feet.

Crack! Bang! Bang!

****

He opened one eye. Black boots with braided laces, the hem of a black trouser leg with a red stripe. Now, with both eyes open, he turned his head and looked up. A black tunic with brass buttons, a face with a square chin, a jarred nose, two sly blue eyes, and a police officer's cap.

Cops!!!

He got on his knees, on the wet ground, feeling the dampness of the morning; he had slipped from the bench where he had made a bed for the night. The newspapers he had put under his clothes—it was a trick learned from "Pitt the Fat" as it kept the cold and wetness away; good lesson! What more values had he learned from what they called the "University of the Street"—were now wet and creased.

"What are you doing, you bastard? Don't you know, you're not allowed to sleep in the park at night? You know that, don't you?"

Now, he saw them well; one old, the other younger; as always, there were two of them. What a mistake! How had it happened to him? He never did that—sleep until dawn, when the patrol was passing.

"Good morning, sir! I'm leaving right now!"

Turning his head to the other, the younger policeman asked, "Should we take him to the station?"

"Sir, what's the good of that? I'm leaving now. Honestly, it won't happen again!"

"That's what you should do! Next time we'll take you in! Understood?"

"Yes sir! Thank you, sir!"

"Move! Faster! And let's not see you again!" the young cop yelled.

Gathering his backpack, he hung the little brass bucket on top, dashing quickly through the trees and bushes in the park. When he got a little further, he slowed down, breathing hard. His joints ached terribly. The overnight dampness had flooded his bones. The old wounds bothered him. His wet, disfigured face, hidden by a careless beard, was full of scars—traces of the puck blows received in the full face. Only his violet eyes, hidden under a wide forehead, gave his face a special light. One of his eyebrows was almost missing, cut by a long scar, which continued down his cheek.

"Ah, Jackson, what did you do to me? How can I forget you?" Jackson had pushed him from the back into the iron bar at the side of the goal. Now a goalkeeper wears a mask with iron bars; it used to be just a piece of leather placed over the face, with holes for eyes and mouth. But that's hockey. Don't hold a grudge. It's a rough sport.

He reached into the wide pockets of his trousers and pulled out a piece of filthy cloth with which he wiped the sweat from his forehead, face, and neck, then shook it in the morning breeze. He tightened his faded coat, made of durable, tobacco-coloured canvas. It was a good coat!

It had once belonged to a climber. He had received it when he had given "Two Teeth" a pair of boots in exchange. He hadn't seen "Two Teeth" in a while, since they had last slept in the St. Peter's Church shelter, and he wondered where he could be. He didn't like shelters anymore. Too many weird people had made their nests there. You could wake up without shoes ... or worse. So, during the summer, when it was hot, or during a mild autumn, he made his nest outside, in parks, among the trees.

The coolness of the morning embraced him. In the dim light of the morning sun, he looked at the city that was waking up to life. There was a gentle breeze, raising the last remains of fog that, in some places, stubbornly hid the face of a building. The smog-covered city appeared, clouded now, as if glimpsed through fine silk. To the east, a reddish-yellow accompanied the sun on its way up from the horizon. He took a deep breath, his chest coveting the moment, as if he wanted to absorb all the beauty of life, in one breath. He, Tommy ... God's servant ... the "Manitoba Tiger" ... the "Desert Puma" ... by the mercy of the Lord, was stubborn to live. Homeless. He wasn't exactly sure how it happened. Maybe it didn't matter anymore. What was the use?

Limping, with small steps, accompanied by pain in all joints, he made his way, street by street, to the heart of the city. It was still early, but the world had already begun to move; here and there, a few people, a few cars. That noise specific to the bustle of the city had begun timidly, but it had just begun; in an hour, it would grow, like a volcano of reverberating sounds over the faces of the buildings. He had gone through the narrow streets, crossed by stinky alleys, impregnated with the smell of canal and fermented garbage. The light barely escaped through those buildings with crumbling walls, the colour of filth.

He was heading to Extra Cup on St. Mary's Road, a canteen for the poor, where he hoped to arrive in time to grab a helping of food—usually pancakes and a cup of coffee. As he approached, he saw that a long line had formed. He regretted having slept so long. With bated breath, he lined up in the row of the less fortunate, condemned by fate.

Tired, he threw down his backpack, his shoulders sore from the straps. Leaning his back against the wall of the building he looked at the long line of people … untied string, made of patched overcoats in all the rainbow … greetings with hand, in silence. They were all there: Jim the Fat, Kim the Dwarfed, without legs, Bob Long Neck, a two-meter guy, Crazy Josie, an inveterate alcoholic, and others.

****

"Jim the Fat" … What a man he once was! Years ago, he had worked as a butcher at a slaughterhouse on the outskirts of a city. But one of his bosses didn't like him and was holding a grudge against him. Either he was asked to do overtime, from which he regularly was denied money, or for more or less imaginary reasons: "So many hooks have been lost: $20; A roll of wrapping paper was destroyed: $15; the knives to be sharpened only in places his boss agreed: $40" and so on, until on a winter day, unwittingly, "Jim the Fat" caught him hiding some of the tools. He became suspicious, followed him, and saw him while he was delivering them to some strangers, throwing them over the wire fence. He had followed him through the yard, through the snow, all the way to catch him red-handed. Arriving at the wire fence, which surrounded the enclosure, after seeing what he was doing, he shouted, "You bastard!" The two associates from behind the fence dashed, disappearing behind the trees. Surprised, the skinny man turned his face from the fence with his big, bulging eyes, making wrinkles on his forehead, being overwhelmed by the furious dementia of the man who was no longer able to judge: "Get lost, swollen barrel, or I'll kick you out!"

Usually calm and patient with everyone, Jim lost his mind. To the scrawny man's misfortune, Jim had a knife on his belt, as all the workers wore, sheathed, over their white overalls. "That's it for you, then," Jim said. He reached for his belt, slowly approaching the fence, swaying on his feet, walking hard, pressing, his boots in the creaking snow of the yard. "Don't you dare! Do you hear? Don't you dare! Are you crazy?!" screamed the skinny man, trying to climb the wicker wire fence that surrounded the building. Jim stopped at the fence, pulled out his knife. "Harsh! Harsh!" Two short cuts, in a cross, with the skill of a professional butcher, over the buttocks of the one perched on the fence. The bastard fell like a darted raven, hit the ground, and reddened the snow with blood, flowing in streams.

"Help!"

"That's enough for you!" Jim the Fat said, turning slowly on his heels and wiping his knife on his overalls. He returned to the building, as calm and quiet as he had left. What a thing! That bastard had fully deserved it, and "Four Buttocks" remained his name, forever, for all who worked with him. Jim had paid; six years spent in three jails. Six years of his life, along with the house he had to sell because of the lawsuits, the wife who had left him, the friends who avoided him, then the prison, the drink ... the darkness.

****

"Bob Long Neck" had come from the States. The mixed-race athlete had been playing basketball since his mother had brought him into the world. All day he shot hoops on the cement court near the miserable block where he lived with his family four brothers, two sisters and the elders. The place stank horribly, the buildings surrounded by garbage. As a child, he had learned to walk on that basketball court, a more open place, with better air. He had played with whoever he met; boys like him from the neighborhood mostly. Especially in the evening, there were real competitions, when their young bodies—shaking, tangling, and shining with sweat in the light of the bulbs surrounding the field—started playing. They played evening after evening, day after day, and then at school.

One day, a sports teacher noticed him and, unexpectedly, he had the opportunity to receive a sports scholarship to a university famous for its athletic program. He had never dreamed of such a thing and the family was on cloud nine.

At university, he had done well, studying and playing basketball for the team. The first year had been the hardest. He made the team every year. In the last year, some team scouts appeared. Bob, who had worked hard and scored a lot for the team, was quickly noticed. In fact, his style of play made a difference; it was unpredictable—each time he played differently, depending on the opponent. He didn't think about it; he naturally sensed the nature of the game—defensive or offensive. One afternoon, after training, one of the scouts, approached him.

"Hi! Can we talk for a while?"

"Of course, sir," he replied. He had recently learned that someone from the team's coaching staff, then from the head coach, had taken an interest in him and had asked many questions about him.

After a short conversation, he received an offer to play, as a test, for a team from the NBA.

He had no words. He could only answer by nodding, his eyes glued on the floor of the basketball court. He struggled to control his excitement and remained motionless like a rock. Time stood still. He felt dizzy. He could feel his heart pounding in his throat, like the beating of a hammer on an anvil.

"Are you okay?"

"Yes ... sir, I'm ... good!"

"Look here. Take this paper. Here's the name and address. There's the phone number. You're looking for Robert Dickens and you say that I, Charles Davis, sent you. Here is my business card. Be there on Friday morning at eight. In the meantime, I'll let him know you're coming. Okay? I need to go now. Good luck, young man!" said the scout, shaking his hand and leaving the room at a brisk pace.

Bob remained seated, still dizzy, not knowing what to do. A short time later, he struggled to move his feet, and stumbled toward the locker room. He only recovered in the shower, when, after a while, he realized that he had used only cold water.

That week, Bob had passed a test game. After the final exams, he signed a two-year contract with the Atlanta Hawks. Within a month he had moved to Atlanta, received a home and an installation check. There, he got to know professional basketball. The game tactics were much more subtle and more elaborate than in school or university; the repetitions of the game phases were practiced to the point of madness. They had to move faster, sometimes feeling their lungs burning from exertion and catching fire in the air of the court, which always seemed as hot as an oven. The sessions in the gym were brutal. There was one physical trainer for four players. The training was scientific, exhausting and long. He was working out with the desperation of a hunted animal. He wanted to succeed... He had to succeed. He wanted it with all the stamina of his young body.

"Work, Bob! Work harder! Do 50!" the trainer shouted in his ear. His blood was pounding through his arteries, his muscles ached and were swollen with overuse. He could no longer feel his hands after the thirtieth lift. His whole body was covered in sweat. With wide eyes, reddened by effort, he completed the last lift to reach 50, and collapsed on his back. This is the life of a professional player!

He had also bought a car, but soon he gave it up, being too tired to drive, being squeezed like a lemon. It was the grueling workouts of next season's preparation campaign. The season had begun, and Bob was used as a substitute; a few shy appearances, especially when his team was playing away. Slowly, he was getting into the team's rhythm. The Hawks was just in the first phase of the team renewing and the new players had to integrate. There was no mercy or compassion. Sometimes there was understanding, but not too often. They were professionals and blunders were not allowed.

And so, Bob climbed, step by step, gaining the trust of his teammates and coach. At the end of his first season, he was considered a promising young man, in the middle of the second he had almost become a star, delighting the stands with the natural way he played and especially with the subtle tricks that accompanied his game. Everything was on his side; he had become loved by the public and the press, he had become a promising star. As the third season began, they had an away match with Dallas.

It was going to be played in a hostile, fiery atmosphere, which only Texans were able to offer and maintain. From the beginning, things had gone wrong; aggressive public, atmosphere, referees, and opponents. The match had started hard, against a team that was famous for the aggression shown on its own field. In these conditions, from the start, they were at a disadvantage, the team had tried to withstand the pressure of opponents. They had been dominated by four points, but then they came back. Then they were out by seven points, yet they came back again. The boos and screams of the crowd rolled towards the huge court, which had now become too small. The referees had also started being biased: reversals of situations, exaggerated eliminations, and all sorts of calls that was not how they arbitrate matches in the NBA.

They were under pressure, but Bob had just put a cap on an opponent, recovering the ball at the bottom of the court. The red-haired giant rushed at him, forehead furrowed and snarling through his teeth, "Black bastard!" Bob ignored him and deftly avoided him, passed the ball back and forth with his teammates, made a sharp turn to avoid another opponent, and started alone towards the opponent's backboard. He had jumped on the ring, when he suddenly felt short of breath.

A hand had grabbed him between his legs and the same voice crackled the poisonous words between the clenched jaws. "Dirty Nig—" He collapsed, his head hitting the floor. A sharp pain seared through his mind, then, in pain, he rolled onto his side, curled into a ball, biting his lips until he could taste blood. Pushes ... a melee ... the late intervention of the referees ... coaches, doctors, physical trainers, teammates and opponents, all invading the court. They were pushing, shouting at each other. A few spectators appeared, cunningly sneaking over the railings. Then others joined them. The security guards intervened late ... It was useless. Everything was lost. Finally, total chaos ensued.

They had forgotten about him. Now they were running over him, stepping on him, stumbling over him. With tears in his eyes, he struggled to his feet, swaying from one foot to the other, completely disoriented. An elbow in the back, then a blow to the ribs. "Dirty Negro!" "Monkey!" "Bastard!" He couldn't take it anymore. The energy of life, accumulated and locked in his body over humiliated generations, was unleashed with the violence of a volcanic eruption. He answered back with his fists, with his feet, struggling to fight the group of teammates, pulled aside. He passed a few. Others appeared in front of him. Another blow to the ear, then a kick to the tailbone, to make him see the stars. Screaming like a wounded lion, he turned. He put his palms behind the young man's head, and ... crack!!! Bob hit briefly with his forehead, at the root of the nose, and felt the bone crack. The opponent fell suddenly and disappeared from his view. He had learned this shot on the street during school when he was a teenager. It was called the "Danish kiss", the name apparently coming from somewhere on a battlefield during World War II.

Eventually, he managed to sneak around the people, until he reached his teammates. Together, fighting, they made their way to the entrance to the locker room, then inside the tunnel, where everything became easier.

This was the only major fight in the NBA that year, and the Federation decided to set an example. Although televised, in the replays and analyzed by the investigation, no one could see the clever blow of the redhead. In the jump, he had been surrounded by a pack of players. And no one could testify about the racist words, even if they had heard them. The fight was followed by suspensions and fines, but very few for the Dallas. The Federation needed to wash its image, and it did; both clubs had been drastically fined, and there were many suspensions for players, accompanied by fines: 2 months suspension and $10,000 fine; 6 months suspension and $ 30,000 ... and so on.

For Bob, it was the end. It turned out that the bastard whose nose he had broken was the son of the former Texas Governor, a lawyer by profession, with a lot of connections in the world of law. As a result, a few days later, he was awakened by the police at his door. He was taken into custody. There was a trial, and then another. Not only did he lose a lot of money, he became indebted. Eventually, all appeals were lost. Later, his mental collapse in the darkness of the prisons. Seven years of strict regime without the right of appeal. Justice had wanted to set an example and had succeeded. For Bob, it was a total loss. He destroyed his life in detention, where, in order to survive, he had endured unimaginable humiliations and acquired bad habits. After his release, he hit the street ... the abyss ... the darkness...

In the queue at An Extra Cup, "Bob Long Neck" was dancing, spinning on his heels, swinging back and forth and humming a song from his imagination, hidden in an unknown memory of his brain.

"Bob Long Neck" was dancing......

****

In the dim light of dusk, among the hills covered with patches of forest, the roof of Bill Henderson's house could hardly be seen, the walls quietly out from among the trees. Below the edge of the forest, stables and outbuildings were scattered around, and further down the valley, there were fields covered with crops, and grass for the animals. Only a stream, guarded by a few willows, interrupted this abundant overflow. Every evening, ritually, as if chiseled in the seal of ancient times, the animals were taken to the stream. With their hooves in the water, their necks outstretched, their muzzles barely touching the shiny surface of the stream, the herd of cattle were drinking unabatedly. A gentle evening breeze waved through the leaves, then down over the barley and wheat fields. The light was falling sideways now, lengthening the shadows of the trees and all the other plants in the household. It was an amalgam of light and shadow, detached, as if from a dream.

As the shadows stretched out around the house, a woman appeared on the deck. A white shirt, with tight-fitting sleeves, and a brown plaid skirt, with wide folds, covered a healthy body. A wide-brimmed hat allowed only a few locks, the colour of tobacco, to flow rebelliously. Stepping out, she walked towards the railing, grabbing it with her hands. She looked down the hill towards the stream. Her round, rosy face, guarded by two beautifully arched eyebrows above azure-blue eyes and a tiny nose above fleshy lips, stiffed motionless. Her eyes pierced the horizon until she found what she was looking for. She cupped her hands and shouted, "Michael! Michael!"

"What is it?"

"Come faster with the cattle up the hill! Don't waste time!"

"Okay!" A young man on horseback, wearing a weather-worn hat and leather chaps, turned his horse, leading him slowly toward stream. His shirt was wet on his back, and sweat ran down to the back of his pants. Flies and mosquitoes swarmed around him and the animals. He chased them away from time to time, with sudden movements of his head and hands. Michael was still young, just 14 years old, the third child of Bill and Emily Henderson. His two older sisters went to town to attend university. They came home only on holidays, during which time they were not exempted from farm work at all.

Bill was gone to the edge of the property, to one of the plots below the forest. He was driving the tractor along a slope, pulling behind one of the fertilizer machines he owned and scattering the fertilizer; like his father and grandfather before him, he didn't like chemicals, so he used only cow manure. Below the stables, at the other end of the farm, he owned three manure collection tanks. Mixed with water, the fertilizer used in the fields grew fruit and vegetables—the best and most sought after on the market, bringing in a good profit. Every year, customers struggled to buy from him, because organic farming had become a rarity. He also continued the family tradition of crop rotation, keeping a quarter of the plots fallow every year, and using seeds selected by him, according to a technique that he and the others before him had known. The work done with sowing, fertilizing and irrigation was accomplished by the warmth of the sun, the love of nature, and the mercy of God.

Bill was almost jolted out of his seat in the tractor's overheated cab. He was a massive man, always eating heartily. His work was always done, his protruding pouch touching the steering wheel. For a long time, he hadn't been wearing a belt, replacing it with a wide pair of suspenders. The peaked cap hid his curly white hair, his short, fat neck was tight between his shoulders, and the gaze his blue eyes scanned forward restlessly, sweeping the area in front of the tractor. He had a little more fertilizing to do before he finished working here. Once the animals had arrived, he had to go to the stables for evening work there. The work continued in the splendor of the fields and the forest. For the Henderson's, life usually flowed quietly, with nobility and calm.

Something rather exciting had happened that morning at the farm. Lessie, a wolf-dog mix who had lived with them for several months, had given birth to four adorable puppies. Michael had made a straw bed for her at the top of the stable, and the four blind, pink little beings huddled together on Lessie's belly, who watched over them lovingly.

There were several dogs at the Henderson's farm. Lessie had made puppies with an ash-grey German shepherd, Tatter—his fur was always in disarray, in tufts—who was great at herding the animals, which was essential to a farm. Lessie, an alpha female, kept all the other dogs in order. She had been bought from a nearby chicken farm a few years ago, and, although Bill had traded a sheep skin for her, he was not sorry. He had good dogs, of great help, which skillfully returned the animals and kept the house and household safe, especially in the harsh winters. On those terrible nights, the dogs roamed outside, patrolling around the stables, huts, house and other places, only barking for a good reason. Bill had trained them himself so that he could trust them. "A good dog and a hard-working wife at home make your job half as easy," his grandfather would often say; God, how true it is!

****

Gathered there, they all stood in line … the queue of the hungry.

"Crazy" Josie, had had a life that could have been a subject of a novel. She had come from a good, earnest family living in Kensington, a small town on Prince Edward Island. She had spent her childhood with her other sister, Lucy, with whom he had had fond memories. Their parents, Joseph and Elisabeth, had raised them in an atmosphere of love and respect, honour, and common sense. Her memories of her father depicted him as a tall man with a broad forehead and bushy eyebrows, hiding a pair of grey, warm, gentle eyes, with a look full of compassion and understanding. She remembered that, being an accountant, he always came home late at night, working overtime and trying to cope as well as possible with the family's needs and daily expenses. The mother worked as an educator at a kindergarten a few hours a day, and she sewed and repaired clothes for the clientele she had formed. Of medium height, with long golden-brown hair, an oval face, with sensual lips and blue eyes, she was cheerful and had a contagious good mood.

In this pleasant atmosphere, the two sisters had grown up. Josie had done her regular schooling in her hometown before leaving to attend a university in Montréal, eventually enrolling in the Faculty of Marketing and Business Administration. Lucy, in turn, attended college for two years. She had opted for the Faculty of Journalism. The parents made substantial efforts to support them in their studies and the young women did their best. Some part-time jobs had been welcomed. They rented room in the house of a teacher, a former schoolmate and a good acquaintance of their father. They were on a good track until Lucy fell seriously ill. Investigations after investigation, analyzes, hospitals and every test imaginable. She had lost a lot of weight, was weak, her bones pierced the skin of her face, and her eyes were sunk deep in her head. With a white face, bluish-grey lips, she looked like a being from another world, her gaze begging for kindness and pity.

Finally, came the verdict: cancer, in a phase of acute metastasis. Her suffering was enormous, there was a rapid evolution, and in a few weeks they all walked, heartbroken, behind Lucy's coffin on the paths of Kensington Cemetery. The shock had been strong. The family was devastated. Although they were the same people, without Lucy's presence, everything was changed. Nobody wanted to admit it, nobody wanted to say it, but everyone thought so.

Josie delved deep into her studies, trying to cram her first two years of university into one. And she did it. Then, she met John Wilson, a charming, fine-featured, and attentive young man from one of the old traditional families of Ontario. She met him in one of the university libraries when he had politely stepped aside to let her walk down the narrow aisle between the tables of a reading room.

"Please, miss!" he whispered, motioning.

She passed down the narrow aisle between the shelves, then turned.

"Thank-you. You are very kind, sir."

"John. John Wilson. With whom do I have the honour?"

"Josie Creston, sir. You're very kind."

Then they headed for the library exit. In the huge hall, with a mosaic carpet on the floor and tall cathedral-style windows, stepping side by side, John addressed her:

"I have never seen you here. And didn't have the pleasure to meet you. If you don't mind my asking, what are you studying?"

"It's no secret, sir."

"John. Please call me John."

"All right John. I usually take my books home. I study at home; I like the comfort."

"Of course, you're right."

"But you, John, what makes you come here? What degree are you getting?"

"Commerce, focusing on Trade. Very much related to your area of study." They went outside, going down the long staircase, when he dared to ask, "What about a coffee? It fits well now and will keep us awake until late in the evening; you can still study something tonight, can't you?"

Now they stopped on the sidewalk. Josie felt confused, but relented.

"Ok, fine. But only a coffee."

Within a few short weeks, it became so much more than that. He was charming, always attentive, made her very emotional, and that affected her deeply. Meetings, walks, hugs and hopes, all took place at lightning speed. They felt strongly attracted to each other. They saw each other every day. He insisted she be introduced into his circle of friends and she eventually accepted. She accompanied him to several parties, usually with music, dance, champagne and caviar—fine, educated people, elevated discussions, always polite. That's how he met John's friends, George and Lynda, Helen and Joel, and Ron and Margaret, all couples; the latter two danced wildly, recklessly, with abandon, delighting the audience. They were at Rhonda, a restaurant famous for its menu and good music. They were sitting together at the table, sipping their cocktails, with some friends in the booth reserved for them for that evening.

"Look at Margaret! What a performance! So is Ron's!" said Helen.

"Honey, these two could participate in any dance competition. Couldn't they?"

"What can you say? Some people have dance in their blood; they feel the rhythm, the music and they move so naturally. But you, how do you move, my tubby?" Helen teased him.

"Ha! I'll show you later, my dragonfly," Joel replied.

Chubby as he was, Joel had a big head, wide jaws, and flap-lop ears. Helen, a short-haired blonde woman of medium stature, with an oval face, two large brown eyes, and beautifully arched eyebrows, had a body like a willow stalk. She was also quite cultured. None of them could imagine what Helen had found in Joel, but it was obvious that they got along quite well.

Josie liked everything about John, and she was aware that she liked him. But she didn't know why, behind the euphoria she felt, an uneasiness persisted. It seemed to be an unknown anxiety about something that was going to happen, or something was to come. She told herself not to bother with it too much, and let herself be engulfed in the arms of passion, with a frenzy she had never experienced.

One day, John put his arms around her, saying, "My dear Josie, we've been together for a while and I want to confess that I love you, and I can tell you that I really love you so very much. I'm thinking of starting a family."

"What do you want to say, John? Are you serious when you say that?"

"Very serious, Josie. It matters that I love you and we get along well. I'm convinced we'll be a great family. And wild!" he added, giving her a charming look. Josie was stunned. She hadn't expected his proposal so soon.

"Well, what do you say, Miss Josie?" he said with a charming voice. A few moments of silence had passed. A dialogue of glances began, continuing under the seal of the same silence.

"Well, I accept. I hope we will be happy together and you will take care of me, darling." They kissed heartfelt. She remained with him that night and after.

She was introduced to his parents at one of the family's summer residences on the shores of Lake Ontario. She would remember that evening for a long time; they had traveled a long way, from Montréal to Belleville, near which was his parents' villa. It was a wonderful twilight of a serene fall day. The sun was above the horizon, dimly illuminating the road and the buildings lined on either side. The sharp smell of algae floated in the air. Not long before they had crossed one of the bridges over the Moira River in Belleville; he had one hand on the steering wheel, the other holding her hand. They were both happy, both hopeful, serene, and confident, immersed in the optimistic silence of their youth and love. As they approached, a kind of fear seized her; it became deeper and deeper, and heavier. After a while, he broke the silence.

"We're coming closer, Josie! It's not far. Look, do you see those docks and wharfs? Shortly after we will turn toward the shore, to the left."

"John! I'm afraid! I don't know why. I'm terribly scared!" Her knees began to tremble, the soles of her shoes tapping softly on the floor of the car.

Passing his right hand protectively over her shoulders, squeezing her softly and bringing her closer to his shoulder, he reassured her, "You have nothing to be afraid of, my dear. My parents will be okay. I just told them we were getting married and they didn't object. They just wanted to see you."

"You see, that's why I'm afraid. They'll see me and I don't know what they will say. I don't know what they'll think of me. What if they don't like me?"

"They will like you, so don't be afraid. Why they wouldn't like? If I like you, they will like you too, for sure. They'd have no reason not to. You are beautiful, full of wonderful qualities, well-educated. Why? How many girls are there like you are in this world?"

"Yes, but what if they still don't like me?"

"Chase away these thoughts, my dear, and have no fear." He hugged her tighter to him. Disoriented, she rested her head on his shoulder. The trembling of her legs calmed down a bit, and she recovered a little ... until the car suddenly turned onto an alley guarded by two rows of sturdy maples, with massive trunks and thick branches. On either side of the road, they covered the view, with the exception of some lawn peeking through. Now, in the fall, everything was wrapped in a cloak of rusty, brown, yellow leaves. At the end of the alley, the silhouette of a modern villa could be seen. Feeling shivers down her spine, Josie detached herself from him, bringing her head closer to the windshield and trying to pierce the view in front of the car as deeply as possible. When she could clearly distinguish everything, she froze, remaining wide-eyed; a lofty villa loomed in front of her, with some wood ornaments, and what she could see was only glass, surrounded by a perfectly maintained lawn in front and on the sides of the building. There were many flowers on the edges of the roundabout where the alley ended. She was out of breath. Petrified, she slumped back on her seat.

"Stop, please! I can't!"

"But you don't have to be afraid, my dear. Please calm down."

He stopped the car in front of the entrance, where a few steps away from either side were decorated with flowers in bright reds, blues, and white. Her head was down, her gaze hardened on her lap, on that skirt in changing shades of brown, prepared for this occasion and which now seemed like a rough cloth that scratched her skin through the nylon stockings that covered her feet. She felt everything she was wearing was ordinary, loose, and cheap. The same was feeling about the tight tailor costume, with two wide lapels, the blouse with fine embroidery and the sharp brown high heels shoes. She felt that everything was vulgar, in bad taste, cheap, and useless.

John stopped the engine, jumped out of the car, and walked around it to open the door for her. When he opened it, he was greeted by two scared big blue eyes in a pale face, wrapped in brown hair that fell over her narrow shoulders. Fine-lined lips, now trembling nervously, guarded over a smoothly curved chin. Her face showed fear, helplessness, and pity. Feeling the moment, John did not press, letting her rest for a few moments.

"Calm down, my dear. I'm here with you. Don't worry! My parents are open-minded people, understanding everyone, don't be afraid. Look, take a few deep breaths and you'll feel better."

Struggling to overcome her fear, she took several deep breaths, turned on the seat with her feet dangling outside the car, and then slowly got to her feet. She felt supported by him, with both hands wrapped around his left arm. It was good that they were on the other side of the car, and no one from the house could see them.

In the doorway, a distinguished couple of an imperturbable calm, with charming, friendly smiles—the same one she had seen at John—was waiting. She calmed down and walked more confidently, still supported by his arm, climbing the long steps. John introduced Josie to his parents. Warm greetings followed then they were ushered inside. In a room with a fireplace, in which there were some very comfortable sofas, coffee awaited them. Josie was reserved, and John often intervened in the discussion, helping her as much as he could. Educated and thoroughly understanding, John's parents, made Josie fell more relaxed and comfortable.

"Tell me, please, Josie," asked Karl, "more about the field of study you have chosen and for which you are just preparing. What's it called ... something with marketing?" Josie was embarrassed. It was obviously an attempt to open a conversation on a common ground, a very polite one. Considering their intelligence and training, they could not help but know about the field.

"Marketing and Business Administration, sir."

"You can call me Karl, my dear. We shouldn't be too official, eh?"

"And you can call me Eva," added her future mother-in-law.

"Thank you, Karl. Marketing and Business Administration has been around since the 1930s, although it has not been viewed as scientific. Marketing for different products requires a direct study, detailed and realistic, of the different segments that determine the distribution and absorption of goods."

"My dear, you certainly understand the concepts," Eva smiled. "It is very important to society. And you talk so passionately! It is obvious that you are very much concerned by this field!"

"Thank you, Madam."

"Eva, my dear, Eva; we don't have to be so formal."

"Thank you, Eva, but I think you are exaggerating."

"All right, all right, Josie," Karl said. "Eva means she's just happy that you've embraced this field with so much dedication. It is very important that you like the chosen profession and that you dedicate yourself to it with enthusiasm. At least in our conception."

"Of course, Karl, that's what I meant," Eva said. "John chose Commerce, although I don't know how determined he is."

"Leave it, mother. I knew what I was choosing, so don't worry! As for passion, that comes with work!"

"So be it, my dear!" Eva casted a meaningful glance at her son.

Finishing this subject, John hurried through coffee. They pretended to have other commitments, and his parents did not insist to delay them.

A few weeks later, Josie's parents met their future son-in-law. In a few months, the wedding was done, then they moved together into a rented house in Montréal. Their starting nest was a two-storey house with a lawn in front of it, a wide driveway running down to the street, dressed in horizontal white planks, large windows, and a gabled roof, the shingles imitating the tiles.

For next few months, Josie had the happiest days of her life there. In the morning, they left together for the University, returning according to their course schedules. On Friday evenings, they usually met with their now well-formed circle of friends, going to dances, restaurants and clubs. Now married, the financial support of his parents had been substantially diminished. John was in his final year of business, being very busy with exams. She was forced to minimize her course load and take a part-time job. Everything seemed to be going well.

Until one day when she got pregnant. She hadn't been sure of the pregnancy, so she went for a test; it came back positive. For a few days, she was afraid to tell him. One night, she decided she had to broach the subject.

"John, I never asked you about children. Do you want to have children? What do you think about this?"

"Dear Josie, of course I want to have children. Children are part of a family's life, aren't they? I want to have children, to enjoy this life with them and with you. But why are you asking me that now?"

"Because, my dear John, it has happened!"

"You mean …?"

"Yes, John, we're going to have a baby. I didn't how to tell you. I didn't know how you would react. I'm glad you're not upset."

"Oh, but it's awesome! Of course, it's beautiful … wonderful!"

"I've decided to keep working. It'll be fine, John."

"Yes, we will manage, there is no other way. A child! What will my parents say? They will be happy, of course. How couldn't they be? A child … our child."

They both decided, although they were both so busy, it was a good time for a baby. He was in the final phase before graduation. She decided to work as long as possible, and at the same time take some of her third-year courses. Gone were the pleasant Friday evenings. Over time, their attention was focused on the same subjects: the coming child and John's graduation. With consistent effort, they both succeeded. Their girl was born on an August morning; everything went well.

"Thank you for the beautiful gift you gave me, my dear!" he had said, excitedly and with tears in his eyes, when he brought a huge bouquet of flowers to the hospital's maternity ward.

"It's the happiest day of my life, other than the day we met!" he added. "I love you both with all my heart!"

He sat holding her hand while she cuddled the child in her arms. They both felt so close to one another, and fulfilled. It was a rare point in time—full of hopes, longings and dreams. They named the girl Charlotte.

In a few days, mother and daughter were at home. John, who had graduated for two months, was in high spirits, but because it was summer and the hiring season was very slow, he decided to take a temporary job. He found it at a store and worked there for a while. In the fall, when hiring started again, he applied for several positions, but did not get any job offers. He found out that his chances for a job in Montréal would increase considerably if he had a Master's degree. He asked several sources and the conclusion was the same: a Master's degree would offer unlimited possibilities.

"Josie, I did some research and this is what I've discovered: the market is very slow now and God knows when it will get better. To find a job, it seems that my only chance is a degree. Otherwise, all the effort made for graduation is pointless. I have no chance. No chance. There's nothing."

"And if you follow that plan and get your master's degree?"

"Then, my dear, it will be much easier. And after that, any advancement is easier. And if I find a job, we will have more money for all of us. It will be better anyway. What do you say? Can we do that?"

Looking away, driven to her thoughts, she accepted his plan. Now, for her, there was no more possibility of continuing her university courses, at least for a while.

They made new some plans. She knew tailoring and embroidery from her mother, and she could start working at home and at the same time take care of Charlotte. Moreover, her mother had offered to come and help her for a week or two, when the business would start. Then, in consultation with John, they rented a room to a niece who was starting to attend high school and who at the same time could help Josie with the little girl.

Within a month, she started the business. During the day, John was busy reading and studying for his Master's degree, and he worked part time some evenings. That's how the next three years passed. Charlotte was older now, walking around the house, playing, filling their hearts with joy. In the evening, they were exhausted, squeezed like wet rags, but they managed to move forward.

The day came when John defended his thesis and was granted a Master's degree. He decided to celebrate and reconnect with some of his old friends. George and Lynda were still together, as were Helen and Joel, while Ron and Margaret were not; they had left Montréal for the West Coast—Vancouver, according to some. The friends met at a downtown restaurant, not so fancy, but chic and discreet. It was a beautiful evening, just as it had been when they were all single. Their friendships were the same, as if just making a leap in time. The jokes, dancing and champagne brought them back seven years. People congratulated John on his Master's degree, for his great academic success. Everyone knew that, from now on, several roads would open before him; only the sky was the limit. They talked and laughed until the morning. Eventually, they parted, talking of seeing each other frequently.

It took a while for John to apply to several companies and finally get a job at a large, reputable company in telecommunications to work in the Commercial Business Department.

They were at the height of their happiness. Charlotte had grown up, too, and soon she was going to kindergarten. When she started grade one, Josie was finally able to resume her courses at the University.

But it wasn't meant to be. Josie's mother got sick and then bedridden and needed permanent assistance and care. Alone, her father could not cope. Josie didn't hesitate a moment, and, despite

John's opposition, took the little girl with her and they went to Kensington together.

****

The dim twilight crept through the windows of St. Patrick's Shelter down in

the Lower City. The room was packed with bunks, and it was filling up fast. Coats in all sorts of worn colors rustled as folks found a place among the rows of beds. Life's hard-luck cases gathered slowly; each one grateful for a cot to sleep in, away from the chill night air outside. It was colder now; you could feel it in your bones. They'd passed the check-in. The guards picked through the lot, only letting in those who wouldn't be trouble—a simple task since they recognized most of them by sight.

"Hey, Kim, how's the day treated you? Hanging in there?"

"Not too bad, sir, but I'm tired," Kim the Dwarfed answered, dragging his small frame forward on two wooden stumps, leaning on planks for support.

"Well, well, Josie, here we go. Still 'numbed up' tonight?" The guard grinned at her.

Josie shot him a dark, knowing look, saying nothing as she passed.

Inside, they each grabbed a bed, eyeing the neighbors they'd sleep beside. Tommy nodded at "Two Teeth," "Fat Jim," "Broad Palm," "Split Lip," and a few others. Looked like it would be a decent night, he thought. Seeing everyone settled in gave him some sort of comfort. In hushed voices, they shared stories of the day or memories from the past. Each laid their bundle beside their bed, then took turns at the showers while friends kept an eye on their belongings.

The light in the big room dimmed even more until the bulbs flickered on, just in time for everyone to see that not a single cot was left empty. They murmured a while, then settled down, knowing the lights would soon go out.

Tommy lay in bed, staring at the ceiling, half-listening to Two Teeth recounting the days near scrape with the cops over a rest stop inside a mall. Lying head-to-head, they talked low, voices drifting off as Tommy's mind wandered.

The lights went out. A soft murmur, then silence. The "cursed by fate" were at rest, sinking into the blank tumult of dreams.

Dawn came, filtering in like the twilight from the night before. They hurried, gathering their things to head out. A shout, then a murmur. Another shout. The guards appeared. Someone had no more headaches to worry about: "Split Lip" lay on his bunk, throat slit. His pillow, the sheets, were soaked in blood. The new boots he'd gotten just yesterday, gone. Someone who wasn't supposed to be here had found a way in.

A slip by the guards? Or something worse? It didn't matter. For Split Lip, the pain was over. Just another unlucky soul gone, a fleeting chapter in the heavy, uncertain life of the forgotten.

****

Josie found her father lost and helpless, and looking much older than he really was. Only his eyes were the same: kind and gentle, enveloping her in their warmth. She entered the house, going straight to her mother's room. Now ill, lying in one of the upstairs bedrooms, her eyes were sunken deep in her head. Without wasting time, Josie contacted the doctor, found out details about the treatment prescribed and asked him to come there the next day, as he had been doing for several days. Elisabeth was suffering from gallstones, with a serious complication that severely affected her pancreas. Until a certain stabilization, it was not possible to intervene surgically, and then some deeper investigations would be necessary.

They spent all winter, spring and part of the summer together. Josie had time to talk to her mother, as she had never done before. She spent many nights in the chair near her bed, watching her. She cared for her, washed her, and surrounded her with all her love and compassion. Later, after the surgery and recovery, they had more time to confess to one another about life.

"Josie, please tell me," Elisabeth had tentatively asked her, "how your marriage is going. What about your life as a couple How do you and John get along?"

"What can I say, mother? I think we are doing well. In fact, we were and are so busy, he with his exams, then with work, in my turn with my studies, Charlotte, and the business, that we haven't spent much time together. But we're going out to restaurants, or dancing, with friends from time to time."

"Okay, okay. How is he as a husband? Is he considerate with you? Does he surround you with care and affection?"

"How can I tell you, Mom, he shows he cares, of course, he's always been that way. We were too busy to spend more time together, anyway, not as much as we would be right. But we've had our beautiful moments."

"Okay, my dear, but what you're telling me worries me somehow. Your father and I, until you went to school and had to work extra, used to spend many evenings together. You know, after dinner, we would sit in the living room by the lamp, me crocheting or embroidering, and he reading novels to me, every night. He stopped, he commented, sometimes we contradicted each other, but we were so happy! You know, his voice is so soft!"

"Okay, Mom, but you can't compare the pace of life back then to what it is today. We live in a different society from those times. The pace is very fast now. Time is not enough."

"You have to make time for your family, Josie, otherwise everything goes awry and you won't have anything in life."

"We're trying to do our best, Mom."

"Yes, yes, try!" her mother replied, at the same time, throwing Josie a significant glance.

They felt close. They loved each other. They revealed the thoughts and feelings hidden in the most delicate corners of their minds. There was one thing they didn't talk about: Lucy, nor her death. It was a taboo subject, hidden in the mother's heart. Josie knew that, and Elisabeth knew that her daughter knew that. It was something like a cocoon hidden in a fine, impenetrable fabric, buried in a corner of their souls devastated by pain.

During this time, Charlotte attended a nearby school where her grandmother once worked as an educator. She lost no time in making friends, continuing her happy childhood. When it was time to go back to Montréal, there were regrets, sighs and hugs. Elisabeth felt stronger now, though she still had a long way to go before she fully regained the sharpness that had characterized her before.

They said their goodbyes, parting as hard as their reunion had been.

Arriving home in Montréal. Charlotte, at the height of her happiness, found her room, with the toys in it, feeling as if she had returned from somewhere far away, from another planet.

And John ... She felt John had changed somehow. She embraced him with emotion, but she didn't get the same feeling in return. He seemed more formal, and he avoided her gaze.

"Is the mother-in-law better now? Can she handle herself? What about Joseph? Does he still work until late in the evening?"

"Mother is better, although she lost a lot of her energy. As for my father, I found him weak, depressed and much affected by my mother's condition."

Conventional words, attentive, but devoid of emotion, the emotion that had bound them before. They did not talk much in the first days of their return. He came home very late, justifying it by claiming that he had a lot of work to do. His gaze was changed, his face stiff, with a metallic look. He wasn't himself. One evening, she asked him why he smelled like alcohol when he came home so late. He answered in a short, disgusted voice, with a hoarse pitch. "Leave me the hell alone! I have business meetings with clients! What do you know?"

He had never talked to her like that before; he had never raised his voice. She didn't know what to do, and said nothing in response.

Although he supposedly earned a good salary now, they were not able to entirely cover the household expenses. She found someone to babysit Charlotte for a few hours so that she could resume her classes in the evening. During the day, she worked on her business as before, tailoring and embroidering for the clientele she was trying to win back. One day, as she was preparing to clean and iron one of John's trousers, she searched his pockets, checking for forgotten things. Her fingers reached something: a few small packets of paper, which she pulled out. She looked at them, turned them around, but they meant nothing to her. She put her hand in his pocket again, and, at the bottom, felt plastic and something like dust between her fingertips and under her fingernails. She pulled out her hand and ... white powder. A terrible suspicion seized her.

She said nothing. She cleaned and ironed his trousers, but kept one of the packets.

The next day, she went two blocks away to her usual pharmacy. She knew Ted well, a kind young assistant, who had helped her several times in the past. Showing him the packet, she asked him if he knew what it was. Ted's eyebrows raised, took it and carefully opened it and put the contents on a lens screen. He took a small portion of it with a spatula. He kneaded it between his fingertips, examining it carefully, then smelled it. He went in his back office, returning with a bottle, from which he poured with a pipette, a few drops on the powder. Upon contact with the drops, it turned brown.

Looking up at Josie, he smiled, embarrassed. "Where did you get the packet, Josie?"

"I found it on the street and I was curious about it," she replied hesitantly.

"Well, Josie, that could be the finest cocaine you can buy on the street from dealers."

Shocked, she turned and went outside. She walked along the sidewalk, along the boulevard, pacing nervously, her eyes to the ground. She felt tears running down her frozen cheeks from the gusts of wind. She got lost on the streets for a while. Then, hopeless, she headed home.

And so, it went aimlessly for months. Josie took care of her little girl, work, her classes, and John, who was more irascible and more incomprehensible. He went from a state of euphoria, talking long and fast, to states of silence, nervousness, or irascibility. Josie concentrated on her last year finals. She refused to think about what was going on with John, and he hadn't told her anything. She stayed at the University, sometimes until late, trying to prepare for the final exams. She was studying, wanting to finish once so that she could hope for a good job or a change. All she cared about was the girl's future. After school, Charlotte stayed with another family until John arrived home.

One evening, returning earlier than usual, Josie went upstairs to the girl's room. She tiptoed, so as not to wake her. The door was open. She stopped in the doorway. The child was sleeping in her bed, which looked a mess. She took another step forward and froze, petrified. Sitting in an armchair, a glass of wine in one hand, legs relaxed outstretched, a demented look towards the girl's bed, drunk, pants open, and full of cocaine dust, John, delirious, was mumbling something incoherent. In his eyes, she saw the same metallic and aggressive glow that, as of now, she knew: only cocaine could give him that stare. She remained silent, immovable. Time had stopped.

Finally, she took a hesitant step back, and another. Scared, she turned and flew down the stairs and into the street. She wandered on streets for a while, through darkness, until she could no longer keep on her feet. She wandered into a park and sat on a bench. She was not able to think. A train-like roar began to ring in her ears. She couldn't breathe and she felt that there was no more air for her. She felt her heart beating in her throat, like a ram. The rustling in her ears became deafening. Everything was spinning, nothing was in its place. She stood up and tried to take a step, then everything went dark...

She was found in the morning, fallen down on one side, with her head on the grass and her legs in the alley. Two wardens found her. An ambulance took her to a hospital. The police were called and began an investigation. She awoke in a hospital bed. Sitting next to her bed on a chair, wearing a white lab coat, a doctor held a file. Two nurses were standing behind him.

"What's your name, ma'am?"

Looking around, she widened her eyes. Fear seized her. What had happened? What did they want from her? Shaking her head, she began to cry.

"Can you tell me your name, ma'am?"

What did they expect from her?

"Your name, please. Of course, you must have a name," he repeated kindly.

Sitting up, she leaned forward, struggling to think, to remember something, but she couldn't. Nothing was there. She wasn't there ... A terrible fear gripped her, making her tremble.

"I ... I'm ... nobody ... Me, I'm ... nothing ... I ... I don't know who I am." And she fell back on the bed, sobbing.

Finally, they identified her with the help of the police. The whole family had been notified. Everyone came to see her: mother, father, in-laws, John and Charlotte. She looked at them with an empty gaze. She didn't recognize any of them. Two nurses had to take her mother to a treatment room where they administered a sedative to calm her down. The in-laws looked at her with pity and condescendence. Charlotte had fallen on her knees, streams of tears wetting her face, while John looked at her without seeing anything. Josie did not recognize them.

A few weeks later, following the doctors' recommendations, she was transferred to a mental hospital outside the city for a specific, longer treatment. With turrets in the four corners and small, barred windows, that grey building looked like a castle. It had meadows with grass and flowers, and a wide area behind it, where on sunny days the patients could walk freely. The staff were attentive, dedicated to the profession and their patients. All surrounded by a stone wall, flooded in some places with ivy. There, the days passed in a long-established routine, comprising the same activities: breakfast, treatments, meetings with doctors, lunches, and group activities— in a large, bright room, with wide arches over the ceiling, then descending on side walls. Sometimes, when the weather was better, they would go out accompanied and assisted by the nurses who worked there. In the evening, a frugal dinner, some reading, and then it was bedtime. They were all dressed in thicker pajamas during the day, blue for men and pink for women, and blue robes for men and red for women. Only doctors and nurses wore white uniforms.

Josie was shyly accommodating to this new community. She had no preference for games in the great hall and didn't have any friendships with any of them. She didn't talk very much and hesitantly participated in group discussions.

One day, she left. She was near the stone wall that surrounded the enclosure. She got closer, her eyes on some beautiful flowers that had grown next to it. Nearby, an open gate; probably forgotten by one of the gardeners. Serene, absent, she went through it. There was a path that led her along a stream. For a while, she walked on it, among the bushes that marked it on either side, her robe rustling when it touched the tall grass. She was walking faster now and was quite far from the sanatorium building, then met a bridge over the stream and crossed it. She took it to the right, along railroad tracks, looking down and stepping on sleepers. She walked like that for a long time until on her way was a stationary freight train. She walked a while along it until she saw a wagon with an open door. Leaning with both arms and palms on its floor, she jumped a little and rolled inside. She walked around in the car, inspecting it detachedly. Finally, she crouched on a handful of straw between two loose bales, with both palms together and resting her head on them. This is how a good time passed, in the silence of that evening, in which only the buzz of crickets broke the silence. A creak, a slight jerk and the train started moving. With it, Josie, left behind the past, her mind troubled by strange images and hallucinations, a wandering soul travelling into another world.

That's how she got to the city. Wandering on the streets all day, dressed in a kind of shabby trench coat, faded by the weather, with some shoes like ships, much too wide and wasted away. All these were a gift of the mercy of other souls like hers. More valuable ones, such as a woolen blanket and thick socks, she kept tucked in a corner under one of the bridges in the lower part of the town.

One day, one of the homeless had offered her an alcoholic drink. She liked that liquor. She felt better. After a while, she became so fond of booze and looked for it herself, so that soon she left behind any limit and was almost always drunk. She did anything for that drink. Everyone knew her, and some laughed and made fun of her. That's how she came to be called "Josie the Drunkard" or "Crazy Josie." She was drunk most of the time, red-faced and bloated, with sick eyes, their white turned yellow, dishevelled hair and her sly, drunken eyes. She wandered through the town, along with others like her. Now she was standing in the line, leaning against the back of the wall and swaying from one foot to the other. Her troubled eyes, wide open, were raised to the sky, as if dreaming, as if asking for mercy and maybe a crumb of pity. Maybe only up there would she find peace. "Crazy Josie" was swinging. "Crazy Josie" was looking at the sky.

****

They knew one another. Each had his passions and vices; each had his own stories. Walking corpses of city streets; some of them lame, without one or both legs, some without a hand, or simply addicted to various vices—alcohol, cocaine, marijuana, or heroin. Some, beaten by fate, not clear in their minds, with their thoughts carried away to places known only to them. They all sat calmly, some talking quietly, whispering in a low voice. They followed an unwritten law: no fights, shouting, or queuing scandals; otherwise, they would lose food and the canteen would close.

Leaning against the wall, too, Tommy tried hard to calm his breathing. He looked up at the sky, searching feverishly, with a trembling hand, in one of the deep pockets of his overcoat, for the tobacco bag. The lighter. Then he dipped his other hand, the left one, injured and shorter, in the other pocket, after the packet of rolling papers. His fingers played nervously inside the overcoat. He didn't find the papers. He tried once again, with his blunt tips of fingers, sweeping all around. His fingers, bent like claws, stabbed. He rotated his hand in the back of his pocket. His legs began to tremble nervously; he felt that they didn't hold him anymore. "O Lord, have mercy! Not now!" he murmured. With his knees shaking nervously, his back against the wall and his gaze on the sky, he drifted down, slowly, slowly, until he touched the asphalt of the sidewalk. He knew what was coming. He knew the crisis. He saw it. It was bearing down on him. The "White Fog" engulfed him, grabbing him in his tentacles. Crossing the sidewalk, he struggled, convulsively shaking his hands and feet in all directions: "Booommm!!! …Piuuuu!!!...Piuuu!!! …"

****

"Dr. Donald Fredingson! Dr. Donald Fredingson!" came the announcement made by an impersonal voice in the corridors of the hospital, sound in Tommy's brain like the claw of an eagle. Gently swinging his head, he stared at the room bathed in diffused light. He was surrounded by white curtains, other than the small table at the head of the bed, beyond which he could see blinds covering a window. Tommy was lying in a bed, the upper part of his body raised. An IV had been inserted into a vein on the back of his hand, while his left hand rested on the blanket that was covering his legs. He was dizzy and exhausted. A dark, elbow-length sleeved hospital shirt was wet and stuck to his back. He struggled to stay awake, to judge. His mouth was dry. He fell into a numbness, as if gliding down somewhere, attracted by an irresistible vortex. Eventually, he gave up trying to stay awake and let his mind fall down into nothingness.

****

At Henderson's farm, the four puppies were doing great. Cared for by their mother, Lessie, they were growing up under her watchful eye. After a while, Lessie began to leave them alone once in a while; at first less often, then more and more, often and for a longer time. In turn, they ventured around the den, getting to know the world around them. One of them was especially more daring than the rest; grey, with some lighter areas, with the legs still small and the belly almost touching the ground, he was curious and independent.

His eyes were as big as coat buttons. He looked more chubby than slender, like a ball of fur. Although he could barely walk, one day he headed up the hill, among brambles and weeds. He could not be seen among so much greenery. He treaded hesitantly, as if trying the ground in front of him with his paws. Curious, with his eyes wide open, trembling all over his body, he walked, touching the blades and vines of the grass with his muzzle. He touched a flower with his paw, then with his head, trying to feel it and smell it. He then went on to meet other new things that he encountered on the way. He was not going straight. He made his way in a zigzag, without any target. When he reached some bushes, the way became harder for him; unexpected obstacles appeared: scrub, cut roots, fallen branches. He came across a small puddle. He stepped with one of his paws into the water, but quickly pulled it back and turned around. He walked around the water, then stopped. He stretched his head over the water, curious, stretching his neck. What he saw, that face—his face—made him jump back, scared. He continued his way through the bushes and thick grass taller than him. The ground, as well as the vegetation, became damp and soft under the cushions of his paws. He reached a bank and saw something bright and sparkling running down the hill. He looked around, unsure of his path.

It was one of the streams of clean water that crossed the farm. Only from this crystal-clear water, the farm animals would drink in the morning, before leaving for pastures, and in the evening. The Henderson farm had collection basins for winter.

The adventurous pup stopped on the steep slope, looking at the streams of water that flowed down the hill. Sniffing, stepping forward, he stretched out his neck, his front legs tucked into the loose bank. Unwillingly, he slipped down the bank, trying to slow down the fall with his front legs, but without success; he rolled into the cold and clear water, which, with speed, carried him downstream. He could have paid dearly for this adventure. He could not hang on and jump on any of the banks, the current being too fast and too strong for him. Yipping helplessly, he tried to keep his balance and stay with his head above the water, floating down the river. Lessie heard him and ran, bounding into the water and grabbed him by the nape. She paddled to the side of the river and carefully placed her pup on solid ground. Then she licked his face a few times. Feeling safe now, the little one was whining tenderly, with pleasure. Then Lessie grabbed him again and, holding him by the nape, carried him to the den. There she put him down and began to wash his body, licking it. The other puppies were also snuggling around him, next to the culprit, who was moaning with pleasure. With Lessie, they all felt safe.

After a few weeks, more courageous now, he had another experience; the little pup ventured in the direction of the stables. Right near the stables, Bill had built some hen houses in the yard. He knew what chickens to raise; the beautiful Bresse hens for meat, the golden comet for eggs, and the barred rock, good for both eggs and meat. He used eggs for the house, but he also had several loyal customers to whom he periodically delivered eggs and chicken.

And so, another rebel joined the adventure; a cockerel, which had just replaced its down with feathers, set off up the hill, along the fence, to escape from the yard through a wider hole in the wire fencing. With his head low to the ground, occasionally pecking, he gathered seeds and other grains.

In turn, playfully, the puppy walked beside the stables, avoiding holes left by the animals' hooves and bale wires. He rounded a corner of the stable, and bumped into the chick. The chick, with his long neck, head raised, was a little taller than the puppy. But now, feeling him, stretching his neck, he raised his beak. He stopped in his tracks smelling him. The puppy also stopped, then slowly, half walking and half crawling, he got even closer. Like a stone, head up, the chick stood motionless at first, then turned his head to one side. The puppy stretched out his muzzle, sniffing again. Finally, the chick turned to face him again, and, suddenly, pecked him at the nose turning quickly, it scuttled down the hill.

His second adventure, although not as dangerous as the first, caused him to whimpering in pain. He turned and went back along the stables to find his shelter and comfort. When he found her, he crouched beside Lessie. It felt good there; he felt protected.

****

He heard voices in a low, almost whispered, tone.
"Let's change his clothes!"
"Hold his back."
"Let's increase his dose. Would you give him 200?"
Someone wiped him with a sponge, with warm water.
"See the other foot?"
"Quiet!"

****

Again, low voices. But this time, between two men.
"Too bad about him, doctor. We tried to help him, but his temper … his habits. I say it, and so do others: he's the greatest goalkeeper in the NHL of all time. Then he was a hero in Afghanistan. Who brought him here?"
"A street sergeant called an ambulance and accompanied him here. "I know of him," the doctor replied.
"The management of the Club and the Veterans Association must be informed. We can't leave him like this! We have to do something for him, as we did another time. This time, it's much worse. God, what a state he's in!"

****

That game had been announced as crucial for securing a place in the Eastern Division play-offs. They had, by then, the chance of a whole string of wins. They all hoped for qualification. They dreamed of it, anticipated it and longed for it. All they needed was one last bit of momentum, one last impulse. The Club's management, the coaches, and the city officials all put pressure on them. They had a few days to prepare and they did it with unprecedented ardency and dedication.

There would be three training sessions a day, the coaches decided; one in the morning, on the ice, another in the afternoon, the theoretical session, and in the evening, the third, again on the ice. He remembered how Harrison, the head coach, drew game diagrams on the board, repeating them several times so that everyone would know, learn, memorize, and be able to apply them to their encounters on the ice. Also, Rob and Troy, the two seconds, gave them some videos, to better understand the opponents' games. Again, the opponents were studied, dissected, analyzed, and drew conclusions about the best tactics to approach the match. But the problem was that their opponents were doing the same.

As Tommy expected, things went differently on the ice. Completely different. From the beginning, they had suffered when two of their players were given major penalties at the same time. That was a huge handicap in such a game. The audience booed nervously, especially since one of the penalties was just a stronger check on the opponent, something common in NHL matches. Eager to control the match, the referees blew their whistles at anything. The rage in the stands also went down on the ice, spilling over the players. The game became extremely fragmented. They fought one by one, two by two, forming a few pairs in the art of boxing. Throwing their gloves down, with a hand they grabbed the opponent's sweater, tried not to slip on the ice, and threw their fists at faces, at bodies, whenever they could. Tommy huddled in his goal, trying to cope as well as possible with the kicks that flowed, one after the other, as the opponent attacked in waves. With only three players, they were closely surrounded by opponents. They threw themselves desperately in the path of the puck. A defenseman was taken off the ice when the puck hit him; he had dived in front of a slapshot, and the puck had pushed his visor into his cheek, cutting the flesh to the bone. Bewildered by the blow, he remained on the ice, while blood began to flow. The silky, thirsty ice absorbed it like a sponge. The medical team rushed in, and he was taken to the locker room. Realizing he needed surgery; an ambulance was called.

In the meantime, the opponent had changed all three lines and yet had not scored. Now, the best of the three lines were on the ice. Between the posts, Tommy was doing miracles shot after shot, defending the goal. He gloved the puck to slow the game, allowing frequent changes for his tired teammates. With twenty seconds left until the end of the major penalties, the line change put three rested teammates on to fight together to pass the penalty time without a goal. The opponents' nerves had reached their limit. They had tightened the game even more, pressing a few metres from the goal. Tommy could barely see anything through the forest of feet, both teammates and opponents. He rejected each puck, unconsciously, more out of intuition and reflex. The opponent shoved two of his teammates, pushing them towards him, who in turn had been pushed back on the goal line. Seeing nothing but bodies but trying to look through a lot of legs to see something, he had both legs outstretched on either side, covering the goal as much as possible. He heard the crack of wood on frozen rubber, saw the stick on the left side, at the base of the bar. The puck bounced off the post and was thrown into the air. An opponent hit it in the air toward the goal. Straightening his legs, now on both skates, Tommy volleyed it into the air with the handle of his stick, then grabbed it in the glove of his left hand. With the puck safely out of play, he turned to face the net. Furious, the shooter charged, at full speed, slamming Tommy in the back. Not seeing what was coming, Tommy's head hit the iron bar. Everything went dark.

Part of his forehead, eye and cheek, all on his left side, were injured, his blood spilling on the ice. He didn't know how long did he lay there. A cold seized him, a cold that penetrated him, to his bones. That match cost him dearly. Jackson had taken terrible revenge on him. But he had understood; that's hockey. With hearts racing at over 180 beats per minute, the nerves of some players give in.

****

When he opened his eyes, he felt cold shivers run over his arms, chest and back. He was lying in bed, completely naked, the head of the bed bent upwards, and he was washed by two nurses. A piece of cloth had been placed under him, and the two of them passed pieces of wet sponge along his arms, over his chest, over his whole body, washing him skilfully. He looked at them, dumbstruck, trying to stay awake.

"Could you please turn on your belly so we can wash your back?" Docile, he obeyed, letting them go on. Washed everywhere, then dressed in clean pajamas, he let them comb his messy hair and beard. His bedding was changed, too. Then they disappeared.

Left alone, he now felt a pleasant warmth wrapping his whole body. A sweet torpor seized him. Then he collapsed into nothingness again.

****

Other voices reached him.

"He refused our help. He systematically refused to register. The Veterans' Association cannot do anything without the documents being completed. The money has to be justified. He was injured three times, they picked him up with a stretcher and they took him by helicopter to the military base. He had the right to come back home, but he chose not to, and he returned to the front lines. Sir, what stubbornness!"

"Yes, I know. It was the same way when he was a hockey player. If something went into his head, you couldn't stop him. Like a mule: hard to handle, hard to prepare. But what a show he put on! People were screaming like crazy, and he filled the stadiums where he played. They fought for an extra ticket!"

He opened his eyes. He still couldn't see the ceiling hidden in the dim light. Slowly, carefully, he moved his hands and feet, then his whole body. He felt less numb than before. Using his elbows, he pulled himself up, resting his back on the pillow. As before, he could not determine whether it was day or night; only the pleasant and discreet light wrapped up his cubicle. For the first time since he arrived, he was conscious of reality. He knew that he was in a hospital, but he didn't know why or for how long he had been there. He checked his hands, feet, chest, and his head … He didn't feel any wound. That was good. He tried to look back … The run-in with the cops. The walk to the canteen. Standing in the line … that must have been it for sure; the white fog had covered him. How many times had it happened before? He didn't remember. It had started after Afghanistan; he knew it very well. He tried to remember.

The door opened and two nurses appeared.

"Good morning! Did our young man get up? Did he sleep better last night? We don't need so many sedatives anymore, right?" the nurse assured him. Blonde, short and stocky, she moved with energetic movements on her short, thick legs. Her long hair, pulled tight in a tail, was coming out from under her white cap.

Looking at them, Tommy couldn't help himself; a wide smile grew on his face, while a feeling of warmth enwrapped him. "Good morning, ladies!" he answered politely. "Please, can you tell me when I got here? And what hospital is this?"

The two nurses were doing their work with some instruments, on a table in the corner of the room. The second one was tall, Creole, with black hair like embers. Without turning her head towards him, preoccupied with some syringes, she said, "I don't know when you got here. I wasn't on duty when they brought you in. But all your vital signs are good now. We can't tell you more about your medical status. The doctor will."

"From today, you need to start eating better," added the blonde. "You're at the General Hospital. And one more thing: you have to take better care of yourself. You need to be more careful with your personal hygiene. They have showers at the shelter, don't they? So, at least one thorough shower a day. And clean and cut your nails more often. And your feet look miserable and they could easily get infected."

The other nurse chimed in, "We will put a special ointment on your feet, and when you get discharged, you will receive a tube of it so that you can continue the care."

Tommy looked up, his eyes lost in the hidden ceiling, then he closed his eyes. He thought about how many blows, cuts and accidents his legs had endured. The hockey skates had not always been of good quality and fit when he first started playing. Long before he played the game, they used to be made from ordinary leather, with padding covering all the way up to above the knee. You always had to be careful that your shin pads covered the top of your skates; if you were not careful, and you did not adjust them properly, you could be trampled and injured. Lying on his back with his eyes closed, he remembered, as if it had been yesterday:

He was a goalie playing against a top team. During the half-time break, in the locker room, he chatted for a long time with one of his teammates about a previous play, regarding the fast line changes during switches from attack to defense; the player did not enter the ice fast enough—the change was made late—leaving an opening to set up a one-on-one, and he was lucky to have been able to stop the puck. They debated the line change, each arguing and supporting his own opinion. Finally, it was time to get back on the ice, and he, a pack of nerves, did not adjust his equipment properly; a mere quarter of an inch was left uncovered. A quarter of an inch only. The opposing team was continuously pressing. The Bruins was playing tough, as if they hated their adversary.

"Forward, forward! On them!"

"Let's suffocate them now!"

White and blue figures hovered in front of him. He tried to remain calm, gritting his teeth, and moving his head, up and down, right to left, following the puck. At a crush in front of his goal, with his back to the post, he was hit in the mask with the butt of a stick, at the same time as a skate stepped on his foot. The tip penetrated that tiny spot: a quarter of an inch. Falling on his side, he felt the bone crack. One of the toes gave way under the pressure of steel. He felt the blood flooding the inside of his boot. The bone had broken like a match and pierced through the skin. He had collapsed on the ice, helplessly, while around him the beating became general. The doctor had come in with the stretcher, the ambulance, the hospital. In vain. He had lost the rest of the season!

"My poor feet!" he thought. "Cuts, swellings, abutments ... he'd had them all. On top, they were swollen like two bags!"

"That's it, angel! We need to give you some injections. Any location preference?" the blonde asked.

Lying on his back, he replied, "I don't care. Anyway, I had injections on both sides, it doesn't matter now."

When they finished, he thanked them kindly, especially for the service done an hour before, when they cleaned him, washed him, and changed his bedding and pajamas. They finally went out, leaving him alone with his thoughts.

****

He heard a few knocks on the room door.

Before Tommy knew what was going on, a few people had entered.

"Hello, Tommy! How glad I am to see you again! But not really in this situation."

"Hello, Tommy!" added the other two in unison. Now, he woke up suddenly and could see the three of them better. The first who greeted him was a small, fat, bald man, Richard Cole, the Club's president. He did not know the other two—one tall, with glasses, and another of average appearance; they were perhaps two of the Club's current administrative assistants.

"I found out late about the circumstances in which you got here," Richard continued. "I brought these two gentlemen, Mr. Moos and Mr. Hall, who are two of the current Club Secretaries. You have to know that everyone was worried when they heard about you. There are many of your old teammates who still keep in touch: Carlson, Charles, Hubbert, Lee, Daniel, and others. They all sent you their best wishes over the phone. The phones have been ringing off the hook these past few days with people asking questions. The office staff are overwhelmed and don't know what to say," Richard added. "But man, what happened to you? Do you really live on the streets? Oh, forget it! Look, Tommy," he said, "everyone wants the best for you. We know how much we owe you and we want to see you well, recovered, and back on track."

"We're glad you're feeling better," said Mr. Moos, the taller. "Recovery should go well and we hope you are going to be back on your feet soon."

"Everyone is asking about you," Mr. Hall added. "At the Club, there's been a lot of worry when we found out the news. We've lost track of you for several years. We were amazed when you were picked up from that part of town."

Lying on the bed, Tommy looked at the three of them with a kind of half-detachment, examining them one by one. He knew Richard for a long time, from the time he was president of the Club. Together they had had good times, a few famous successes in the NHL, but also some direct confrontations—especially regarding money matters. Richard had been very mean, going so far as to save money cutting the free pop the players consumed in the locker rooms. That was the turning point when he turned the whole team against him. They had had some harsh arguments. And now, Richard claimed he wanted to help him! He didn't know the other two at all.

"Tommy," Richard continued, "we have come here to see you, to wish you well, because, whether you know it or not, you continue to be one of the top members that our Club has produced and one who has fought for the colours of this organization."

"Just look at you. How much compassion you show!" Tommy mumbled. "Where were you gentlemen when I was starving on the streets? Where were you when I was wounded in the fighting in Afghanistan? Maybe you were playing golf!"

"Now that we found you, we can report to management about the whereabouts of a famous Club member," Hall continued emphatically.

"And we will find the necessary means—funds, so that we can help you," continued Mr. Moos. "It's a shame to let you live on the street."

"Tommy, first you have to get well. That's the most important thing," Richard said. "You shouldn't worry about anything. Just think about recovery. Leave everything to us; we will take care of it. We will also contact the people from Social Assistance, to see what they can do, too. We will work together. We put you up in social housing, and the Club will discuss an application for a lifetime annuity. This way, you will be safe. In the meantime, we will contact the War Veterans Association to see what they can do to help you. Why didn't you make a request to them? You were justified—you were wounded in battle, weren't you?"

He looked at them, trying to stay calm. He mumbled, "Thanks."

Suddenly, they were in a rush. Richard stood up, hat still in hand, saying, "The doctor says you're on the right track. You just get healthy!"

"Get well soon, sir," said Moos, approaching the door.

"You'll be well, soon, Tommy! See you soon, no worries." Hall said as he closed the door. And as quickly as they arrived, the three of them disappeared.

"What a nerve! What condescending bastards!" Tommy mumbled.

****

Above Henderson's farm, only a few white clouds laced the dome of the blue sky. Although still early, the sun had begun to warm the air, predicting another hot day. The dew, which had covered the ground in the morning, making all the crops, grasses, shrubs and forest shine, was gone by now. Above, on the hill, the dogs roamed among the stables, wandering near the buildings, or lying down and sleeping in the sun. Michael was already in the field taking care of the cattle. The peace and quiet that reigned over the farm was the same as every day that flowed over this oasis of beauty.

Emily was bustling about in the kitchen making fresh bread. Already a few loaves were in the oven. With her sleeves rolled up to her elbows, hands full of flour, she kneaded the dough on one of the wide wooden planks placed over the table. Finally, she opened the oven door and placed the last pan of dough on the rack, then carefully closed the door. The burning fire and the hard work kneading the dough lit her cheeks a ruby red, which then spread down her neck.

They had a good oven and the bread made on it, for good reasons, melted in your mouth. The house was well-built, although it had been modified several times. It had been built a hundred years ago, when things were done with patience and great care.

Picking up the cutting board and the other used utensils from the table, she washed them in the sink. She turned and wiped the table, then looked at the oven once more. She grabbed a sleeveless jacket and covered her shoulders and went out on the deck.

She took a good look down the valley, as she had done so many times before. Everything was peaceful. Michael could not be seen anywhere, being on the pasture up near the forest. Searching the horizon, she knew that it would be another hot day. She headed up the hill toward the henhouse to feed and fetch water for the chickens. She had asked Bill so many times to fix some of the henhouse boards, but, stingy as he was, he refused as it was not necessary to waste money.

She changed the chicken's water, taking a few bucket journeys to the tap. Grabbing a bushel of grain, she spread it throughout the yard. The birds rushed over and started pecking, gathering grain by grain.

She entered the stable where Bill had gone in the morning to scatter some bales for fresh bedding for the animals. She climbed up the ladder to the loft where they kept the straw. Standing near the top of the ladder, she stopped to listen for him but heard nothing. She carefully stepped around some bales, then she froze.

Curled up, on his side, his hands outstretched in front of him, Bill lay motionless. Covering her mouth, she went closer, holding her breath. With trembling fingers, she knelt and touched his face, and checked for a pulse at his neck. Bill's body had already begun to cool. A sigh escaped her. Taking his hand in hers, she looked at him, her eyes watering. A life together. A beautiful life they had had. "Why did you go right now, Bill? Why did you hurry?" Streams of tears were running down her cheeks while her mind rummaged through the clutter of memories. Lumps of feelings and thoughts were travelling through the mirror of her mind. Bill had gone……..

****

She first met him at her parents' farm. It had been a scorching day. The stifling heat had finally passed, and they were sitting on the porch on the wicker chairs and sipping their tea. Breathing out smoke treads, with the heels of their boots on the railing, her father and brother were smoking pipes. The sweet smell of tobacco floated around. Everything was quiet that evening, as it should be after a working day at a farm.

Suddenly, the silence was broken by the sound of an approaching car, until a pickup truck appeared and stopped right behind the house. This is how she saw him for the first time: massive, with broad shoulders, he slowly stepped out of the car and headed towards the porch. He was wearing blue jeans, fastened over his shoulders with suspenders, cowboy boots, and a tan wide-brimmed cowboy hat. Under it, a face with prominent cheeks burned by the sun, and two piercing blue eyes, completed the figure.

"Good afternoon, gentlemen! I'm on my way to town and I thought I'd bring the vegetables I talked about. There are a few boxes in the car."

"Of course, Bill! Terry and I will unload them," replied her father, shaking his pipe and tapping it on the back of his palm. Emily remained mesmerized. Like a magnet, her eyes were drawn to him. He had an air of health, energy and life, which she had never experienced before. A strange heat passed through her body, and nervous chills ran down her cheeks, arms, and breasts.

Their first formal encounter was at a county fair in Dowson, a nearby town, on Farmers' Day. There were many people, fried sausages on the BBQ, country music, and beer—lots of beer, as usual. She danced with him for the first time. He had come to her, piercing her with those playful blue eyes. She had seen him from afar, approaching with his slow, solid steps.

"Do you dance, young lady?"

Again, the same feeling of warmth all over her body. She didn't know why, but she blurted out, "No, thanks, I'm not dancing."

"But let me introduce myself, Miss. My name is Bill Henderson, and I live on my Deep Valley farm."

"Delighted, sir. I know who you are. We met at my parents' farm. You came with some vegetable crates promised to my father."

"Miss, I admired you even then, even if I didn't know your name. Now, would you like to dance with me, please?"

"I'm sorry, sir, I have to refuse you."

"Miss, people have gathered here, to eat, to party, to drink beer and to dance. Why did you come? I hope you have no hesitations regarding me."

"No, sir, it's not about that. I just don't want to dance."

She looked up at him. Her face turned red. Then she felt his determination and sincere joy of living and loving. His eyes continued to pierce her deeply, while his strong cheeks and neck reddened.

In a flash, she realized she had risen in the air with her chair. With a few steps, Bill reached the middle of the dance floor, carrying the chair in which she was still sitting above his head. Soon people gathered around, dancing and clapping. Then he gallantly lowered her chair, kissed her hand and asked her, "Do you dance, young lady?" She couldn't hold back her laughter. They danced till morning. Within six months, they were married.

Now, looking at him, she felt her soul full of gratitude for the years spent together, for the care she and her family had received every moment. He had been a righteous man, vigorous and attentive at the same time. He had always surrounded her with tenderness. His being exuded an air with a noble warmth of soul. Now he was lying on his side, with his ruffled white hair free from his cowboy hat. She caressed his cheek with her palm, then grabbed his hand in his, kissed it, and pressed to her own cheek.

****

He knew it was night; he had learned to orient himself by the sounds in the corridor. The night was not so hectic. In the hospital wards, the same diffused light. He had woken up suddenly, with his nightgown completely wet from sweat. He had been dreaming. It was like yesterday.

"Tommy, you're trying in vain, I'm faster than you!" shouted his brother over his shoulder, skating on the ice of the lake, playing hockey with other children. They used some blunt sticks, and instead of a puck, a piece of rubber. The children were divided into two teams and played every afternoon after school. His brother, Kenn, with his back to him, sometimes playing the puck, part holding his hand to one side, was unstoppable. Feint short to the left, then turn sharp to the right and easily outrun the two opponents, scored in the opponent's goal. In vain, Tommy had pursued him, desperately trying to catch him, but he could not reach him. His brother was so good that no one could stop him. He outshone everyone in speed, and his technique was flawless. Somehow, he was proud of him. The team he played on always won. That's why they all fought for him, when choosing the team. Tommy, who was strong but not as talented as Kenn, was once put in the goal to defend.

Then came that damn day. There were a group of children running up the hill on the street, noisy and mischievous, like all children. They were pushing each other, trying to be the first. Of course, Tommy was in the lead. At the intersection, he didn't see the delivery truck. In turn, the driver was surprised by the crowd of children in front of him. Something hit him in the left shoulder, throwing him into the snow. Although wounded, he hid it from his parents. For several days and nights, he had unimaginable pains and couldn't sleep. Like a mule, he gritted his teeth at them all. He was careful not to scream, biting his lips and the duvet. He could not feel the upper arm on his left side at all. From time to time, pain shot through his shoulder blade. Eventually, his parents realized that he had been hit badly. He didn't admit where it happened, thinking he would be in trouble for not being careful.

Since then, Tommy had a shorter arm. He had learned over the years that he had fractured his upper arm bone and that the bone had not fused together correctly; it was bent, so it was also shorter.

After the accident, they only let him play as a goalie. The left hand held the catching glove. With a short, precise movement, imitating a hook, he was able to grab pucks that other goalies couldn't handle. He stayed in the net for his entire hockey career.

Despite this accident, he had a wonderful childhood. Together with his older brother, Kenn, he met after school with the boys' team, starting the frenzy. Of course, as it was Canada, they played hockey in the winter, and the winter lasted more than half a year! They played in any weather: with or without wind, but also at -35 degrees Celsius! At that temperature, ice and even snow squeaked like the bow of a violin, sometimes mimicking the cries of a rock guitar.

During the summer, they 'borrowed' a boat from someone they knew would pay little attention to it. For a few hours, they went fishing on rivers or lakes, or sometimes they had short expeditions, in out-of-the-way places.

God, what a wonderful childhood they had …

****

He tried to fall asleep again, but he couldn't. For a long time, he tossed from one side to the other. Exhausted by so many attempts, he finally succeeded.

"Good morning! How did you spend the night?" The nurse's words greeted him when he had just opened his eyes. Rubbing his eyes, he blinked, trying to adjust his vision. The nurse had come with a syringe kit and placed it on the table. On the nightstand, breakfast was waiting for him.

"Good morning Ms.! I slept well, thank you." An alluring smell of toast was coming from the bedside table on which the food tray was placed. "If you don't mind, I'd like to eat something."

"Of course, my dear. But first, go to the bathroom. When you're ready, I'll help you wash." Sitting on the edge of the bed, he let his feet slide into his pants.

"You know, talk is circulating around here that you were a star in the NHL. They say you're that Tommy, the goalkeeper of goalkeepers, who was talked about so much. I heard that you also fought in Afghanistan. Honestly, no one recognized you."

"Yes, ma'am. Isn't this life strange?" he replied, and disappeared into the bathroom. Washing his hands, then his face, he looked at his face in the mirror. He let his hands fall. His long hair, black as coal, fell in disarray. The scar that started from the forehead, descended over the eyebrow, eye and cheek, stopped a little above the jaw. What a strange creature! Man of the street. Homeless. He was almost 45 years old, hardened by the fights on the ice, Afghanistan, and the streets. Although he had endured a lot, it was always his choice; he never owed anyone anything. He leaned closer to the mirror, looking into his own eyes, he said, "Never, Tommy! You never gave up and you never will! You will never humble yourself to beg!" Slapping his cheek sharply, he wiped his face with the towel, combed his beard and hair and returned to his bed.

"I see you've arranged yourself. I'll give you the injection, and then you can eat."

After the injection, sitting on the edge of the bed, he tried to start breakfast.

"I don't want you to get tired; Stay in bed. Here, I brought a special table for eating in bed." She cranked the bed to a comfortable incline.

"Yes, ma'am. Thank you very much!" He stretched out and, leaning back against the pillows, received the table kindly offered by the nurse. On the tray was a plate of toast and a cup of coffee.

"Press the button when you're done. Someone will come to take the tray." The nurse disappeared out the door. He ate alone, in silence. After they had taken his tray and lowered the bed, he laid down on it, trying to clear his thoughts.

A short knock on the door and a nurse slipped inside, accompanied by a person dressed in a long raincoat. The man was tall, had white hair, and was holding his hat in one hand.

"Tommy, this gentleman wants to see you," said the nurse. Of course, with your permission."

"Gerry Thomson is my name, sir. I'm the president of the War Veterans Association in this city. Nice to meet you, Tommy!" In two steps, the man was next to the patient's bed.

"Sit down, sir," said the nurse, placing a chair for him near Tommy's bed. Then she left.

"Hey, Tommy—I can call you that, can't I? Well Tommy, the organization I represent has lost track of you. And that was quite a few years ago. No one knew the situation you were in, the way you were living, or whether you recovered after you came back from Afghanistan. From the data we have, it indicates you were hurt. You had the right to return home after your injury, but you chose to return to the battlefield. Impressive. Few people would have done that. Beautiful gesture of sacrifice and patriotism. We will take a look and see what can be done for you. We will definitely help you, but we need all your current information, as well as a written request signed by you. When I come to visit you next time, I will bring you a form to complete. Do you think you can do that?"

The rigmarole continued, sounding like the words of an auctioneer. Tommy could no longer follow him. His thoughts flew away to the time he was voluntarily enlisting in the army. The words seemed familiar ... as if he had heard them before. The same bombastic twist, the usual propaganda, with the emphasis on uplifting, noble feelings and on the patriotic duty toward the nation. With his gaze fixed on the door, he could no longer hear him.

When the speech stopped, he just muttered, absent-mindedly, "Yes, sir! Do as you wish. I'm glad you're interested in me and my fate."

"Of course, Tommy! As soon as the Committee meets, we will start the process. Once the documents are signed, you will receive everything I told you about."

And the tirade continued. Eventually, finishing his plea, they parted cordially, Thomson leaving in a hurry.

Tommy repeated, "The patriotism and sacrifice you have shown will surely be rewarded. Our organization will do everything to help you. We will fight for a medal of merit!"

What did he know? Had he been there? In the filth and dust of the desert? Had he known the fetid smell of swollen corpses from the heat in just twelve hours? Did he know what it was like to defuse a bomb in a minefield, surrounded by corpses that had not been picked up for days, in that heat and smell that made your eyes tear? And you weren't allowed to go wrong by even two millimetres!

"Office mouse! Walking locust! Circus jester!" Tommy muttered aloud. He rolled onto his side, trying to calm his thoughts. His feet began to tremble slightly, some scattered convulsions. A memory from Afghanistan! Eventually, he calmed down.

****

Shortly after Bill died, according to custom, he was buried in the land he had worked so lovingly and diligently and in which, eventually, all mortals go. It had been a dignified procession, with all the loved ones around, as well as many friends, farmers from the community and people who had known him and dealt with him on various occasions. There were also the Simons, the Pattersons, Redford, Jackson, Roberts, and many, many others. They all surrounded the coffin, dressed in dark clothes, some of which were a little out of fashion, but farmers didn't give in to buying new clothes for such occasions. In the town cemetery, they stood around the grave with bowed heads, respectfully and deeply in remembrance. The pastor, dressed in ceremonial robes, read from the Holy Book. "Pray for the sleeping soul of God's servant, Bill, to forgive him the sins done willingly and unwillingly ..." sounded the words, carried by the wind, which had intensified. They all reflected deeply on the life of the deceased, on the meaning of their lives, from father to son, the number lost in time over generations, like grains of sand.

Emily, standing beside her son and two daughters, were next to the pastor. They were a family devastated by grief. Trembling slightly, she sighed, with a handkerchief in her hand, her gaze fixed on the coffin. She was haunted by the thoughts and memories of their life together. She had cried so much that she had no tears left; her eyes were dry. She was tired and worn out, and pale as a piece of paper, ready to collapse. Michel supported her discreetly, with one arm around her waist.

When it was all over, the convoy of people headed for the church, where a few dishes had been prepared for the family and those close to them. They would all eat, then have a glass of wine or a lemonade, mentioning Bill ... and talking about their problems. By late afternoon, it was all over.

Emily stayed with her family for three days, away from the farm. This was left in the care of some of their neighbours, also reliable farmers. When they returned home, it was evening. They were all gathered around the kitchen table, silently eating homemade biscuits and sipping from milk cups. The silence became overwhelming. Only the ticking of the old pendulum clock in the living room in the next room broke the silence. Getting up, Emily picked up the plates from the table and put them in the sink.

With her back still to them, she said, "You're leaving tomorrow morning."

Her chin trembled a little; she could not be seen alone here, only with Michael.

"I talked to Tom. He'll come with the truck and take you to the train station." Then, hesitating, after a few moments, "Don't think about anything now. Take care of your business ... take care of your school work. Michael and I will stay and take care of the farm. We'll finish it somehow. You just have to finish school."

"Yes, Mother," said Sarah, the older of the two. "We can work, too. I and Emma thought about taking some part-time jobs. We can cover at least some of the expenses."

"That's right, Mom!" added Emma. "We both talked about it and decided we can—"

"Listen, girls!" Emily interrupted. "Don't worry. Just go on your way to school. Don't worry. There is enough money. You just need to concentrate on learning. Are you listening to me? Believe me. Just learn. Especially now, when your father is gone, be more responsible to make a future for yourself. Otherwise, you will be overwhelmed by life's troubles. Be strong! You worked on the farm since you were children and you know what work is. Now, you should work to make a future. Do you hear me?"

Eventually, Emma said, "Yes, Mom."

After a while, Sarah also muttered softly, "Yes, Mother."

They felt awkward. The silence was broken—Tick-tock! Tick-tock!—only by the ticking of the pendulum. They avoided looking at one another. They were living a new experience, each realizing that they would never be able to fill the void left by their father. An atmosphere of insecurity had nestled in their souls. The silence became even more oppressive. Tick-tock!

At last, Emily broke the silence. "Go. All of you, go to bed. I'm closing the stables. You have a hard day tomorrow."

They got up slowly, one by one, heading for the stairs that led upstairs to the bedrooms. Standing in the kitchen, still with her back turned, Emily let out a sigh. She didn't want to tell them she wanted to be alone. Alone with her thoughts. She then got up, put on a pair of shoes, put aside the black fur she had worn to the funeral, and picked up a coat from a peg, at random. She threw it on and stepped outside, climbed the hill to the stables. She walked mechanically, staring at the ground. She did everything without thinking, as she had done many times before. She cut open a bale, added a handful of straw here, another there. Once the animals were in their stalls, she suddenly became alert. She looked around in the semi-darkness, not knowing what she was looking for. There was a deep uneasiness nestled in her soul. She needed a support from somewhere. She was waiting for something that was not coming. She entered one of the other stables. In the darkness inside, she searched desperately, looking around her. And she found nothing. There was nothing.

Falling to her knees, holding her head in her hands, she unleashed her soul in a cry of despair and helplessness. "Billye! Billye!"

But there was no answer……

****

"Have you had a better sleep during the night lately?" the doctor asked Tommy when he came for the morning visit. He was accompanied by other staff, including a primary care nurse.

Looking at Tommy's latest lab tests, the doctor shook his head.

"Honestly speaking, your recovery is remarkable, considering the critical condition you were when you were brought here. Now, you, young man, you are not an ordinary case or patient. Your whole body is so affected, as if someone knocked off each side of it. Let's see; your head has traces of wounds and contusions. One of them was so serious that it affected your whole nervous system."

"That one was an explosion, sir, while I was on duty in Afghanistan. It happened near Kabul. A passive bomb exploded nearby and I was hit by a plank or bar detached from the roof of a house."

"Plank, or whatever, you could have ended up paralyzed. Did you know that? And the danger hasn't passed yet.

And furthermore, your scalp was cut ... by a farmer's harrower? You have numerous cuts and blows, some of which have penetrations quite deep into the skull bones."

"Those are cuts from skates, sir, from that time when I was playing hockey."

"Only skate cuts? No, Tommy. And then your cheek is jagged, cut several times, as a sausage before it's ready to fry! And that ugly cut from the forehead to chin has damaged your eye; I have examined it and your crystalline lens of your eye is not, you know, quite fine."

"They are also from hockey, sir. Some of them are from right in the face puck strokes, and the cut is from the goal post. My eyes were also injured by a mortar containing phosphorous."

"Sure Tommy! Hockey and war, but these two do not make the situation easier.

"You have broken bones everywhere—ribs, pelvis, shoulder bone broken and wrongly sutured ... the reason why you have a shorter arm."

"It was a car accident, sir. I was a child then."

"Yes, car accident. How many accidents does a human being need to reach such a state? And your legs are cracked everywhere, crooked and lots of outgrowth. I also think that your blood circulation is another issue. Just tell me how long your feet have been this dark colour?"

"I don't remember sir. I think that this has been for a while."

"Oh, yes," the doctor mumbled, flipping through the file containing Tommy's medical tests, "for a while. This also indicates poor blood circulation.

"And your heart, Tommy! Did you know that you have an enlarged heart? Perhaps because of too much effort. What are we going to do about it? Do you see, we have to work here, too? I am going to prescribe a long-term treatment." He leafed again through the file, then he closed it suddenly, its covers banging with a dry thud. Then, looking down, he was thoughtful for a few seconds as he looked at his patient.

"Tommy, you have to know, that all the staff here is happy to take care of you. They all have found out who are you. We all are proud of you and what you have done for the country as a sports figure and as a soldier."

After a few seconds, he continued, "But for God's sake, to end up on the streets to be picked up and brought here in such a state. Why didn't you ask for help? You are not just anyone. Any insurance company would advertise with your name, would do anything for you." The doctor looked down again.

"Let's say, 'that was then' and see how we go from now on. That's important now. Isn't it? "the doctor said.

"Well, he concluded, we'll take care of what is left together. You shouldn't have a care for anything. You should just stay calm and take care of yourself. Have a great day, Tommy. See you soon!"

The procession of doctors and nurses disappeared down the corridor. Tommy was left alone again, staring at the ceiling, although he actually couldn't see it. He closed his eyes, thinking, listening: "We are proud of you! You are a hero!"

Proud my foot; hero of nobody. I used to play hockey because I liked playing. I did it since I was a child. That's what I knew to do, since I was a child. I started playing in the winter, on the ice of the lake and then I continued at school, on the ice rink.

He remembered those days. It was just after his brother had passed away. He died young due to lung cancer. He was diagnosed, and, in a few weeks, he was gone. And now he remembered that upon returning from the funeral, in the corner of the room they had shared, he had seen his brother's pair of skates.

He had burst into tears and fallen down on his knees, with both skates in his hands, he kissed them one by one and swore he would play hockey in such a way as to honor his brother's memory. Then he continued, "Yes, my dear brother, you had always been better than me, more alert and more talented. As for me, well, I went into the goal and I don't think I made you ashamed. I played for you, for your memory. Yes, you were great, Kenn, my brother. You played great, always!"

He remembered himself as a teenager. He was in secondary school. Word got around that he was the boy who could defend the goal and no one was able to score on him. He had been contacted by a sports teacher and it was in that way he went for the first time on the ice of a skating rink, dressed in complete hockey equipment.

After a few minutes warming up, the coach asked to be the goal-keeper, and the team, one by one, started free shooting.

If at the beginning the coach was skeptical regarding a slightly hunched boy, with an arm rather shorter than the other, after several shots he began to be more interested, and, with widening eyes, the coach followed his performance. He almost couldn't believe his eyes; the strange boy in the goal was defending everything from all distances, not only with his stick, legs, pads and shoulders or elbows, but even using his butt end.

"Holy cow! St. Thomas and St. Patrick, Jesus and all Saints! Where did you come from, boy?"

He has never seen anything like this in his life.

Yes, Tommy thought, those years in school had been beautiful. They had won the city championship three years, and then the Provincials' two years in a row.

You were with me everywhere, my dear brother Kenn. I wanted so much to be proud of the way I played. I couldn't as an offensive or defensive hockey player; I did it as a goalie.

Oh yes, what beautiful years! It was like yesterday. When the hell did, they pass?

****

It had been three weeks since old Henderson had passed away, and the work at the farm was following the same pattern. Emily consulted with Michael and her neighbours and decided to reduce the number of animals. In this way, she tried to be able, together with her son, to cope with work at the farm.

Unfortunately, their neighbours could take just a few animals. They had their limits and their stock was already full. Patterson took three cattle, two pigs and a few hens. Redford couldn't afford more than two cows, and the others, a few hens and some rabbits. And it was a lot of work for them at the farm. Too much.

She remembered how all three of them used to work late in the evening and used three milking machines, barely able to finish. She couldn't afford to hire anyone, and the girls had to be kept at school, and their taxes had to be paid. It seemed that only selling a part of the animal stock could be a solution.

One evening, when Emily and Michael, exhausted, were having dinner, sipping milk and eating toast, she said, "You know, Michael, about animals; I talked to Redford and I asked him to take you with him when he next goes to the fair, so you can go to the animal auction; he can teach you what to do and how to do it, so that you know the business, and can sell part of the stock. I will call my cousin to take care of the cattle for a day."

"Yes, Mom, but I can sell even now if I have too. It's no big deal to sell some animals!"

"Now get your mind off that idea, Michael! There are all kinds of hucksters and charlatans. They will sense immediately that you are new and they will fool you. My dear, open your ears and listen to what old Redford has to say. He is a farmer with a lot of experience and has seen so much and gone through all kinds of things. Your father and he have helped each other so many times. And he is honest."

"Yes, Mother. I just wanted to say that I am not afraid to go to the fair to sell. I can do that."

"I know, my dear. That's why I am sending you. I am not afraid for the pigs, a few hens and rabbits left; in time we can share them with other farms. But there are too many cattle for the two of us. I can't hire anyone, and we need money to be able to work the land. The small tractor needs to be repaired, we have other tools to repair, and anything and everything costs."

"Oh God, how did Bill do it? "She thought as she let out a sigh.

And so, they consulted all evening, like two good householders.

But God, apparently, wanted things to be different.

Although Michael had accompanied old Redford to the animal fair, learning the secrets and subtleties of cattle sales, he had no chance to make any sale: the animal market was down due to a massive import from Argentina and the prices were very low.

Emily felt trapped. They could not keep them all; to sell some of them at the current market price would be a great loss they could not afford, and they could not afford to hire someone either. Day after day, she thought about all these things without finding a way out. Until, one evening, exhausted from hard work, she fell asleep dressed. She stirred from one side to the other, tortured by muscle cramps until she fell into a deep sleep.

She had a dream. It was Bill looking at her with his blue eyes, this time a bit worried. He was wearing his cap with peak and his blue overalls with the suspenders over the shoulders. She heard him say, "Take great care of our children, Emily. They have to build their futures. This is more important than anything else! We worked as slaves on this land just for them to have a better future. The children Emily! Take care of the children!"

With pains in her bones, she woke up. Yes, she will sell the farm and will send Michael to school, then she will move to the city and will open a store—a vegetable store. She had some knowledge in the business and she had close connections with the farmers. And, besides the vegies, she could sell other things, too.

So, in the morning, she was already determined. She would sell the farm. That was the way shown by Bill, which was the best thing to do.

****

Of course, no one knew this yet, and neither did the few dogs in the farm yard. Just like the puppies' mother, or Rex, or any of his other brothers, nobody knew.

Rex had grown and didn't look like a puppy anymore. He had strong jaws and two pairs of fangs. He had tall legs for a puppy under one year of age.

With gray-brown fur and ears raised up looking like the tail of a swallow, he greeted everyone with sparkling eyes. Young and full of life, he was running up and down on hills all day. He had adventured even further, crossing the river with his mother and his brothers, when he had swum for the first time. He was a gifted swimmer, and he liked beating the water under him with his paws, his neck stretched ahead and his muzzle above the water.

One night, he raised his nose to the sky, sniffing the air through his nostrils. He smelled a rabbit and heard it moving in the bushes. It was then when he barked for the first time. At first, it sounded feeble, but, eventually, he managed a strong howl. He succeeded in what nature and his senses demanded from his species.

****

As usual, shortly after lunch, Tommy was lying on his bed, staring at the ceiling. Partly due to medication, and partly due to the rest and lack of stress, he felt much better now. When he was not sleeping, he riveted his look at the ceiling—far from everything, only he and his memories.

With mind's eyes, he remembered the end of his career as a professional hockey player. They had had a difficult match in Detroit.

The game had gone well; they were already leading by two goals. Obviously, the fans were not pleased and they became agitated, nervous and finally aggressive, throwing various objects onto the ice, even a few cans of beer. The referees extended the playing time due to the numerous interruptions. They had no choice. And then, the ice had to be cleaned. Back then, there were no rules so clear and strict in the hockey championships as they are now. Everything was interpretable and debatable, usually in favor of the host team.

The anxiety in the stands spilled onto the ice. The players also became nervous and irascible. The game was interrupted by many incidents. The opponents rushed to attack without a coherent strategy, playing what might be called 'swarming'—throwing the puck into the opponent's half and everyone rushing across the blue line in pursuit of it.

"Hold on, John, cut it once," said his teammates, correlating their actions.

"Henry, you double!"

"Don't go ahead!"

"Come out, Tommy! Stop him!"

"Put him in the curb!"

Going easily and elegantly from defense to attack, they were playing wonderfully. They could play for hours without making a goal. In turn, in the goal, with much experience now, Tommy was doing miracles. For many reasons, he continued, at his age, to be looked at by many important clubs. They knew why.

Again, on defense, in front of his goal, too many feet in front of Tommy's crease; he rejected with his chest a shot from two meters, was pushed aside by a bunch of players, had his hand caught under another player's stick, and lost his own stick just before another shot. Trying to guess the track of the puck, he bent down, put his face on the ice and tried to stop the puck with his mask.

The mask's grid of steel wires was there for protection. However, to no avail; in a few seconds, Tommy no longer had his front teeth and the ice was getting blood-red in front of him.

"For God's sake! He is not a goalie; he is a demon! Do something for him!"

He didn't hear more. As he was face down on the ice, one of the opponents jumped with both skates on the back of his legs on the unprotected part. It was the end. He fainted.

What followed? Well, what could follow, but a general fight? And for him, the end of his career. He couldn't recover; his legs were so badly damaged: the bones were crushed and couldn't be fixed well; several very painful surgeries were required; many months of hospitalization, and almost a year and a half before he could walk again.

He had lost everything. It was over.

Obviously, mass media made a lot of fuss about his games, especially the latest. More than that, in the history of hockey, such a story had never been mentioned: a goalie catching the puck with his mouth. Taking advantage of the story, some companies grabbed the opportunity to advertise different products, from healthy and strong teeth to various ointments for broken lips.

It was the usual media attitude, but for Tommy it was the end. He had given everything on the ice hockey rink.

"Yes, I did everything for hockey, I played for you, too, my dear brother. You didn't get to play anymore. And I promised to play for you. I also played for honour, for the beauty of the game, and for … God knows what else. And I liked doing it. And the applause and cheering, thousands of voices; shouts and roars from the stands, and the media, with its glamour.

After every game, his mind revelled in flash backs, the most beautiful or tense moments of the game that had just finished. Yes, he thought, I had a beautiful career and a beautiful life!

And soon he slipped into a peaceful sleep.

****

A bright light was coming through the bedroom windows. Dawn crept in. Leaning against the back of the bed, she looked out of the window while the light was shyly flooding the room. On the opposite wall, light spots were dancing like leaves in the wind.

Thinking of her life, it was like some spots of colour, impressions, feelings and longings, a dream inside another dream, spots of coloured light on the wall of life.

Those rays gave her hope. Thinking back to the dream she had, she felt better, and somehow safer.

"Yes Bill, you always have taken care of us and you are still watching over us; from where you are, from up there, you have thought of us. Your good thoughts have been sent to me in my dream, so we could move on. Thank you, my dear. We all thank you for your love and care. You care after death, as you did in life."

That was what Emily thought before she got out of bed.

There were so many questions waiting to be answered: "How will she sell the farm? And, if they sell it, where will they live for a while? Of course, they would go to her cousin Paul's place. He couldn't refuse her. They have helped each other so many times. Then, they will have to buy a house.

What about the children? She won't tell them anything yet. There's no point for them to bother now. There will be so many things to do." Once the decision was made, she started another day of work—this time, more determined.

****

Crouched on his knees, with his whole body in that pit, he was trying to disarm a bomb. How many so far? The canvas kit holding his tools was unfolded near him. There were all sorts of pliers, spatula, mirrors with different handles and dimensions, larger or smaller rods, and many more. You could think they belonged to a dental surgeon.

The noise and the heat around were terrific. Over 50°C.

Now on his back, the sweat-wet shirt had glued to his skin. On his forehead, the sweat was dripping on his eyelashes into his eyes and then on the stones, where it was evaporating instantly.

He couldn't afford to wipe his face right now. He had to defuse the warhead. The bomb was not in a comfortable position, if you could say so. They couldn't dig too much around it to make the job easier for him. So he had to dig around it. For that, he had to use a chisel and a hammer. He had to, somehow, get closer to the warhead. With chisel and a hammer, like a sculptor!

Sculptor of death in a stone! The stone sculptor of destruction!

But he had done it. As he always did. He had persisted in doing so. Once he started, nothing could stop him. Like a mule! Just as he had been when he was a hockey player. And now, here he was crouched down, without caring about anything. It was just him and the bomb. Only the two of them; to talk, to exchange impressions and to understand each other ... or not. He had been working for four hours, with others waiting far behind him, hidden among the rubble.

The other soldiers waited to transport the "monster" once it was defused. It would then be detonated on some special lands used only for this kind of operation.

And now they were waiting. They've been waiting for four hours. Four hours in that hell of heat. But none of them dared to rush him, or press him in any way. He wanted to finish faster, but he could make a mistake. A fatal mistake.

With his teeth clenched, as if he were in the goal, he worked, sometimes holding his breath. He was under pressure, but he was used to it. Moreover, he enjoyed it. How many times had he felt the pressure of the public? It was good for him; it kept him awake and in a good shape.

It was the same now. The pressure was immense. All or nothing. Life or death. It was lonely, only he and the bombs ... and maybe his thoughts still there.

Bent down, he tried to touch with his fingers, deep in the bottom of the pit, and feel a loop of wires. He couldn't see it. Could be a fake loop?

Maybe, but he couldn't take the risk undoing it. He knelt down again and rested, wiped the sweat from his face and mounted the lamp on his forehead. He chose one of the mirrors from the kit, the one with the slightly arched rod. Then he leaned his chest into the pit, practically hugging the bomb. He felt the cold metal through his shirt. He turned his head against the steel surface and tried to light the pit as well as possible. For a few seconds, he saw the loop on the mirror surface.

"Damn it," he said to himself. It was a conventional loop, the wires tied with blue adhesive tape.

He leaned back on his knees. He had pains in the muscles of his neck and back. He moved his head, trying to relax his muscles. Then he went back to his work. This time, he chose the long-mouth cutting pliers from the kit. With the mirror in one hand, the pliers in the other, he went back into the depths of the pit.

He hugged the bomb again and felt the cold of the metal through the shirt. He tried again to reach the bottom of the pit with his hands.

He felt a painful prick in his left hand.

He opened his eyes. The room in the hospital where he was lying was immersed in darkness. A dim light let him see the nurse who was just giving him an injection on the back of his wrist.

The bomb thing was a dream, like many others that haunted his nights, especially since he returned from the battlefield.

"What time is it?" he asked.

"Three in the morning. Relax. I am finishing right now."

Trying to follow the nurse's advice, he calmed down, but he couldn't go back to sleep for more than an hour. That's how his nights were in hospital.

****

That morning, Emily started her work as usual. Nothing in her manner revealed her decision. She worked all day, thinking how to do the things she needed to do. She supposed that it would be difficult to sell the farm and the stock of animals together.

The only chance was to talk to her neighbours and some other farmers and to hire an expert in animal sales. Once the stock was liquidated, she could move further on to the sale of the farm.

"Yes, first the animals and then the farm. Tomorrow I'll harness one of the horses to the gig and I'm going to Simon's farm to talk to him. I'll go to Redford, too … maybe to others. They have a lot of knowledge about such things and they have close connections with people in the animal industry. Then I will see what I have to do and how I am going further."

It was most important not to hurry. She couldn't afford to make mistakes. The farm was all they had.

"When the time comes, I will tell Michael, too ... after the sale of the animals he's been arranged. I will tell him first."

So, the next day, she harnessed the horse to the gig and said. "Michael, today I have something to do on Simon's farm. Take the cattle to the pasture near the house. There are other things to take care of today. I am going to feed and water animals first, but the rest you'll have to handle yourself."

"Don't worry ma'am, I will manage. But, what do you have to talk to Simon about that you have to go to him?"

"Well, some old accounts," she said, hurrying out of the kitchen. She felt guilty for lying to her son.

Michael had been raised on the farm for the farm. That was what Bill had thought for him. He was mostly home schooled.

Not much later, Emily got on the gig and headed off to Simon's farm. She was lucky; he was still at home, working around the house.

"Hi Emily. Nice to see you ... but what brings you here? Is everything okay with you, at home?"

"Good morning, Ned! Everything is fine with us, don't worry. I would like to talk to you. Forgive me for rushing like this."

"Oh, no problem. I'm glad to see you again. But, please come in!"

Ned Simon was a tall man with white hair, a beard, and a long mustache. His wild green eyes gleamed from beneath the faded wide-brimmed hat he was wearing—as all farmers did. He let the hammer slip from his hand, and rushed briskly to the gig and helped Emily to get down.

"Donna! Donna! Come out of the house, woman; look, we have a guest."

Soon, wiping her hands on her apron, a short woman appeared. On her head she wore a white cap, as did every other self-respecting farmer's wife, a few white curls rebelliously sticking out, and protruding cheeks and a small snub nose completed the portrait.

Obviously, she had been interrupted from some work, but her face radiated joy. Guests on the farm were quite rare.

"Hello, Emily, please come in! Come in, please," she said again, holding out her hand to the guest and inviting her into the living room where she offered her a chair at the table.

"Please have a seat. I'll make a coffee immediately. You are drinking a coffee with us, aren't you? And I'll bring some biscuits I made yesterday. Come on Ned, sit down. I'll be right back," said Donna, pulling out of a drawer a large cloth, embroidered in vivid colours, which she laid on the table. Spreading her palms with rapid movements, she smoothed the tablecloth. She disappeared into the kitchen.

Nat, after throwing his hat in a corner, sat down. Then he ran his fingers through his hair several times, followed by his mustache and beard. Once the ritual finished, he relaxed and leaned his back against the chair. Keeping his eyes on Emily, he said "It's been a few months since Bill passed away; I heard you did a good job with your son, Emily. Your farm has kept going all this time."

"Yes Ned, I and the boy have done our best. But that's not what I want to talk about. You know that our farm cannot be held with only two pairs of arms. It's too much work, and I have no money to hire workers. And the girls have to finish school."

"I meant you and the boy did well. That's all I wanted to say, Emily. We all know how much work there is on a farm, right? We have been doing this for as long as we know, and so did our forefathers."

Meanwhile, Donna appeared with a wooden tray on which were placed coffee cups and a plate of homemade biscuits.

"Here, Emily. Grab a few biscuits and coffee," Donna said in a familiar tone—they had known each other since childhood. "So, what were you talking about?"

"We were talking about work on the farm, Donna," Ned explained. "I told her how well she and her boy have managed since Bill passed away."

"Oh, yes, we were pleased to hear how you are doing. I was talking to Ned about it, admiring Michael, although still so young, he must be damn hardworking since you managed to do so well."

"Yes," added Emily, "yes, he looks like his father. He is his son, certainly. He knows all the things at the farm from his father: the tradition with animals, the pastures, the fields. He doesn't know as much as Bill knew, especially with tractor repair and other machinery needed for working the land.

What can you do? He didn't have time to learn all of them. And as Bill is no more ..."

There was an oppressive silence. The three of them, looking down, stopped talking. The memory of the departed Bill lingered in the air, too noble to be ignored. He had been working in such a way, with dignity and respect for life, land people ... everything. After a while, Emily broke the silence.

"You both know that I can't go along like this, with only Michael, at least not for a long time."

"Yes, of course, we know that well enough, Emily, that's why we have been so happy to see the way you and the boy kept your farm going."

"And you both know that when we have to harvest, there are not enough arms and I cannot afford to hire because I can't pay them."

"Yes, damn it," Ned concluded. "From whatever side you look at it, you still need people at work, otherwise you will lose all this year's crop."

Thoughtfully, looking down, Ned, took out the bag where he kept his pipe and tobacco. Slowly, with movements that betrayed concern, he stuffed tobacco in his pipe. It was an old pipe, yellowish-brown, stained by the tobacco smoke gathered along the years. Like the farm, he had inherited the pipe from his grandfather. Ned seldom smoked—usually in difficult moments, when he had to make an important decision, or on holiday-like celebrations. His grandpa raised him. His father had been in the military and had been away most of the time. He had died quite young, and so Ned remained to live at this farm, to love it and to give it all the sweat of his brow.

Trying to ease the tension, Ned commented, "Damn good coffee, Donna. Why don't you make me such a coffee every morning?"

"How can you say that? God forgive me! Don't I make it and put it on your table? Yes, but you jump out of the house like a bullet and disappear. I don't see you until noon."

"You are right woman! Too much work to do, and I forget about coffee!"

"Well, do you see? Then stop teasing me," added Donna, smiling. Turning to Emily, she continued, "In the morning, he is like a madman. He has no time for anything. He rushes outside and is gone for the rest of the day."

They chatted for a while longer, Ned puffing from his pipe, all sipping coffee and eating Donna's honey-biscuits.

Eventually, Emily put down her cup of coffee, and choosing her words carefully, said, "Ned, I need your help. That's why I am here now."

"Sure Emily. Sure. Anything. Just let us know and we'll try to help you. You know that."

"Oh, well, my dear," added Donna. "We are honoured that you came to us for help. We are going to do anything. Just let us know."

"Look what is about: I want to completely sell off the animal stock, but I want to make a good price on them. You know better than me how these kinds of businesses are going. You, Ned, have good contacts with a lot of people in the field. And this for years. I hope you can recommend one of them, maybe the best and most trustful you know."

"And then, with the land, what are you going to do?"

"I said and you know it too well, the farm is too big to be worked by only two people. So, I want to send Michael to school. I want them, my and Bill's children to have a better future. Let them look for an easier life in a city. Let them all go to school. I don't know … that's what I think now. Two nights ago, Bill appeared to me in a dream. And he said the same: sell the farm and take care of the children and their futures."

"Well," said Ned, deepening in his chair. "Difficult business. As far as I understand, you want to first sell the cattle, horses and so on, then the farm. Is that right?"

"Yes Ned. Animals first and then the farm. Yes, I don't want it to be heard that I am selling everything. That's why I came to you, because I know I can count on you—on your discretion. I also need a fair price. I've been working hard all my life and I can't afford to give it away for nothing."

"Of course! Well, so that's decided." Ned puffed away. "But where are you going to live, once you have sold the farm?"

"I'm going to town, Ned, to be close to my children. I would like to buy a house there, and I can open a grocery store. I'd know what to do."

"Oh, my dear!" exclaimed Donna, clapping her hands. "I can really help here, as I have a good acquaintance who works in the branch. Yes, I know lots of distributors in the fields. And also, we could ask around. Don't worry. We will think about this, too." She continued, "I find the store an excellent idea. So, you really want to open a store?"

"So, just like that? Do you want to open a grocery store?" Ned chimed in.

"Yes, Ned. I am not quite new with this business. I used to work in a shop like that when I was young. Some things may have changed, but a lot of things have to be like they were in my time. I am not worried about purchasing the vegetables; I know lots of farmers who deliver produce to shops. We've done the same thing ourselves many times, too."

"Oh, yes, Emily. I know you've delivered fine vegetables to stores," Ned added.

Again, there was silence around the table. Everyone was with his or her own thoughts about all these things and their lives. Ned broke the silence.

"So, this means you are going to start a new life. Yes, the kids need your support now more than ever. The loss of a parent must have left a deep wound on them. What we are doing here? We are left here to work the land; our children have made their own way and do not want to know about the farm. Julie, our eldest daughter, works in a New York law firm. She called us last week. She says that everything is perfect for her. The boy, Nick, is settled in Vancouver and has his own business there. When was the last time he called us, Donna?"

"Well, a few months ago. When he called for your birthday, Ned, don't you remember?"

"That's right. Yes. Both children scattered like grains of sand in a desert. We'll stay here until the end," said Ned thoughtfully, closing his eyes.

Again, a heavy silence fell over the group.

Eventually, Emily rose slowly.

"Thank you for the coffee and biscuits, my dear. Also, for your advice and support. I knew I could count on you. I and Bill owe you a lot."

"Don't say that, dear Emily. What have we done over the years but help each other ... as our parents, grandparents and those before them did? As farmers do, right?" She paused before continuing. "And I know who should I talk to; and you are right when you say that this matter should be done with patience and wisely".

"Look, next week I am going into town and I'll stop by the Farmers' Association headquarters. I know who I should ask to recommend someone honest and qualified in the sale of husbandry stock. His name is Jeff. He is the best to recommend someone for this. I will tell him it'll happen in a fortnight; I think. Actually, I will tell him to contact you personally, so that you can set up an appointment. So, don't worry, everything will be fine. Go on with work as before. It seems you will have a good harvest this year."

"I wish you the same—have one of the best! And now I have to go. Forgive me for keeping you from work!"

"No need for excuses," interrupted Donna. "How many times do we see each other in a year? We've been glad you came to us and we want you to know that we'll help you. We are honoured to do it, as among friends."

All of them went out. There, Donna and Emily hugged tightly. Then, holding hands, they looked at each other and drops of tears were gathering in their eyes.

Emily's chin was trembling with emotion. "When I will see you again?"

"Soon, Emily," replied Donna, and then added, "and we will have somewhere to stay when we come to town."

"Oh, Donna! We'll be looking forward to seeing you!"

Now they were really crying. Even Ned was obviously touched.

Turning to him, Emily said, "Thank-you, Ned. Many thanks ... from Bill, too. I know you were lifelong friends."

He couldn't answer. With a lump in his throat, his cheeks trembling nervously, eyes from under the brim of his hat filled with tears, he was only able to mumble:

"Go Emily. Go carefree. We will help you with everything we can. May the Lord be with you!"

With that, he offered his arm, helping her to climb onto her cart. Emily took the whip and started the cart on the road back home. In the doorway, two figures were waving at her, leaning shoulder to shoulder, as they had done all their married lives. With wet eyes, they both peered at the cart that soon disappeared among the wheat and sunflower fields.

****

In that darkness, he lay on his stomach in a sort of trench, trying to defuse the bomb. Around him, the explosions did not cease, and pieces of earth fell on the back of his neck and back. Keeping his chin on his chest, he was trying to illuminate the target object as well as possible. He pointed the beam of light at those wires, at the same time, trying to identify them with his fingers.

He had volunteered for the army, and then had spent a few weeks in the unit's barracks. He had joined the Bomb Detonation Service, being intensively prepared for it.

Their training was structured on the information gathered by "Intel.".

There were many kinds of places handmade bombs could be hidden—on a bicycle frame, or in a wallet "carelessly" dropped on the street.

Their commander, Colonel Steward, loved authenticity, and wanted to train the team in conditions as close as possible to reality. That reason made him always "slip" a few real projectiles among the training ones. No one knew which of them the real ones were, and some trainees had been injured, but the Bomb Disposal Unit was seen as of utmost importance for the commanders, regardless of those minor details.

Their training sessions were so close to reality with whatever they were defusing, which resulted in broken bones, leg amputations, or even worse.

In Afghanistan, the enemy was fighting a fierce guerrilla war and they had to be prepared to face it, no matter what.

His group was scheduled to enter the field in a few weeks, and the pressure on them was enormous. They had to learn in a terribly short time and to be the best if they wanted to survive.

For Tommy, all these conditions seemed normal. He was used to long arduous training sessions in the hockey league.

Hockey! It was like yesterday.

He had been badly injured, and his recovery took far too long. Despite the doctors' efforts to put him back together, he couldn't go back on the ice. Refusing any kind of help, he tried unsuccessfully to do other things, wasting a lot of money without finding his place. Eventually, he went broke. Suddenly, he enlisted in the army. A few hours later he was inhaling the dust from the training ground, marching somewhere in the tail of a platoon.

But he didn't care. He had to do something. And then, where should he go?

He looked intensely at the pile of threads in front of him. With two fingers, he removed two wires. He pushed back his helmet, to protect from splinters. With his left hand holding the wires and leaning on his chest, he was groping in one of the pockets looking for the special pliers, to cut and take off the insulation and bypass the circuit.

The blasts were continuing through the night.

"Lord! That had been close," he thought. "I bet this time the "butcher" has hidden several real projectiles. That's for sure." That's what they called Steward, the commander of Bomb Disposal Unit. He wasn't content until he put a few recruits on a stretcher every week.

"Listen to me, you ducklings! You will thank me, once you get there!" He used to say in his speeches in front of the troops. "Pay careful attention to instructions and swallow the training ground, otherwise it will gobble you."

At the beginning there were one hundred of them. In the first two weeks, thirty-two gave up, seven of them were wounded, and some of the others scattered to other fight units. They had not met the requirements; it was not for them there. But for Tommy, hell was normal.

Military training and playing for the NHL had been hard and long. Every few days a match and, in between, exhausting trainings. They were part of his life. To feel squeezed like a lemon when you fall on the bench after training sessions and a few hours later muscles and whole-body ache as if you had been beaten. For him, pain was perfectly normal.

For these, compared with his mates, Tommy did not suffer at all. Only this time, it was different.

He had managed to remove the insulation off the wires. He put the pliers aside, leaned back on his belly and chest, and started looking in his pocket for the shunt wire. With his fingertips, he carefully pulled one of them. He put it between his lips, and with the back of the other hand, he wiped his forehead, covered with sweat. He started working again, keeping the two threads apart. Red and blue; these had to be cut. If he was wrong and made a mistake, he will not sleep this night; troubled, tormenting work waited for him.

The cannonade was ongoing, almost breaking his eardrum. He overlapped a piece of wire over the uninsulated part and sealed them tightly. Then, with the other hand, using his fingertips, he tried several times to tie the other end to the bare portion of the red wire, but each time, he dropped the threads. He tried again, desperate that he wasn't able. He touched again the strings with heis fingertips...

He opened his eyes. He caught himself touching, with his fingertips, the perfusion tube. So then, he dreamed. He was still in the Emergency Department.

But, when did they put in a new drip? Anyway, there were still a few hours until daybreak. He knew it. A few hours alone, with himself and with his thoughts. Alone ...

****

At Henderson's farm, everything was going as usual, the same beaten paths: Michael taking care of the animals, Emily with the chores around and inside the house.

As if more determined now, after the decision had been made, Emily was working harder than ever. Everything had to be perfect and look good when she was to sell the farm. Their future lives depended on it.

Michael was amazed how his mother became lately, paying attention to all trifles.

"Michael, did you open some new bales for the animals?"

"Yes, mom. Haven't I been doing this for a while, twice a week? You know I do, don't you?"

"Don't be upset darling. I just asked."

It was something different every day.

"Michael, it's time to clean the fountain pool. It's summer and this needs to be done."

-"Yes, Mom, I already did it two days ago. Don't worry."

- "Oh, good; I just wanted to know," she replied.

At the beginning, Michael was a bit surprised by her reactions and tried to understand or find an explanation. Finally, getting deep into work, he left her alone and forgot about it.

Life continued its apparently quiet course at the farm. When people have animals and there is a demand for quality and quantity of the production, care of them must be taken seriously, like they were precious children.

Every evening, they put the milkers on the cows, and then later, when they finished, the milk was put into a cooler. The next day, a cister came to take the milk after the amount of fat was measured. For years the milk they provided had a high amount of fat and they were trying to maintain that standard. That meant more money received on the milk delivered. Their farm had a little of everything.

Besides the quite large number of cows, they also had a few horses, goats—not too many and kept around the house—and a lot of chickens, ducks, geese and turkeys. All these animals required a lot of work.

In the evening, exhausted, it was so hard for them to keep their heads up when they were trying to eat something; usually a slice of toast with butter and a jug of milk. Then they fell into a deep sleep, so that next day they could start all over again. It was Bill who knew the purpose and time of every thing.

None of them said it, but there were times when each of them waited for Bill to appear in his blue overalls ... from the corner of the stable, at the edge of the wheat field, or anywhere. That was harder to take than work.

****

Less than two weeks later, they received the long-awaited phone call from Mr. Jeff, secretary of the Farmers' Association, telling them that Ned had asked to recommend a specialist in the sale of animal stocks. He had found someone, talked to him and left them his phone number. They had to phone him; he was waiting for their call, and they would agree on the procedure for liquidating the stock. First of all, he wanted to see the animals.

Upon hearing the news, Emily suddenly became alert as a sort of tension grasped her mind. Now that the plan had started to unfold, a kind of fear—more an anxiety, crept into her soul. She began to have doubts about the decision she had made.

"It's got to be a good plan," she was telling herself. "What else could I have done? Bring my girls here ... ask them to leave school? And what would their futures be? Should I hire more workers? No! That's the way!" she told herself. "We are going forward. Bill told me to do that in a dream. It wouldn't have happened like that, without a reason. Everything makes sense. Doesn't it?

But I have to tell the boy. I can't avoid it. And then, the animals have to be prepared".

On Sunday, she told Michael to bring the cattle to the pasture near the house and to leave them there. Michael was not surprised to hear that. He had become accustomed to his mother's way of life lately, so he complied without comment.

He finished moving them and was about to go to the stables, when he heard his mother call again: "Hi, Michael. Michael, come home please. I need to have a word with you."

This time, the boy couldn't help himself: "Yes, Mom, what's the rush? I was going to the stables to change the animals' bedding."

"Come in, please, son. I need to talk to you inside."

The boy felt the change floating in the air. Something was going to happen. He slowly went down the valley on the path that led to the house.

He left his boots outside and went into the house. A strong smell of baked dough made him stop.

"Ahh, the smell of sponged cakes in the oven! What had happened to my mother? Cakes just for the two of us? Waiting for someone?" He entered the kitchen, wondering what was going on.

The cakes were already on the table. Michael looked at the beautifully embroidered tablecloth; he hadn't seen such a lavish kitchen table in a long time. Emily showed him a chair to sit down.

"Have a seat here, Michael. In a few minutes, the cakes will have cooled and will be ready to eat. Pour some wine into glasses, please."

Obediently, Michael poured wine from a glass carafe into the two glasses. Eventually, Emily sat down at the table in front of the boy, and, lifting one of the glasses, looked briefly at Michael and said, "Let's toast to the good times, Michael. To times spent in this house. To the honorable and beautiful life on our farm!"

"Yes, Mom, but what's happened?" he looked rather scared.

"Nothing, my dear. God, I wish Bill were here, God rest him in peace!" and then she continued. "Michael, you have your own path and destiny and you have to follow it. Working on the farm is no longer an option for your life."

"But, Mom, I like it and you know, I can work the way Dad did."

"That's not the point, my dear. Times have changed; everything has changed lately. Being a farmer is no longer a life to be proud of. Corporations have swallowed farms, one by one. We've been lucky for a while ... coped as best as we could, and we've been able to keep our customers.

"Listen to me, Michael. Your father and I wanted a different future for our children. That's why your sisters are at school in town. Bill wanted to keep you near the farm for a while, to help him and to teach you how to manage a farm, as a man in our family. Then we were planning to send you to school to choose your path for the future."

Michael snapped, "But Mom, I don't want to leave!"

"My dear, listen carefully, please; and I am not going to say twice: poor Bill is gone, the harvest season is coming. The two of us can't do all the farm work anyway."

"We could hire a few seasonal workers," replied Michael.

"We can't do that, my dear. There is no money. And I don't want to hire seasonal workers and get into debt. If Emma and Sarah would leave school and come to help us ... But this, won't happen. You know, my dear, your father modernized our farm, bought equipment every year to produce more and cheaper and we saved some money, but he didn't have time to do it. And we had just finished with investments this year. He didn't have time. Oh, God, give me strength to do it!"

"But, Mom, what we can do?"

"Michael, listen to me! We are going to sell our animal stock and then the farm. Then we will move to the city. You will go to school, and your sisters will continue their studies. I am going to open a grocery store. This is the plan, my dear." She continued, "I had a dream, and in the dream, Bill was telling me to take care of the family, and that's what I'll do. But don't say a word to anyone. A lot of things depend on that. We have to sell everything at the best price for us. We cannot afford to waste a cent."

For a while, Michael remained silent, then he poured himself another glass of wine, which he drank in one gulp. He was staring at the tablecloth embroidery. Emily felt that he was at the point of making a decision.

She reached out her hand over the table and shook Michael's hand affectionately.

"Please, Michael, try to understand. We didn't want you to work on the farm forever."

She got up, turned her back, grabbed one of the cakes, and cut it into slices. Then, still with her back turned, she said, "And then, you can help me at the grocery shop from time to time." She was relying on his pride as a young man—the man of the family.

"Yes, Mom, I will definitely help you. I already have some ideas."

At these words, Emily closed her eyes and breathed deeply ... "The boy had agreed." That's what she feared the most. He was still too young to think like a man. With shaking hands, she placed the slices of cake on the plate, and returned to the table

"Come on Michael, take a bite. This cake is the best when it's warm."

For a while they ate in silence. Suddenly, Emily broke the silence. "Michael, I have all my hope in you; I am depending on you."

"Don't worry, Mom!" the boy answered hastily.

Emily smiled to herself. He warmed to the idea due to the wine. I have to bring him back to reality, she mused.

"Listen, my dear; I have already talked to Ned and Donna Simon about the plan. Ned has some acquaintances in the meat industry. I asked him to find someone—a professional in selling animal stocks—to help us. Michel, dear, everything should be done quickly, quietly, and without much publicity. No one should know that we are going to sell the farm, too. That's why we'll liquidate the stock first. And we have to get a fair price for whatever we sell. We can't afford otherwise. This is our lifelong work—mine, Bill's, and yours."

"Yes mother, but can't we sell the animals one by one?"

"We don't have that much time, Michael, having the harvest on the field. We have to sell it in a few weeks and for a good price. That's it. Do you understand why, my dear?"

"Yes, Mom. Then as you say. When are we leaving?"

"We don't know that yet. One step at a time. We'll see. That specialist will tell us soon. He will want to see the stock and then he will tell us what to do. Until then, not a word about it. And we are working as before. That's why I turned to Ned for help, as I know he won't tell anyone … neither he nor Donna. We have been neighbours for decades and we have always helped each other".

"And now that you know everything, what do you have to say?"

"Mom, I can work and keep the farm. That's what I mean. Maybe I'll need a few extra-arms at harvest, but I can work it!"

"That's not the point, my dear. We wanted something else for you; another life and another future. That's why we are selling everything and will move to the city."

"Okay, Mom. But you have to know that I am going to help you with the store," he said in a determined voice.

"We'll see how we'll deal with the store. Until then, please go and feed the chickens, and then move the cattle to another pasture, one not too far from home. We still have a lot to talk about tonight. Come home as soon as you finish, my dear."

"Okay, Mom. Now, I'll go to change the bedding for the cattle, then give the grain to the poultry, and then I'll move the cattle."

He went to change his shirt. Soon he left the house and started climbing the path to the hill. Emily looked after him for a long time, thinking, "It's good I told him the truth and he understood. I have him on my side. I don't know what I would have done if he were against the idea. He is the same as his father. And if he's committed to something, he gets it done. Just like Bill. My dear Bill! Where are you? Where are you?"

****

With his sack slung over his back and his coat belted with a scrap of rope, Tommy turned the corner of the narrow alley, dim and littered with trash, and
    stepped out onto the boulevard. He was on his way to the park, looking for a quiet place to spend the day until nightfall. The boulevard was buzzing with activity. Cars jammed the street, the sidewalks were packed, and people bumped into each other, trying to weave their way through.

Not fifty yards down, shouts, whistles, and a murmur of voices gathered in front of him, drawing his attention. Tommy edged closer to the crowd, rising on his toes to see what was happening.

There was Josie, the madwoman, swaying from one foot to the other in her boat-like shoes, dressed in rags that made her look like a walking rainbow. She was yelling at the onlookers, cursing them with fiery insults. Her face was lushed, her eyes wild—she was drunk as all hell, and it was plain as day.

The scene grew uglier as Josie got more worked up. A few young men started taunting her, throwing scraps of bread, tomatoes, even bits of asphalt they found on the ground.

"Boooo! Boooo, you drunk! Careful skating on the asphalt, or you'll fall and crack yourself open!"

"Pigs! Lice-ridden scum! Kiss my ass, all of you!" Josie shot back, swaying as she turned to glare at each heckler around her.

Tommy carefully inched forward through the crowd, trying to get closer to her. Just then, Broad Palm appeared from nowhere, stepping into the circle. He grabbed Josie, lifted her off her feet, and, with Tommy's help, they pulled her away and down one of the dark side streets, out of sight.

Josie screamed bloody murder until they finally set her down between two big cardboard boxes. She quieted down for a bit, only to flare up again at odd intervals, her mind spiraling.

"I haven't seen her this bad in a long time," said Broad Palm.

"Yeah," Tommy muttered. "What do we do? If we leave her here, she won't make it to morning. They won't let her in the shelter like this. Hell of a thing."

"You know what," Tommy continued, "let's give her a ton of water to drink. Even if she wets herself, we'll change her clothes and try to get her inside. We'll prop her up at the door. It'll pass."

They got to work. It was a struggle; she fought them, but they managed to get enough water into her to sober her up a bit. Changing her clothes was easier. Fat Jim showed up in the meantime, and together, they'd done it—rescued her from her own demons, the hard hand of fate, pushing her through for a few more days in this wretched life...

****

One morning, he received a strange visit. A man of average height, dressed entirely in black, with a round face, fair hair, black eyes behind the glasses with a wire frame placed over a snub nose, stepped hesitantly into the room.

Slightly hunched over, he was holding a book with black covers against his chest.

"The man in black," Tommy thought, lying on the bed and leaning on one elbow. He had just finished his breakfast and, seeing the unexpected guest, he widened his eyes, without hiding his bewilderment.

"Good morning, sir! I am Chaplain Peter, and I serve at St. Andrew's Chapel in this hospital," he introduced himself, bowing politely.

Looking closer at him, Tommy noticed the collar of his robe. He understood. This time, a Pastor. Why not? He had had many "counsellors", so "well-intentioned" that he was systematically deprived of his income. Now, he was as poor as a church mouse. Like any of that mattered now. Let it be, a Preacher, if he wants!

"What can I do for you, Priest, if necessary? How can I help you?"

"Hearing from the hospital staff who you are and how you got here, I thought that I could help you, in my way, sir. That's why I'm here. You have gone through terrible trials!"

"The man is onto something; like a hyena sniffing a prey!" Tommy thought.

"You say you want to help me, Father? Very nice, but you see, I want to stay this way, as poor as I have always been."

"I didn't mean material help. In fact, my powers are quite limited in this regard. I myself live a modest, pure life protected by the teachings of the Holy Gospel. I am talking about the spiritual help I could give you, sir."

"You see, Father, I don't remember asking for such help."

"'If you can help, don't wait for requests. Do it!' teaches the Holy Gospel."

"You have an answer for everything, don't you, Father?"

"I strive as much as I can to guide and to bring warmth and comfort into people's souls, sir."

"Warmth and comfort," Tommy thought, and then he said aloud, "Where these were when I was starving and getting lost in the cold? How many times when I lost consciousness did, I wake up robbed of the few things I had? Warmth and comfort? Where were all these treasures then?"

"You must not lose hope, son. God is great and you will find Him if you know how to look for Him within your prayers."

"You amaze me, Father! You really have an answer to everything!"

Shyly, the Minister looked down at the floor. For a few moments there was an embarrassing silence, while the Priest, still standing, was holding tight the book with his hands at his chest as if he were afraid to lose it. Tommy also noticed a cross that hung from a gold chain around his neck.

Eventually, the Priest broke the silence:

"If you don't mind sir, can I ask you a question?"

"If you are here, why not? Shoot."

"Can I ask you how long it has been since your last confession?"

"Oho!" exclaimed Tommy, embarrassed and scratching his head. "Let me think, yes ... Hm! Well. It should be some time. As far as I can remember, I was in high school. Should be a couple of decades back. Satisfied?"

Taking a step forward, the Chaplain said, "And you wouldn't want to do it now?"

Bending his head, Tommy reflected for a few moments, then looked inquisitively at the Minister and said, "No, Father. Not now, anyway. You took me by surprise ... a little fast. I don't know, maybe another time."

"Well, son, if you are not ready, I'll come and see you again, another time. Maybe then?"

"As you wish, Father. We'll see."

The priest bent and headed for the door, where he turned to face Tommy again and lifted the cross saying, "God bless you!"

He walked out as quietly as he had entered.

"Whatever you say, Father" whispered Tommy, and he sat back again.

That night he couldn't sleep.

****

"Hello Ms.!" said the man, getting out of the car and slamming the door. "I'm Thomson, Neil Thomson. We talked on the phone about liquidating the stock. As we agreed, here I am to evaluate the animals."

At first, Emily didn't know how to take the tall man, dressed in a navy-blue jacket, dark trousers, wearing a yellowing cowboy hat, and genuine cowboy boots. With thick eyebrows, a rich black mustache, and two piercing brown eyes, he reached her in few steps, grabbed her hand and shook it vigorously.

"Of course, Mr. Thomson. Can I call you Neil? It's more convenient for me. I'm Emily, by the way, the owner of the farm."

"Sure, ma'am. Call me Neil, if you like."

"Well, what do we start with, ma'am?"

"You better call me Emily."

"Well, Emily, what would you like to start with?"

"With a cheesecake and a glass of wine," she said.

"Oh, thank you! I certainly won't make the mistake of refusing a cheesecake made by a genuine farmer!"

"Please, come inside, Neil," she urged him. She invited him into the living room and, while Neil was enjoying the dessert and a glass of wine, they started talking about the cattle stock. Then they went outside and headed for the stables on the path that went up the hill. She had not taken the animals out of the stables, knowing that Neil would be interested to see them and their level of care.

"But you have a very beautiful farm here, Emily, really beautiful," said Neil looking around at some combine harvesters.

"Yes, I and my late husband, Bill, did our best to have all the equipment needed to work properly at our farm, but he has left ahead of time. Now it's just me and our son. But the two of us can't hold the farm; we can't go on like this. We have to sell. That's why I asked Ned to recommend someone, a specialist to help us. That is how I got to you."

They continued to climb the path.

"I've worked hard all my life, Neil, and now that I am closing out, I want a fair price for the animals. I think I deserve that. Ned said that you were good at these things and he recommended you."

"Emily, please, you have to know that right now the market is very volatile. A good price is probable, but not guaranteed. And you want to do it quickly and well."

They reached the stables and stopped at the entrance of the first of them, looking at each other, both serious and focused.

"Yes, that's what I want; quickly and well. And for that, I will pay you as I said: a percentage of the sale price. I hope you will be satisfied, and I want to be satisfied as well."

"Emily, I have to say once again: the prices on the market are not steady, but I didn't say we can't make it. We will have to increase our area of selling, maybe to go to other states. I will investigate with my contacts. But, first let me see the stock, to see what you have to offer."

They entered the first stable. Meanwhile, Michael arrived and Emily introduced him to Neil:

"This is my son, Michael, my only helper at the farm."

"Hello, young man! But I have to recognise you are hardworking and industrious; you have the courage to watch so many animals alone. Ned told me what a great boy you are. A real cowboy!"

"I'm trying to do my best," the boy replied modestly.

The dim light inside the stable didn't allow Neil to immediately see things around him, but as soon as he got used to the light, he couldn't help but notice the order and cleanness inside, and he had seen many stables. He was very impressed.

Michael had been in charge of cleaning the barns, and he did a wonderful job, cleaning the stables and all the manure forks and other tools, putting down fresh straw for cattle bedding, and tidying up all around, like in a shop.

Neil went from one stall to another, inspecting animals, and cages as well. He entered some of them and checked the animal from head to hooves. In front of others, he spent only a few moments. He wrote in his notebook.

Old Bill had wanted every animal to have its own stall, and he didn't save anything for their comfort. Only a few animals were kept in larger spaces, four in a stable.

After Neil finished the examination of all the stalls, accompanied by Emily and Michael, they stopped outside and Neil, looking at his notes, said, "It's too soon to discuss details, but what I saw, I liked. Emily, it would be great if we could bring potential buyers here. I have some contacts. I have ideas and I'll sleep on them. In a few days, I will call you and follow up."

"Tell me, do you have any papers from the veterinary checks? Do you keep a record?'

"I don't know where the records would be; I am not sure where to look. Bill took care of that."

"Michael, do you know anything?"

"Nothing, Mom."

"Damn it," said Neil thoughtfully.

For a while, Neil didn't say anything and continued to keep his eyes on the ground. Finally, raising his gaze, he looked at Emily.

"Look, Emily, this is my advice: I'm sending a veterinarian from our organization. You'll have to pay him for the services, but I assure you, it's worth it. He will examine your stock and will write a certificate for each animal and he will evaluate them. You will not be sorry for the money spent. When he buys something, the customer wants to have a warrantee that what he buys is in good condition. It's exactly what we offer in order to get the best price. What do you say?"

"Of course. As you advise, Neil. You are the specialist, and I trust your experience."

"Emily, I can't guarantee you great prices, but I can tell you that if you don't have health certificates for any animal, you cannot ask for a good price. You have to believe me."

"I understand perfectly. I am not as ignorant as you think. Send him here, and just let me know when he's coming."

"Ok, we have a deal; it remains to wait for my call!"

Saying goodbye, he climbed into his car and left.

Mother and son were left behind in front of their home, worried about their unsure future.

****

The convoy of armoured vehicles passed through the gates of the military base in a cloud of dust. The base had been built a few months earlier, housing special units operating in that region of Afghanistan. Turning around the corner of a barrack, they stopped in front of a large hangar, built of special materials, where embarkations and disembarkations of those who left or returned from missions took place.

Gracefully, like in a ballet, the line of cars unfolded, each car stopping parallel to the next. At a signal, a handful of men dressed in camouflage uniforms, covered in desert dust, spilled out. Their helmets, goggles, faces were the same—covered with the same dust, yellow and slightly reddish in places. Only their eyes, protected by their masks, were clean.

In small groups, men carrying weapons and bags with equipment on their backs, were walking towards the hangar. They were agitated, shouting, joking.

"Hi Tommy. You've added more victory on your line?" a short man in an immaculate uniform, without a helmet, greeted him.

"Yes, Jimmy, I was lucky this time, too. As you can see, I am back. What about you? When are you leaving?"

"In about half an hour or so. I still have some things to fix and then we're gone. We're heading north. Well, what's it like up there? You have to know; you swallowed desert dust longer than me."

"How is it? The same shit, Jimmy, but you don't work in open field; there are many large rocks, and those mountains could hide an entire army ... even the devil. I never liked when I operated there. Too many ambushes. But what's the rush in that part now?"

"Word is that we must clean up a road, a vital one for our convoys."

"And does your shit freeze in your ass there."

"Hey, you, philosopher, kiss my ass!"

"And you, artist, and you! But listen, Jimmy, be careful there. That's all I'm saying. Don't expose yourself too much. Take care of yourself, cover your back permanently, especially for snipers."

"Now I see why you're so scared!"

"As you say, Jimmy, as you say. Yes, but still; be careful there, that's all I am telling you."

"'Bye samurai! See you in three days!"

"'Bye, desert ferret!"

Round-shouldered due to his backpacks full of equipment, Tommy joined the others entering the hangar. Inside, there were long tables where they unloaded their backpacks. Specialized personnel checked the packs and placed them in special cabinets.

The men were happy to have a shower, a clean uniform, and the lunch at the canteen, sprinkled with some beers; never enough.

Next, they went to their bunks, where sleep would come or not. Many times, Tommy couldn't fall sleep, was troubled by nightmares, or slept with frequent interruptions. From some reasons, when he returned from a mission, he was haunted by the most terrible images possible. He often woke up, drank a lot of water, and then went back to bed trying to fall asleep again. The images of the last mission kept coming back to his mind, like a playback. Sometimes he was tormented by terrible leg pains.

As usual, he entered into the routine of coming back from a mission; lingered in the shower, trying to wash all the dust gathered on his skin and pores, and if were possible, in his thoughts. Standing under the running water of the shower, he thought how wonderful it would be if the water cleaned not only the body, but also the soul. In the shower, his thoughts flew freely.

Yes, that last mission had been a rather difficult one. While they were cleaning a minefield, the enemy was putting them back in the same operating place. It was an epic struggle. Sisyphean job. So, the mission was extended to the upper limit allowed by their equipment and supplies.

The last two days, he had chewed only chewing gum. Although rationed, the food was gone. The same with water, but after a day without water, he felt his throat dry and his tongue swollen. He couldn't stand when he swallowed; he felt stings. He was lucky with Uncle Sam gum; it helped somehow.

Eventually, the withdrawal order arrived.

They had followed the road with frequent search stops for detection of possible mines placed in the way of their convoy.

All of these demands stretched their nerves to the limit.

When they got closer and saw the barracks, the reunion with their comrades and removal of the equipment slowly took them back to their normal lives. But then they started feeling the tiredness. It was like someone had poured lead on their legs.

Mission completed and still alive, this time too.

It was what Tommy was thinking of while he was lying on his bed in the ward of the hospital.

He remembered how he struggled to fall asleep on the first night after a mission.

The morning had come and they had gone to the canteen for breakfast. They had just started eating when the news arrived: Jimmy was gone. The car he was in had been blown up by a mine, well hidden among other fake mines. The enemy was playing with them a hard and dirty game.

Now, lying on the hospital bed, starring at the ceiling, he was thinking about all his comrades and Jimmy ... especially Jimmy. Tears flowed down his cheeks, leaving two wet traces, and then landed on his pillow. Tears in the memory of fallen comrades, fighting oblivion.

****

Unable to help herself, Emily was in a constant state of alertness, and it seemed to her the days were flying by. In all that time, many people passed by Henderson's farms.

The first was Neil, who came with a vet and his assistant. The matter lasted several days, during which time each animal had been carefully examined, and then a certificate was issued. It was as if it would never end.

Finally, the last animal was examined and the last certificate issued. Dr. Adams didn't like wasting time at his office, so he completed all certificates, as well as the necessary stamps, in the field. He had just finished all the work when Neil appeared. He and Emily carefully examined all certificates, one by one. Emily signed a check for the doctor, who raised his hat politely, shook her hand, and left.

Left alone, the two look at each other and Neil said: "Emily, I saw the certificates and I have to congratulate you. I can say that for a long time, I have not seen such a healthy stock of animals. Just a few small insignificant injuries normal for such a big farm. Now I can bring you clients; I will come with them personally. In the meantime, you prepare the animals for each visit. I will give you a call beforehand. So, keep the stables clean, with fresh bedding at ..."

He stopped.

"Oh, forgive me. I forgot. I didn't have to remind you of anything; I didn't mean to offend you. You know very well what you have to do."

"Don't worry, Neil, it's okay; let us not forget anything we have to do. I want a good price on animals, you know that."

"I guarantee it will be a fair price, Emily."

After that, like the vet, he said goodbye and went away.

Left alone, Emily was overwhelmed with thoughts of severe hopelessness and heaviness came over her. She had lost her confidence. The snowball had begun to roll down and could not be stopped. The fact that the money had begun to slip away through her fingers made her feel insecure. Although she knew it was necessary, she couldn't get used to the thought. She felt uncomfortable and vulnerable. She had known that a moment like that was coming, but she was not able to see the outcome.

The check she had signed to the doctor seemed to burn her fingers, but she hoped the trembling of her fingers had gone unnoticed.

There was nothing else to be done. She was alone, a little scared, and yet still very eager to succeed. She had to spend sparingly, but these expenses were absolutely necessary, she reminded herself.

Days were passing and lots of potential buyers began to come to the farm, sometimes alone, or accompanied by Neil. All of them looked at the animals—examining them, evaluating them with knowledgeable eyes.

But certainly not one of them knew or cared about the dogs roaming the paths of the farm or around the house. Nor about that naughty puppy, who had grown up now, with strong legs and wide chest.

He had established himself as a leader among his brothers and sisters. This sense of superiority was coming perhaps from his ancestors through natural selection. Even the oldest dogs on the farm avoided conflicts with him. He made his den in the farthest corner of the last stable, up the hill close to the forest. Always far from the others dogs, showing some tolerance only to his mother. He used to come down when food was brought to them either by

Emily or Michael. On these occasions, real battles had taken place, and after them, the toughest and strongest left with the best and biggest piece. Most of the time, he had been that one.

He, Ruby, as his masters had named him, attacked any dog who had grabbed the best piece of bone or meat, to make it throw it in a hurry to escape Ruby's ruthless attacks. He would bite in a flash, above the snout, sometimes aiming for the jugular, after knocking him down, hitting from lateral. Thus, he had become the alpha dog, and the other dogs accepted him as such.

Their lives at the farm unfolded beautifully for them; free dogs— free to tread any path, explore the nearby forests, and be regularly fed. Free and happy.

****

A light knock on the door. Another one ... and again. "Who the hell is it?" Tommy thought. "Come in" he said.

"Forgive me, but the door was ajar." The round head of the priest, nose adorned with glasses with silver frame, appeared.

"May I?" he mumbled shyly.

"Yes, do come in. Didn't I tell you already?" he answered, a bit surprised by the Chaplain's humility.

Eventually, he was in. The same black suit, black shoes, and the same black book with black covers, in one hand at his chest.

"Since you have come, take a chair and sit down, Father," Tommy invited.

With slow movements, the priest moved a chair near Tommy's bed and sat down. He was holding the book tightly, as if clinging to it and what it was inside of it. His other hand caressed the cross hanging at his neck.

"What do you have in your hand, Pastor? I see you with that book again."

"It's the Holy Bible, son. It gives us our Christian stories and parables. Every good Christian should respect and cherish it."

"Well, well. And the cross?" Tommy pointed to the priest's neck.

"This is the cross that I wear permanently. I use it in the holy liturgies, as well as in confessions of the faithful."

"I see. That's why you brought it with you! You want me to confess!"

"No, sir. I told you, sir. I wear it almost every moment. And about your confession, of course, if you are ready."

"What do you mean, 'ready'? Do I have to do anything special first?"

"There are many and various conditions, sir. One who prepares for confession must really be ready to receive the Lord in his soul, confessing his human sins, with a sincere and humble desire to correct and be forgiven."

"You sound like you are reading, Father. What else do I need to do first? To fast, or to prostrate? To pray? What else?"

"Hm," the priest cleared his throat. "As I said, there are different situations, sir. Fasting before confession is welcome, but not always decisive. The desire to correct sins and faith in God are especially important when someone wants confession."

"Well, I have eaten today, Father. Can I still confess?"

"It's up to you. Do you nurture the desire for purification of your soul, to come closer to God in the forgiveness of your sins?"

Looking at the wall, Tommy reflected.

Had he ever had that sincere desire to be close to God? Had he ever wanted to confess, to pray, to ask God for forgiveness?

Bits and pieces of memories rolled out before his eyes ...

The dim pre-dawn light contoured the silhouettes on the battlefield: contorted armored vehicles, charred bodies—others swollen from the heat.

And the smell, the same; that sweeten, rotten when far away and changing when approached. It was sinking deep into nostrils, bringing him close to vomiting.

He was lying among corpses after the ambush had cut off any possibility of retreat. He knew there had to be others, too; they were not all dead, but he was not sure ... He could not shout; the enemy was nearby. He could sense it, and there were some suspicious noises ... he was sure that it was the enemy searching for survivors. There had been more explosions, and the flames continued. So far, he could say he had resisted. He had run out of water.

He crawled and took a few cans with water from the fallen ones. But now, he no longer dared to move. It was almost morning light. He crawled near a "cleaner" corpse, which he thought might be useful to him.

His throat was swollen, but he did not dare to drink. With his eyes looking to the heavens, collapsed on his back, he watched the dawn break. He remained lying that way, waiting, listening to the faded noise of footsteps. The sound came closer and became louder. He tried to guess their movements. They seemed to be walking in zigzag. From time to time, there was a dry sound.

He froze and a cold shiver ran down his spine. He understood what it was: an enemy group coming to liquidate the dying soldiers. Every now and then, with a blow, they stabbed one of the fallen bodies with bayonets attached to the end of their weapons. Thud. Thud.

The panic was so great that he could not move a single inch. He was paralyzed.

The footsteps were approaching. He could see them now. One of them was carrying a flamethrower, and intermittently scattering flames in one direction or another.

He lurched closer to the body beside him, gripping the belt; with the other hand he seized the collar. Slowly, half an inch at a time, with breaks between movements, he covered himself with the corpse as well as he could. The footsteps were coming closer and closer.

Petrified, he suddenly thought intensely of God. For him it was over ... the end. He thought of His power ... how much he could do. He could do everything. If you pray and believe.

He asked God—from his heart, as never before—to let him live for a while ...

Thud, thud, thud ...

The footsteps were so close to his ear.

Then he felt God closest to him, and the footsteps moved away until he could no longer hear them. He had listened to his prayer and let him live.

He returned, looking away from the wall and, as if awakened from a dream, looked at the priest. He had asked him something ... what had he asked him? Oh, yes, something about confession.

"Father, I think I will want to confess someday. But I don't feel ready today."

"No hurry, sir. I said it and I will repeat it: when someone feels ready, with an uplifting desire to come closer to God, he can confess for the forgiveness of his sins. Then is a good time to do so."

A few moments passed in silence. Then they start talking about other things.

"Are you well taken care-of here, sir?"

"I can't tell you about that, Father. As you know, for several years the street has been my home and table. For me, a hospital room, with a clean bed, bathroom and shower seems like the realm of the impossible. It's like I'm already in Paradise."

"Yes, it is good for a person to keep clean—both outside and inside."

"Look, sir, if you want, I could bring you some books with religious themes, books you could read when you feel like it. They will calm you and give you that state of mind and the willingness to come close to God."

"Of course, Father. I'd like to read. Unfortunately, I have to wait. My eyes were affected during fighting in Afghanistan. I am under ophthalmic treatment. The doctor promised me that soon I would have a pair of good glasses for my eyesight. Right now, I can't read and I can't stand the bright light."

"Of course, you have to recover. I was not referring to a certain 'moment'. Anyone must be prepared to receive nourishment.

"But, in general," he continued, "I see that it's going well. You know, I permitted myself to talk to the doctor who takes care of you and he says that you have done amazing things. He had never met anything like it in his career."

'Recover', Tommy thought. What did the priest know?

Blows, contusions, cuts, broken ligaments, having to recover in two days ... otherwise you would lose your place on the hockey team.

Recovery meant intense sessions of physio to recover from a heel, or a dislocated shoulder, elongations, hanging in the belts and many more.

He had gone through many such "recoveries."

"Yes, in my career as a professional hockey player, I went through so many unpleasant events."

"Go forward with the same strength," the priest urged him. "Now, I am leaving you," he said, getting up from the chair. "The hour of the Holy Mass is approaching. I'll come to see you again if you allow me."

"As you wish, Father. I am here, and I am not going anywhere."

"Then, the Lord be with you!" The priest made a cross in the air with the Bible.

And Tommy, without wanting to, whispered, "God help us!"

****

One day, accompanied by Neil, another potential client arrived at Henderson's farm.

Rodrigues was one of the rich, ever-expanding farmers who had bought land in the neighborhood and wanted to increase his stock. He was running a big business; he was not content with a few animals of poor quality—and he was willing to pay top dollar for it.

So far, Emily had had two offers, and Neil hadn't stepped in, which she appreciated. The offers hadn't been bad, but she expected more. The price was good, but just not good enough.

As she agreed with Neil, he and Michael would lead the customers and accompany them to the stables.

"Hi," Rodrigues exclaimed, shaking the lad's hand. "Yes, I know you are strong, boy. I've heard that you and your mother take care of all your animals alone!" He slapped the young man on the back with his huge palm.

"I need people like you at one of my ranches. Ha, ha," he laughed and hit him on the back once more and then he turned around.

"Yes, Neil, finding qualified personnel in this field is increasingly difficult. The young people are heading to the cities and no longer want the hard work to cultivate land and take care of animals."

"But this is the future … the fate of progress. We need to rely more on technology and machinery."

"Leave me alone with machinery; I have enough of it. In the end, a man has to get his hands on it, otherwise the job will not be done."

"Well, you are right. The diligent and intelligent man is, after all, the key to success," Neil added.

"Ha, ha! You caught the idea, didn't you?" Rodrigues said cheerfully.

The three of them were now at the entrance of the first stable.

Señor Rodrigues, a massive man, tall with broad shoulders, wore blue jeans, cowboy boots with pointed toes, and a fine, white shirt showed under a velvet, light brick-coloured coat. Under his white cowboy hat, you could see an authentic Mexican face, with prominent cheekbones, and black eyes under bushy eyebrows covered by a pair of gold-framed glasses. Thick lips, above a thin, black, "Mexican" mustache, and a dimpled chin completed the portrait of this colourful character.

Attire, accent, and behaviour indicated his origin. Noisy of his kind, he had a baritone voice, which would have honoured any respectable opera house.

"And now, let's see what we have here, boy!" he urged Michael, pointing to the door of the first stable, and went inside. The man examined a few cows and then said, "Can we have more light here, boy?"

Michael complied and opened a few windows. The man entered into each box, stroking the animals, talking to them, examining their mouths, eyes, and hooves. He carefully inspected them everywhere, talking to them.

"Wow, my mother! Yes, you are so cute. Why are you so anxious? Let your dad check you. You are a good girl! Ha! Ha!"

Then he moved on to the next stable, with the same scenario. Neil and Michael were surprised when the Mexican came out of the stable with a thin stick and began to dig through fresh manure, examining it, and smelling it here and there.

It took more than an hour before they were finished seeing all the animals in the stables. Then Senor Rodrigues asked to repeat the tour; he wanted to see some of the stock again, especially those with minor wounds.

He was just examining the foot of a cow, where a healing wound was visible.

"This one fell down on a slope and slammed her leg into a cut stump. I kept her in the stable for a few days only," Michael explained.

"I can see, boy. Yes, I can see that. I have a tallow-based tincture. A miracle!

Leave it … it will be fine."

Letting go of the animal's leg, he raised himself up. The rest of the time went the same way. All in all, the man was an expert at cattle.

He had taken off his coat, hanging it at the entrance of each stall. With the sleeves of his shirt rolled up, he examined each animal zealously, with the experience of a specialist.

Sweaty, with perspiration running down his cheeks, on his neck and back, and his shirt no longer white, he got up, pushed his hat back, and methodically started down the hill to his truck, parked in front of the house.

Neil stayed with the boy. He felt that Rodrigues was at the point of making a decision, maybe making an offer, and Neil thought it better not to intervene.

Senor Rodrigues reached the car, opened the door, took a bottle of water from inside and started sipping tactfully. He wiped his face with a handkerchief, then he took a few more gulps.

Finally, he waved to Neil, who understood the message and walked to the truck.

Looking down, Rodrigues started, "You are right. The stock is in a very good condition, but there are many animals. I understand that the woman wants good money for them. I want to solve my problems and help her, too."

"All right. What are you thinking?"

With his hat on the nape and his hands on his hips, he stated his offer.

After the Mexican left, Neil and Michael headed for the house. As soon as they stepped on the deck, Emily arrived in an instant.

"Well?" she prodded, coming to the point immediately.

"Emily, we need to talk. You have an offer. It seems a serious one to me," Neil smiled.

"Perfect! Have a seat you two. I am going to bring some cake and blueberry juice."

When she returned, she sat down, looked at them, and waited.

"What offer? I want to hear it!"

"Well, you see, he knows that you want to sell the whole stock. He also has guessed that you are in a hurry and somehow you have to do this fast. But he also has some problems that he needs to solve before he takes possession."

"What do you mean? What kind of problems?" she asked in hoarse voice. "Firstly, I would like to know how much he offered."

"Emily, his offer is $200,000 for the whole stock. To me, the price seems good. It doesn't even compare to the other two offers you had."

With wide eyes, surprised, but also thoughtful, Emily said:

"Yeah, it's a sum! What is your professional advice?"

"First of all, let me tell a few details of this offer. He also has some problems, as I said, with the construction of new stables. These are delayed, and he offered you this price with the following condition: he gives you all the money right now, provided you keep the animals for a month and a half until he finishes his stables. You have to keep all the animals as healthy as they are now, as he has seen them. If one is missing, ill … or something else, you have to give him $800 per head."

"And how … I mean … I keep them on the farm at my expense for another month and a half?"

"That's right," Neil nodded. "Listen Emily, you have to make some plans and some calculations. This helps you. If you find a buyer for the farm soon—although I doubt it—you must put the farm in possession after the term at which the Mexican has to take his animals."

A deep silence settled upon them for some time.

Nervously, turning the fork on the empty plate, Emily was looking out at the horizon, as if preoccupied to find the answer there.

Turning to her son, she asked, "Michael, what do you say?"

"As you say, Mom."

"Well, the price is good. Michael, I don't think we'll have feed problems for another two months, will we?"

"No, Mom; not for four, at least."

Closing her eyes and turning her head back, Emily reflected. She remained like that for about half a minute. Then she straightened her head, opened her eyes, and said in a serious, grave voice, "So be it. We will close the deal. There is no point in waiting for better deals or customers. I do it because the price is good and because it is as we hoped it would be."

"And we'll keep the cattle for another month and a half."

"We will also forget about some worries and those who will visit the farm, will see how many animals can grow on it."

" Neil, could you please call Senor Rodrigues and inform him that I accept his offer?"

Just as seriously, Neil stood up, holding out his hand.

"Congratulations, Emily! I can say that you made a good and very balanced deal. I know the market and what you can get at the moment. You couldn't find a better offer. You've seen how much the other two offered you. As for the phone," he continued, "I will call him tomorrow before lunch. The offer is valid for a week, he told me. Usually, these kinds of deals are valid for three days. The fact that he said 'one week' means that he wants the deal to be made. And it looks like he got it. We don't have to show him that we are in such a hurry, although I am convinced, he guessed it. He is a very good farmer, very skilled and very good with people, too. I had taken references about him as a possible customer weeks before, and look, it's almost done."

"Yeah," Emily said with a deep breath. "It's done."

****

She was staring at the front wall, with both elbows on the table and holding a glass milk in her hands. Two pots on the stove, sizzling lightly and raising steam to the kitchen ceiling, were the only noise that broke the silence of the house.

Her thoughts were far away … worries of her mind … worries about existence … and the future.

With her blonde hair flowing in disarray down her shoulders and back, a brown coat hastily pulled over her clothes, she looked beyond the wall, into a sphere of turmoil and uncertainty.

'Have I done well?' she was asking herself. 'She had accepted Rodrigues's offer. Now, slight doubts began creeping into her mind. Anyway, she reminded herself, the price was very good—much more than the other previous offers. And more, he bought all the animals at once, taking a lot of worries out of her hands. Yes … minus the maintenance for the animals for another month or two. Here, the Mexican had been clever. Well, let's see what two extra months mean: the barn was almost full with straw and hay. Michael had taken care that it was replaced as soon as it was used. Good move! Bill's school of thought! The rest of the fodder wouldn't be too much money either; they had enough grain, and any that remained would be sold with the farm. However, it would not make a significant difference to the farm price.

So? Well, in addition, it will only be her and Michael's work. That won't be a problem. Just as long as they keep themselves and the stock healthy'.

She was lost in thought and remained at the table, motionless, until the sizzling pots got hot enough to spill over onto the stove. Finally, she got up, went to the stove and stirred the two pots with a wooden spoon. She stared out of the window at the fields, like a naval officer inspecting the open sea. She sat back down. She was waiting for Michael to return with the cattle. Today he was a little further, on a plot of pasture at the edge of the property. She felt tired. That day, she had cleaned the stables and sprayed them with lime solution.

She sat back down and, with her hands wrapped around her milk cup as if in holy prayer, she continued to think about what she needed to do in the coming weeks.

Okay, the sale of the farm was next on her agenda. She needed to find a realtor, but she was sure the other farmers didn't know any realtors, so they couldn't help her. And they wouldn't sell their farms for anything in the world. The farm is in their blood; that's their life—their way of being.

She had to find a contact. She thought about Neil. He said he knew the animal market … but not everyone sells their animals only; some of them sell their farms, too. Maybe he knew other farmers who had used. He hadn't mentioned it to her because he is a professional. He only solved his slice of business; no questions, no indiscretions.

She decided to ask Michael in case he had heard of anyone. These young people, she mused; you never know when they have the best ideas.

How easy would have been if she could have asked Bill!

But Bill was not there anymore. He's gone forever.

"Oh God," she said aloud, "Please help me!"

****

In the evening, later than usual, Tommy once again received the priest's visit.

"Good evening, sir! I hope I'm not bothering you," said the Father, stepping shyly through the ajar door."

"Not at all, Father! You never bother me. Come on in and get yourself a chair."

"Thank you, thank you very much!"

"But what happened to you that you came so late, Pastor?"

"I chose this time, so that we can speak privately."

"And what would you like to talk about?

"It's up to you, sir. First of all, I have to ask if you want to have a conversation."

"On what topic, Father? Religion, isn't it?"

"We could talk about anything you want, with or without a religious theme."

"I assume you would like a religious topic, wouldn't you?"

"Sir, scientists use their minds to improve life for humanity. We Priest Ministers seek to help our fellow humans in discovering and smoothing their way to God—in bringing them closer to Him."

"Beautifully said, Father! We can talk about everything you want. I'm in a good mood, so take advantage."

"Thank you, sir. I would like to know more about your life as a professional hockey player. Then, about how you fought in Afghanistan. I understood that you defused bombs there."

"Oh oho, Father! Well, it seems that you want to know everything! It will take me days to tell you."

"No sir, I wasn't thinking of that. Only general aspects. In this direction, my knowledge is very limited; I don't know anything about the life of a hockey player."

"I can tell you Father: difficult, but beautiful. A lot of hard work, a lot of physical and mental effort, at training and in games. A lot of pain, then a short time for recoveries. What can I say? A very intense life. I don't even know when it was over. It was like a dream."

"Our whole life is like a dream, son. Materialism seeks to tempt humanity with immediate and easy pleasures and it is certain that such a life cannot bring lasting happiness. It is the same with the situation when a child does not stop crying until he gets what he wants. Then he starts wanting something else and starts crying again. It is also an adult attitude, concerned only with the material world. Once the desired thing is obtained, it is abandoned and something else takes its place. Achieving inner health, tranquility, lasting joy and happiness is impossible for those dominated by sensual or material pleasures.

"Endless happiness is found only in the knowledge of God. Sooner or later, every human being must learn the lesson. Son, the true aim of life is to know God."

"Okay, Father, I understand. I understand. Let's go back. What exactly would interest you about my life as a hockey player?"

You said that you had hard workouts, involving great physical and mental effort. What exactly is the difficulty?"

"Well, Father, imagine that we started with the so-called "warm-up," which consisted of skating at least 50 laps around the ice, among which were dozens of sprints. When I had just started my career, after the first 20 laps and 8 to 10 sprints, I felt tired—very tired. I had no air, and I felt like I was suffocating. But, over time, I got used to it."

"Habit is one of the attributes of the human. Demands on the human physique and mind get easier once it gets used to it."

"The same is true with the idea of looking for God. Once you get used to looking for Him, you will find Him everywhere, every time."

"I didn't think of that at that time, Father. But in a short time, I managed to keep up with the others. After warming up, I was trained as a goalkeeper. Two were attacking, trying to score, while I had to go out of the crease to stop them. The attacks came in waves, one after another. They wanted to improve my exit speed and reaction to attacks one-on-one. After that, there were shots from everyone, from any position. Sometimes they fired two or three pucks at the same time. Sometimes I was so exhausted that if I dived on the ice, it was difficult for me to get up again. Then, one of the coaches used to scream in my ear: "Up! Where do you think you are, at the beach? You are a pro! You never get tired, you never feel pain, and you never give up. Jump faster on those skates."

"They made the speakers very loud so that we got used to the noise of the stands. It seemed too loud. The rest of the time, the coaches screamed in our ears. Our headaches and pains remained in our ears hours after training. They only stopped the loudspeakers during the explanations. That's how it was then … that's how the training was done."

"And the games?" the Minister asked.

"Father it was wonderful! We usually played a few games on home ice, followed by a few away. At home, when we played good matches, beautiful phases, the people in the stands roared and seemed to pour over. But when we played badly, they booed us. But it was great. The audience, the lights, the colours … it was like a dream."

"Yes, son! Man's whole life is a dream. This world seems real because God created you in His "Cosmic Dream." Wake up to the "One Reality"—God, and you will discover that life is but a miraculous spectacle, a divine play of lights and shadows."

"Is that so, Father? Actually … what exactly is God?"

"Oh, son! How can I tell you? God is consciousness. Regardless of the nature of matter, it was created by God through an act of His consciousness.

"Let me tell you a parable. Once, a scientist, adept at the theory of materialism, told a sage that it was beautiful to represent flowers, trees, rivers, mountains—in fact the whole Universe—as a dream of God. But all these objects were identical, being actually made up of subatomic particles. 'Yes,' replied the sage. 'But you see, if you let a pile of bricks and mortar fall to the ground, do you think they will form a house? Of course not. Intelligence is needed to do something coherent with them. Protons, neutrons, electrons, and all other particles are those bricks from which the Universe is built. But intelligence is needed to give the form that they each have."

"So, this is God: consciousness?"

"You can call it that, in a simplistic way. It is not only consciousness. He is beyond causation, and humans, in order to be happy, must look for Him."

"So, you mean, I have to look for Him, and if I find Him, I will be happy?"

"Look, I can ask you, sir, what can you lose if you try? What have you got to lose?

You see, unfortunately, people are not happy because they go all their lives for something material; they chase after illusions."

"Here's how it is: I'm going to tell you another parable to make myself understood. A dog owner had devised an ingenious method to make his dog pull a very heavy sled. With the help of a stick tied to the sled, the man suspended a large and appetizing sausage, close to the dog's snout. Lured by the sausage, the dog almost did not notice that during this time he was pulling the sled. And regardless of his effort, the sausage remained at the same distance from him.

"The same goes with people. They believe that if they get something material and fulfil a desire, they will be happy. But, once they achieve that, another one appears, and then another, so that their whole life they will not be happy, just always chasing after something else. In this way, 'the bait of happiness' will be unreachable, and they will be overwhelmed by the sufferings generated by the effort to achieve an illusory happiness."

"Oh! That's it. I've got it. Now I understand, Father, what you mean. But where do I look for God, and how to look for Him?"

"Why don't you start with yourself, sir?"

"With me?"

"Yes, with you. Seek first to analyze yourself. Seek to look at the world differently, beyond material concerns, beyond your everyday interests. Imagine, during the night, several containers are full with water, and the Moon is reflecting on the surface of the water they contain. The image of the Moon will be different for each of the containers, although they reflect the same Moon. More broadly, God is distinctly reflected by every human being, but He is not affected by them. Even if the containers are destroyed, the Moon will remain unaffected.

"Try to find the manifestation of God in all that He has created. Seek to change you vision of this world. Look for the beauty of God in a sunrise, His tears in the form of raindrops, his tenderness in the love of a mother for her child.

"Different religions are just different ways to reach God. The real foundation of a religion is not only faith, but intuitive experience. Intuition is the ability of the soul to know God. To know the object of a religion, you must first know God."

"Father, I am speechless. No one has told me about these things before. At least, not as you see them. They were presented to me differently. I don't know how to say it ... perhaps more dogmatically. You see things completely differently."

"Don't try to flatter me, sir! It's all about the way you look at and feel things ... the perspective from which you look, seeking to increase your awareness."

"Look, only shallow people claim that their religion is the only true way, and all other ways are false. I say it out loud and I have constant disputes—disagreements with Brothers in the faith, of the same religion as me. "

"Why I can say this is because I have been seeking with all my heart to know God. Religions are many, and they appear and disappear over time. God is the same.

"Here is another parable, so that you can understand:

"A famous priest of a certain Christian religion has died. At the entrance into Heaven, Saint Peter did not want to open the gates for him.

"'How is it that you don't want to let me in? Me, who in the course of my life sent thousands of sinners to Paradise, converting them?' he asked Saint Peter."

"'Perhaps you sent them, but I can tell you that none of them arrived here!' replied Saint Peter."

"Do you understand now? The closeness to God is not dogmatic. There must be a sincere will to know Him."

"Time for treatment! Excuse me, gentlemen, for the intrusion, but the patient needs to have his treatment."

A tall, thin Sister in a white robe stepped inside the hospital room.

"Oh, sure, sure!" said the priest, rising. "Now I leave you, sir. You have to follow your treatment."

"Thank you for visiting me, Father!" Michael replied.

"I'll stop by to see you again."

"Any time. You are welcome any time."

At the door, the priest turned, and, cutting the air with the cross placed over the Bible, made the sign of the cross. "God, bless you!" he exclaimed, and disappeared.

Michael remained stunned in his bed, while the nurse came to tend to him.

****

At the headquarters of the Association of War Veterans, there was great agitation. Although they had initially thought of something small, a small circle, a kind of briefing, that circle widened so much that they had been forced to prepare the large meeting room.

The theme was well known: "Helping Tommy."

Garry Thomson, president of the War Veterans Association, was to chair the meeting.

Meanwhile, guests gathered in the lobby in front of the meeting room, grouped in clusters, talking, while other people were smoking, and drinking coffee.

Donovan, the former president of the Hockey Club where Tommy had played, was also there, along with his two Secretaries. Also present were the other Secretaries of the War Veterans Association, other influential figures, and some of the City Hall leadership.

No one had expected such a turnout, and Garry, red-faced and agitated as he was, walked like a prairie bird through the bushes, guiding the employed staff to put more chairs in the meeting room.

Out of the blue appeared a few cameramen.

'Who had invited them? And where should we put them?' Garry wondered.

"Damn it!" he murmured. "They'll find a corner." The building was old and funds were limited.

"But the air conditioning? It was repaired? It didn't work a few days ago." He disappeared through a side door, looking for the building administrator.

As the guests arrived, the space became too small. Because the appointed time was approaching anyway, they were let inside. In the hall, changes had been made: the oval table had been drawn at the front, taking over the role of a presidium table, and chairs had been arranged, forming a few rows.

All this time, the cameramen were looking for sockets to keep their batteries charged.

"Listen, Ken, I didn't expect so many people. Who should we invite here in the presidium?"

"I think it would be good for us to be the only ones—the ones from the Veterans Association, and then to listen to the questions in the hall. We will vote by raising hands."

"Great Ken, I don't want to have troubles with the media."

The meeting began. The proposals for presidium were collected. However, a few people from City Hall, from the hockey club where Tommy had played, and a few journalists found their place at the table.

To Garry's delight, everyone seemed satisfied. So, the formalities began with speeches, the inventory of resources, concrete measures of action in fundraising.

Local TV stations recorded everything, everyone trying to be as generous as possible, waving their pockets and talking more and more "precious" and "patriotic."

In the long run, it was decided to open a bank account for Tommy in order to make donations, in addition to the cash offers from the War Veterans Association, the Red Cross, and City Hall. The latter announced that it was offering Tommy social housing. Speeches continued in a cascade, journalists struggling to take notes, cameramen recording. Everyone happy ....

****

Emily had guessed correctly. Neil knew a few of realtors who were able to sell farms. She also understood correctly that, as a professional, Neil was not going to get involved in anything else without being asked.

So, she fixed an appointment with him and visited him at his office. It was very kind of him, she thought, that he had introduced her to the realtors. At her request, he recommended one; the best and most expensive realtor in the market. He also told her that Robson was well worth his fees. Emily didn't hesitate and took his word for it.

She got in touch with Robson two days later, and in another two days, he came with one of his employees and saw the farm. He had also been informed that the possession could take place in two months.

To her surprise, Robson offered Emily a much higher starting price than she had hoped. And so, a few days later, customers began to roam the farm, accompanied by Robson's office assistant. For her and Michael, these visits became annoying because they were supposed not to be there, so they were taking the gig and disappeared from there for a while. Usually, they went to the pasture to stay away from visitors.

After a few days, they had the first offer. Robson recommended her not to rush, and to think well. Emily declined the offer, but a few days later she began to have doubts and regrets. Everything had calmed down and no other potential buyers appeared. But Robson assured her that the real customers would soon appear.

For a short time, Emily went from a state of calmness to one of anxiety, until one day a whole family arrived, interested to see the farm. They were from the west and wanted to relocate in the region. This time, Robson accompanied them. They made an offer on the spot, a little lower than she had initially asked. They bargained a little over the delayed possession. Robson ran the negotiations going from Emily to the family, communicating conditions and offers. The two had retreated somewhere, at the edge of the forest, while customers were waiting on the deck of the house. Meanwhile, Robson used his jeep, running from one to the other, like a ping-pong ball. After a series of adjustments, they closed the deal.

****

God, how fast and easy it had all been! Now, Emily congratulated herself on choosing Robson, and Neil had been right this time, too. Robson had been rather expensive, but he deserved it. Thinking back, she thought again how lucky she was to have such a friend as him.

Now, she felt released from the tension and burden, and yet…

In the evening, when Michael came home—tired, sweaty, and full of dust, as usual—she told him the news. Michael's eyes widened.

"So, is it done? Is it sold?"

"Yes, Michael. It seems so."

"What do you mean? It is possible for the buyers to change their minds?"

"As Robson told me, there are a few more steps to follow with their bank, mortgage approval, and other things. They can change their minds within 10 days. That's the legal term."

"So, it's not ready yet."

"How can I tell you, Michael? Robson told me that this was the procedure. He also told me that he had checked them before bringing them here and everything seemed fine to him. If they weren't reliable people, he wouldn't have bothered to come here with them. So, we can't do anything but wait. Just in case, let's not be joyful too soon."

"But when are they supposed to have the possession permit?"

"Two weeks and three days from now."

"That's a long time. Hmm!"

They sat down at the table and had their supper in silence.

Abruptly, Michael broke it. "Mom, I'm going to help you in the store when I am not at school; I can unload the goods and arrange them on shelves. I can also help you with the sale. I would also like to deal with the customers."

Emily was taken aback. "So fast! These young people are so different. They adapt so quickly and forget so fast. No memories and already thinking about the future."

"We'll see, Michael. You focus on school; that would make me happy to see from you."

"Yes, but you know, I can help you and I would love to," he replied enthusiastically.

"Look, my dear, I don't want to say that I don't need your help. You have to know that your first duty is to learn very well at school."

"Sure, Mom. I can learn. You know that if I start something, I will always work hard and do a good job."

"Yes, I know, my dear."

Her thoughts were wandering far away ... but with lots of worries close by—very close.

Dawn had caught her with eyes still open. She couldn't sleep. Terrible doubts that had seized her. She had sold the farm. She knew that she couldn't keep it, with only the two of them. To call her daughters back home to help them wasn't a solution. "I don't even want to think about it," she said aloud.

Selling it had been the only way. And yet, she was still in doubt.

She had lived on the farm as a child with her parents, then with Bill. Why was she afraid? Why?

Sitting down, she was rocking forward thinking and trying to find the source of her anxiety.

Suddenly, the reason appeared to her like a lightning bolt. "I am afraid of change. And I am afraid of living in a city."

One of the following nights, just after midnight, a great uproar was heard from the stable. Almost as if on command, all creatures on the farm voiced their fear. The horses were neighing, hitting the walls of the stables with their hooves, the cattle were bawling, and the dogs were barking like mad.

In an instant, Emily jumped out of bed, ran to the door and down the stairs, where she met Michael, who already had a wind lamp in his hand.

"Leave the lamp, I'll take care of it. You load the rifle and take a few more bullets with you. There's something near the stables."

"Yes, mom."

From the hall in front of the kitchen, Michael grabbed the rifle off the rack, tore the cardboard of the bullet box, loaded the rifle and stuffed a few more shells in his pajama pockets.

They met on the deck, Emily in a long pajama shirt with boots on, hair dishevelled, holding the lamp and Michael with the rifle. They headed up the hill, walking at a brisk pace.

Meanwhile, the racket grew. The barking of the dogs became more and more hysterical, accompanied by banging on the door of the stable.

"Come up the hill, among the huts and stables. I want to take a pitchfork too," Emily said to Michael.

As they were getting closer, they heard some growls among the dogs barking.

"It might be a bear, Michael."

"Wait for a second. Hold the lamp," she said, pulling a bale of straw from the stable, cut the twine and spread the straw with both hands. She took a forkful of straw.

"Light the straw, Michael. Don't move far away from me and don't shoot it; if it's hurt, it will kill us".

They turned the corner of the barn. A large brown bear, surrounded by growling dogs, was pounding around with its paws as a reaper. The dogs were pulling out of its way, then threw forward again, their lips drawn and showing their white fangs.

Stepping bravely forward, holding the fork in her hands with the burning wisp of straw, Emily swayed back and forth, shouting with the boy:

"Get! Get out of here!"

Michael fired twice into the air. The bear jumped into the massive wooden door, almost knocking it down. The dogs, feeling their masters, became bolder and fiercer. Emily was pushing the burning straw back and forth toward the bear's head.

The bear jumped to the side, sweeping at two dogs, when another jumped on its back. Shaking violently, it got rid of that one too, throwing it a few yards away.

Eventually, the bear turned, hesitantly leaving the entrance, heading for the forest at a gallop, grunting, and quickly disappeared into the darkness.

Emily stomped on the remains of the burning straw. "Let's go check the animals." She entered the stable, holding the lamp high.

They talked slowly and softly to the animals, getting them to calm down. Emily and Michael checked everywhere. They found no wounded animals. Emily had been afraid of that. She didn't want to pay Rodriguez a penny for an animal.

Thankfully, the damages were minor. Only a few planks needed to be replaced; the frightened animals, throwing their hooves, had broken them.

Once outside, they searched the dogs to see if they were injured.

"Hi, my dear ones," Michael called them, crouching in the middle of them and running his fingers through their fur. Suddenly, he realised that one was missing.

"Mother, Rex is not here!" he shouted.

"Look there," said Emily, showing the direction with her head. Michael found Rex, standing on his hind legs, whimpering, panting, and full of blood around his neck. It was obvious the dog was suffering.

"Hold the lamp, please," Emily knelt beside Rex, who, sensing her, wagged his tail.

"The bear scratched him from the back of his ear to the eye, Michael. We have to carry him home."

Michael knelt down. "You tough dog; to jump on the bear's back! I said it before, you're like a devil. You're so smart and able to protect the cattle. Good dog!"

Leaning the fork against the wall of the stable, Emily said, "I will take the rifle and the lamp, Michael, and you take Rex in your arms and let's get him home."

Rex had been taken care of, bandaged in rags soaked in potions Emily had known since she lived on her family farm. In a few days, Rex was much better and out of danger.

****

After a few days, after the evening liturgy, the priest came again to visit Tommy.

"What do you want to talk about tonight, Father?"

"You see, sir that depends on you."

"Father, please don't make me feel bad by calling me 'sir'. Just call me 'Tommy'."

"Very well, son, I will call you Tommy as you wish me to. Well, it's up to you, Tommy. We can talk about anything you want."

"Would you like to talk about people's sins, Father? Or about their virtues? In fact, what's a sin?"

"A mistake, son. A mistake born of ignorance."

"A mistake? Ignorance? What are these?"

"Ignorance, from a certain point of view, can be called a lack of knowledge of the realities of the spirit, and their replacement with an illusory dream. A mistake is always based on distorted understanding or a misunderstanding."

"Is that all?"

"You see, Tommy, we are all sons of God. Sin can be perceived as a disobedience to His law. So, we could imagine God's answer, His anger, and His severe judgement, and punishment, which will endure. In fact, we are the ones who judge ourselves at that moment when we know we have committed a sin. But if we consider a sin a simple mistake, we will assume we can correct the mistake."

"Interesting, Father! But who commits a crime, commits a greater sin? Is it a sin a crime?"

"By all means, son. That breath of life, which is in us, is the same as that which exists in all beings. To suppress the right to life of a being means to deny the reality of universal existence, we being an expression of it. Murder is suicide."

"Impressive! I have never thought of that! Dear God! You really shocked me, Father!"

"No, Tommy. These are truths."

"But a thief, Father? Does a thief commit a sin when he steals?"

"Definitely. It is the same thing. What he takes from others is identical to what he takes from himself. The self from others is our own self."

"A liar, Father? What about a liar?

"Lies separate us from the true reality of God, which is the ultimate truth, as Jesus says. Through lying, the one who commits it isolates himself from the loving help given by those who live in harmony with their realities. A liar destroys the fundamentals of whatever he wants to create in this world."

"Brilliant! Father, you have answers for everything ... answers that will keep my mind busy for a long time. The truth is that we are all sinners, Father."

"How can I tell you, Tommy, sin tempts people, showing itself in different forms, and shines. Let me tell you a parable.

"'A man was walking through a place in a region famous for its diamond resources. He discovered many small shiny pieces, but they were only pieces of glass well-sharpened. Despite the fact that he hurt his hands and fingers, he didn't stop from rummaging; he didn't stop, searching each piece of glass, hoping to find diamonds.'"

"It is the same with sin; it's its false radiance which lures us, but it does not make us happier. Such experiences will always lead to disappointments. The pleasures of the senses can end only at monotony and disgust. By identifying with your senses, you will not discover the truth about Him, the Almighty.

"But sin can be removed through right thinking, prayers, and with the help of God's grace and power."

"So, can sin be blotted out, Father?"

"I wouldn't say that. Rather, it can be forgiven. You are a child of God. Do not identify yourself with the mistakes you've made, but relate to your eternal relationship with Him.

"Considering yourself a sinner, you open the door and invite sin to enter and encompass your mind."

"Rather, remember your good deeds and seek to keep it that way. See if your love for God is sincere and deep. God is bothered by your indifference rather than your imperfections or mistakes."

"Is that so? I don't know, but it sounds nice, Father."

"Look, Tommy; here's another parable.

"'Let's say we have an object polished with gold and we cover it with a black veil. Are we going to say then that the object is black? Certainly not. We will always know that behind the veil is a golden object.'

"Likewise, when we remove the veils of ignorance that cover the spirit, we will discover the unchanging beauty of divine reality. Don't be afraid of God. Talk to Him; tell Him the things you did wrong. Don't forget that you are His child. Talk to him with much love.

"In this way, regardless of your mistakes, He will help you to eliminate your imperfections, considering you as one of His children, in His Divine House, where, in fact, is your place.

Spiritual ignorance is the greatest sin, making all other sins possible …"

"Are you okay, sir? Tommy!" The priest asked, seeing Tommy lying on his back, his hands under his head, and staring up at the ceiling."

"Oh, yes, no worries. I'm just thinking about what you are saying."

"I hope I haven't tired you too much," the priest told him, standing.

"No, Father, no worries."

"I'll come to see you again, Tommy."

"Thank you, Father. Yes, I know you've been giving me a lot of food for thought."

When he reached the door, the Father turned and blessed him, and Tommy replied with "God help us, Father."

The priest disappeared behind the door.

****

The next morning, as soon as he had finished his treatment, another nurse entered. She had been trying to stop a group of noisy people in the hallway. Closing the door and panting, the nurse apologised.

"I could barely keep them out, sir! Please forgive me. But there are a lot and they want to see you. They are very insistent, and I cannot let them in here all at once. They are journalists."

"Journalists? God, what do they want?"

"I don't know, sir. I tried to talk to them, but they talked all at once and almost pushed me through the door, sir."

Only now did Tommy notice that the nurse with bright red cheeks was standing with her back to the door, leaning against it with her hands at her side, trying to bar the door.

"Listen to me, dear! Tell them I don't want to see anyone. Is it clear? No one!" he shouted, emphasizing each syllable.

"I beg your pardon, sir! I am doing what I can, sir! You know what the media is like. You can't mess with the media. They are very strong and very insistent. The director of the hospital himself sought to calm them down. They threatened him—"

"But who do they think they are? Almighty?"

"I don't know, sir. Could you still see some of them? It would calm them down."

"Well, I don't want to see any of them. What do they want to assault me with? What's going on in this hospital?" Tommy snapped angrily.

"Please sir! Please, I beg you!" prayed the nurse, who already had tears in her eyes.

He was perplexed. Tommy had never expected something like this. Only now did he realize how terrified the nurse was and how acute the situation had become.

"What is your name, please?"

"Valerie, sir. Valerie Dawson."

"Well, Valerie, if you can't do otherwise, please go back and tell them that only one of them is allowed to come in. Let them choose a representative, anyone they want.

"And, Valerie, please tell them that I'm tired and under medication."

"Yes sir, I'll try. I'll tell them that your state of health does not allow other people to visit, and you must be careful and avoid any kind of stress."

"Very well said! I have to be very careful! Go ahead and don't give up, don't let them in. Do you hear me?"

"Very well, sir."

She turned and opened the door, trying to say something, but in vain. No chance! Without any trace of embarrassment, she was pushed inside and a lot of people, like cattle in a stampede, rushed inside. Some of them carried spotlights that flooded the room and made Tommy look for shelter under his blanket. Dozens of voices speaking at the same time erupted in all corners of the small room.

"Pull the cable!"

"Microphone test! Test ... Can you hear me?"

"Tommy, how are you?"

"Are you grateful for what City Hall did?"

"Go ahead with the camera. Where are you?"

"Contact me."

"We are starting to record!"

"Grab a chair, man!"

And so on ...

The noise was deafening. A few cameramen had climbed on some chairs and had their lights aimed at Tommy, who, with the blanket drawn to his chest, his palms in front of his eyes, was trying to protect himself from the lights focused on him.

A bundle of microphones had been placed in front of him, and the questions were flying at him like arrows at the same time.

"You say you don't know anything about the noble gesture the City Hall made?"

"What noble gesture? I don't know anything," Tommy defended himself.

"Where have you been so far?"

"Is it true that they picked you up from the sidewalk?"

"Have you lived in the country all these years?"

With both hands in the air, as if defending himself, he shouted, "I know nothing! I don't understand anything, but absolutely nothing! And yes, I lived on the streets. Because that's what I wanted. What else do you want to know?"

"I am in hospital and I want silence. Can you hear me?" he began to shout "Silence!!!"

Taking advantage of the few moments of shocked silence, the nurses intervened.

"Please, you have to stop. The patient needs peace and rest. He is under treatment."

Meanwhile, the Head Physician and the Director of the hospital appeared.

"Gentlemen, please! You are invited to the conference room of the hospital. There we will give any information you want. This is a hospital room and patients cannot be recorded in any way here. More, this patient fought in Afghanistan and suffered physical and psychological trauma and needs rest. Please leave now and meet us in the conference hall. We are going to answer all your questions. Please."

The journalists tried to ask more questions but were firmly escorted out of the ward and taken to the hospital conference room. Soon the last cables were unplugged and last cameraman was out of Tommy's room.

Left alone, Tommy felt slowly out of breath, convulsions coming slowly to grip him. "White Fog" wrapped him gently in its arms. He was found one hour later, unconscious on the floor near the bed.

****

A few days after the bear visited the farm, Emily and Michael had a talk about what they had to do immediately and in the near future.

They were in the kitchen having dinner.

"Michael, we need to talk," she began. "Things will go very fast from now on and we have to be prepared. We need a good plan."

"I thought about that, and I wanted to talk to you, but I put it off because of too much work."

"Listen, Michael, Rodrigues is coming in a week to take the cattle. In another two, there is the possession of the house. We have to move fast."

"Tomorrow morning, bring the cattle to the pastures near the house. Then you can take an hour or two to help me pack—I can pack the small things in boxes, but I can't do the big ones. And the furniture has to be ready for transport."

"Yes, mother, I know and I will help you with everything."

Emily put the fork on the plate and looked at him, weighing his resemblance with his father.

"Tomorrow, I will pick up the buggy and go to town to arrange transportation. I am going to buy some cardboard boxes to pack some stuff. I have no idea how many we need.

"We are going to live at my cousin's place for a few weeks until we find a proper place for us. I don't want to rush to buy a house. We need one in a good commercial area. I want the store on the ground floor, and a first floor and maybe second for living space for all four."

"That's great, Mom! We will stay together as before."

"Yes, Michael, it will be great," she said, stealthily wiping a tear.

For a while, they were eating silently. Suddenly Michael broke in, "Listen, Mom. We have already sold some hens and chickens. There are not many left, so we could cut and freeze them. But what are we going to do with the dogs?"

"Sorry, I overlooked it, Michael," she said. We have to give them up, too. Neil and Donna have already asked about Ella and Betty. What about the rest? Talk to people … your friends, and I will talk to acquaintances in the city, and let's see. I don't think we can get some money for them. Nobody will want to pay for them, but maybe we can give them away. Some people love dogs."

"The Thomsons want Ella and Betty? Well, Neil wants them because they are the only who knows. But, you know, Rex is the best."

"My dear, of course we are giving them what they asked. These people have helped us so much. And it's none of our business what dogs they choose."

"What do you think, mom, about the new owner? He might want to keep a pup. It's worth asking."

"Michael, my dear! How come it didn't cross my mind? I'll talk to the realtor tomorrow to ask them. Good idea Michael! Wonderful!"

They had finished eating and got up from the table, washed the dishes and went to bed. Strange feelings overcame Emily: the same fear of the unknown.

****

Tommy recovered in a few days, but heated discussion took place between his doctor and all the other staff involved in what had happened. The interference of media in midst of the medical treatment had been so great that it was almost compromised. The recovery of a war-traumatized patient was delicate and long lasting.

"Listen, Tommy," the doctor said, "From now on, we won't let anyone in, without the approval of the chief doctor or me. So, don't be afraid. We'll guard you with the police if necessary."

"Well, yes, but, please, no police. I can't stand police. I am sick when I see cops in uniform."

"Okay, Tommy. No police then."

"And now, try to rest. You are again ascending on the recovery slope. The crises you have, and we have discussed about, when you feel what you call "white fog", are because of the stress and traumas gathered in time during the war. What you need is lot of care and rest in order to get better. Try to sleep," the doctor said, leaving the room.

But sleep didn't come to Tommy as soon as he wanted. It was only very late that he managed to fall asleep—a troubled, broken sleep, often waking up with his shirt wet with sweat.

The war with its horrors was always at the back of his mind. Those who do not know what war is like, should never know. Everything is pain, suffering, irrational, and crooked. Actions are beyond any reason, attitudes, senses, thoughts, all life is distorted.

A cold sweat had awakened him. With goose-bumps and cold with fear to his bones, he stared helplessly at the trembling of his feet sticking out from under the blanket. He had dreamt of a mission, one of those you never want to remember. You want it to be deleted from your memory—and even your subconscious mind, so it can never bubble up to consciousness.

Their team had already been on a mission for a few days, working in a minefield. One by one, mines had been defused, the land checked and checked again, and now they were waiting for the withdrawal order. They had already loaded the tools and materials into trucks to go back to the base, when the news arrived like a shock, he and a few others were asked to travel 50 miles to the north, where, according to information, a railway bridge might have been mined.

"Listen, Bill! Do we really have to swallow this lie? What's this bridge about? We did our job. We're going to the base, aren't we?"

"Tommy, hold your horses and don't rush," replied Bill, the captain. He was a skinny man, medium-sized, with light blonde hair, brown eyes under discoloured eyebrows, strong eyebrows arches, and a prominent chin.

"Hold your horses, Tommy" he repeated under his breath, pushing his chin forward. The order came from a higher level, so, 'no comment.'"

"Okay, Captain. Looks like I have no choice. And how many do we have to go?"

"A small group. You, as a leader and choose two more. Your choice. Take a jeep and go. You will receive the data in half an hour; maps and everything."

"Why, didn't someone go by chopper? They would move faster, do the job and return quickly."

"It's not possible, Tommy. I don't have the maps yet, but as far as I know, the area is very rough—only sharp cliffs. The landing would be extremely difficult. Even so, you will have to walk a few miles to the target. So, grease your boots, dessert rats that you are."

"Anyway, we did our job. Why do we have to go? They could send a crew from base."

"The order came from the highest level. General McGregor himself requested 'a team to be sent there urgently.' It looks like a hot potato and we need to deal with it. We're closest to the target. So, keep your mouth shut, take two people, the jeep and load the materials you'll need. See you in the armoured car in half an hour. I'll give you all the details there."

"No chance to ditch it, nah?"

"That's right, no chance. Go, do the job and return to the base. Do not communicate anything by radio or phone until you return; you are many miles far away from the base. That's the order!"

"Yes, Captain. It means it's serious!"

"Yes, Tommy, very." Bill turned on his heels and left him alone.

Tommy hesitated for a moment, weighing the situation, and then started walking along the row of trucks. He stopped and shouted two names, "All and Pitt, to me, the assembly!"

"Hello Tommy. Did the scorpions invade you? Why are you shouting like that? What do you have in mind?"

"Where is Pitt? Where are you, baby eagle? Where the hell did you hide?" Meanwhile, he was walking along the trucks, calling him, when they almost collided. Pitt popped up between two trucks, with an open can of pineapple in one hand and a bayonet in the other. From time to time, he was picking a piece of fruit with the bayonet.

The strap of his helmet was loose, his shirt out of his trousers, his boots with laces hanging on either side.

"So, what's up Tommy? Why are looking for me?"

"Gather your equipment and we'll meet at the commander's armoured."

"Whaaat?"

"As you heard. Get your kitbag and we'll meet there. You have five minutes, you coyote desert!"

"I am not going anywhere. We're returning to the base."

"Look, Pitt," Tommy said, this time in a firm voice, "I don't like it either. Yes, we have to go. We are going on a mission about 50 miles from here. Order from the highest level. So, calm down, tighten your gear and move your ass to Bill's armoured as soon as possible."

"It's not true!"

"Five minutes, Pitt. You are wasting precious time talking. Can't you hear? Move your ass at once!"

Behind Tommy, All asked again, "Do we really have to go, Tommy?"

"Yes, All, so don't comment anymore. Same orders for you."

Turning on his heels, All walked away, grumbling and with his hands buried deep in his pockets.

Yes, there was nothing that could be done about it. Someone had given an order. Crooked or straight, it didn't matter anymore.

Orders had to be executed. No comment. Without resistance. Just in time to be executed.

They had camouflaged the jeep about 5 miles from the target, hiding it among some cliffs.

Guided by GPS and with knapsacks on their backs, they walked on an almost invisible path, climbing towards the mountain peak.

"What a shit hole! Why did we have to go up here?" Pitt wailed, carrying the heavy backpack filled with materials.

"They probably thought it's better for us to mountain climb to maintain our weight and physical condition!" replied Al.

"What a load of crap! Complete a mission and they send you immediately to another. They've gone completely crazy at HQ."

"Shut up! Both of you! The enemy can be around. There is information about the guerrilla troops in the area. From now on, we are going to speak only by signs; you have been trained for this."

"Oh, my! Well, it can be dangerous with guerrilla troops around, huh! As for speaking through signs, look at my language!" and Pitt turned his back and slapped his buttocks with his palms.

"Silence, both of you! Enough! Quiet! That's an order," Tommy added.

In the evening, they found a secure shelter in a small ravine.

They had a hard time that night. If during the day the heat was stifling, overnight, the air was ice cold, even worse in the place they found. They had already spent three weeks on the first mission, and now they had to continue in the mountains in even harsher conditions.

At first beam of light, they returned to the road.

The closer they got, the more careful they had to be. They spread out, but maintained eye contact. Around noon, they were able to see the target hidden between the cliffs. All around were rocks like needles, and, hanging in a gorge, the railway bridge. There were entrance tunnels on each side. They upraised the situation; very difficult to access, impossible to approach by helicopter, and extremely dangerous. Now they understood why a small team of sappers was necessary, but they were not any happier.

All around them, a myriad of hues, from dark brown to bright white, folded the mountain slopes, hiding the bridge as though it were in a bucket. The light reverberation was so strong that it strained their eyes.

They studied their objective for a while. The railway bridge was built with support structures made of planks in strait and oblique positions, developed into two impressive arches.

Beckoning them to come closer, Tommy whispered "We need to find a safe and secure way to go down. We are looking for a gorge to hide our equipment, and that will be our base. From there, we will start to approach the objective."

"Aye, aye!" the two muttered something sounding like consent.

The descent was another adventure. With heavy sacks on their backs, they clung to the rocks with their hands, often their feet hanging freely, or rested on their toes with a doubtful stability. Tommy did his best to help as much as he could. They had the bridge in sight when Tommy signaled them to wait. He had just seen a small cave a few dozen yards distance. He reached it on his own. It would just fit them and their materials. He motioned to his mates, who arrived safely and dropped their backpacks. The straps had left heavy tracks on their shoulders.

After they had caught their breath, All and Pitt start whispering, "Why the hell did we take so many materials? We are not beasts of burden to carry so much weight through these mountains!" complained All.

"They didn't know what to expect. Their data shows that the enemy could have mined the bridge and we have to check."

"Holy cow! They didn't even know if it was mined or not! What kind of information was that?" Pitt intervened angrily.

"What good is this talk? At least speak in lower voices; you don't know where the enemy is or if they can hear you," snapped Tommy.

"The three of us, the bridge and the enemy around us! Beautiful combination! What can I say?!" Pitt snorted.

After a while they calmed down, and Tommy told them: "I am going down to search the area. You stay here and don't make the slightest noise. Try to eat something. I don't know when I am coming back, but don't leave; wait for me."

Carefully, he chose a few tools from the backpacks and put them in the side pockets of his pants. He placed the smaller items in his shirt pockets.

He picked up a light rifle with collapsible stock, gave his mates a few more instructions, and then vanished through the rocks.

He went down the hill in stages: descending for a while, then stopping, listening, watching, and descending again. Closer to the bridge, he could see it in detail. Even with binoculars he couldn't see anything suspicious at first glance.

He thought, "I have two options. I could go back and the three of us come back, or I could continue alone and finish the preliminary search. Damn it! It's too dangerous to return . . . any more noise involves risk. I am already near the target. I will continue."

He advanced more in a squat position and then crawled, eventually reaching the bridge. At first, he didn't find anything suspicious. He had expected that. If the bridge had been mined, the load would have been pinned down between the steel beams.

He continued to crawl and then he went under the bridge. He squeezed through a myriad of metal beams, like a honeycomb, then he clung to one of them. With binoculars, he started searching through the darkness below, sweeping each beam carefully. He passed an oblique beam and then came back to it. Something was wrong. He adjusted the lens and saw it—a short wire end with black insulation, slightly protruding above an edge. No doubt about it. Good job. The hand of a professional. If he had looked from another angle, he would not have seen anything.

He had to get there to see how the wires were tied. It took him some time to move noiselessly. On the way, he found a few more loads and he decided to make the inventory in an orderly manner, beam by beam, starting from the bottom up.

Twilight found him lying on his back, just below the railway tracks, trying to pull out the fuse of a load fixed to a beam. It was getting dark, and he could barely make out the wires. Obviously, he couldn't use the flashlight. After he finished this one, he'd return to their base in the cave. Tomorrow they'll come together and finish the job, and they won't have much left to do. He had worked well so far. He had begun from below, so that the darkness caught him just below the tracks. The truth is that he didn't expect so many loads. The mining had been well done. Holding a pair of pliers in his mouth, he was trying to feel the thread— "Drrrrum! ... Drrrumm!" Two short bursts of gunfire. Reflected by the rocks, the sound seemed to wake the mountains and valleys. The echo died slowly. Then there was silence. He shuddered. Maybe his mates were gone. .. All and Pitt were dead ... and they would look for him.

He heard steps on the gravel around the bridge. They were coming towards him. In the gloom, it looked like there were five or six. Two of them with heavy weapons took the paths along the bridge. Two others descended on the right under the bridge, while the others did the same on the left side. Luckily, it was almost completely dark, although not enough for his comfort. He slowly slid under one bean, then two beams down. He stuck to it, trying to make himself one with it. He hoped to become a beam, not a target.

Luckily for him, those on the path overlooked him on the right. He watched their silhouettes through the darkness. They wore hats like plates, the attire of the mountain people in the region. After a while, they came back. He didn't blink. He hardly breathed. He waited, minute after interminable minute. Minutes as long as a human life. Minutes twitching his nerves.

Tommy thought they must be professionals. It was dark, and searching was more difficult. If someone was hidden under the bridge, they knew he couldn't last too long without moving. The war between nerves and resilience. Tommy's hands began to tremble; his legs had the advantage and training of the long hours spent between the posts and an increased ability to maintain his tone for a long time.

"No pain! There is no pain!" he would repeat the coach's shouts in his mind during his exhausting training. "Pain is only in your imagination. Turn it into a pleasure!"

He breathed lightly and turned into a bundle of muscles with a uniform tone. A half an hour passed, then another. The enemy gave up first. They retreated rather carelessly, stepping as a group on the rocky path. And then there was silence. Tommy didn't move. He still suspected that they might have left someone behind to watch; he was right. In about half an hour, he again heard footsteps departing. That's why he was still alive. This ability to wait and foresee the adversary's moves, like in a game of chess.

He relaxed a little more, then, with effort, he managed to get above the metal beam. He lay down on his stomach, gasping, but without much noise. He no longer felt his hands or legs. He decided to rest on that metal beam for a while longer, enjoying its coldness, felt through his shirt. He took off his belt and tied himself to the beam with it. A fall into the chasm below in the middle of the night was not impossible if he fell asleep. It was getting cold. He lifted his collar and relaxed his body.

"You don't feel the pain. The pain doesn't exist!" In that position he rested until morning, and by noon, he finished demining the upper part of the bridge.

He could not return to the base. In that cave perhaps there were only the corpses of his two mates. They must have been surprised, and now he could do nothing for them. How did the enemy find them? Perhaps they had tracked them from the Jeep. Anyway, he couldn't go back there either. He took out the map from one of his pockets and decided on an itinerary. He would have to use the GPS indicator sparingly to preserve the batteries.

After three days, he was out in the open, in the middle of the desert. On the fourth, he ran out of water. He still had 30 miles to go to reach the base. He changed the schedule and travelled only during the night. After the sixth day, the GPS batteries were finished too, but he was not far from the base. He was dizzy and his mind was not very clear. He decided to walk continuously, to get as close as possible to the base.

Soon he began stumbling. He fell and couldn't get up. He crawled, breathing hard for a while. It was as if an iron glove was squeezing his swollen neck. A few hundred yards left. Then nothing...

A unit on patrol found him the next day, face down and fist clenched in the sand. He was taken to the infirmary, and there they noticed dashes and dots made with a marker on his left palm. A sergeant deciphered it: "mission accomplished."

****

On her way to town, Emily passed by Ned and Donna. Together, they set the latest details of the move.

In town, she spent a lot of time shopping and making last arrangements. She bought some cardboard boxes for packing, and other materials for packing up. She was able to arrange the move with a specialized company, and she found a temporary storage space, as there was not much room at her cousin's place.

She tried to find some good homes for the dogs, but without much success. Still, she ran into Bertrand, a fruit and vegetable merchant at a farmers' market, who was somewhat interested. She knew him since Bill had done business with him. The Frenchman said that he needed a smart and fierce dog to guard his goods day and night. Emily immediately thought that Rex would be perfect for the job, but she would have to talk with Michael about it. She was trying to finalize the move business and she still had the feeling she had forgotten something. She went back to the farm that evening full of doubts.

Her cousin, Paul, tried to encourage her and calm her down.

"Stop worrying so much! Everything will be fine, Emily."

"God damn it, Paul. It's been our whole life here. I cannot let it go so easily. For me, this move means losing my roots." She paused, searching for words. "I don't know Paul, for me this is like a verdict and I am scared," she said, shedding tears.

Paul hugged her tightly and tried to reassure her, "Trust me! You are not alone, and we are here to help you. Everything will be fine."

Then came the day when Rodriguez took his cattle. From that moment on, Emily and Michael focused on packing.

Ned and Donna had taken the dogs they wanted: Ella and Betty. Rex was promised to Bertrand and, to their surprise, the others were to stay at the farm, wanted by the new owner.

A tractor and a few other farming tools were given to Ned and Donna as a present. They deserved them.

The rest of the equipment and tools were part of the contract with the new owner. Emily did not want to bother with them. The crops, as it was agreed, remained at the farm. In the city, for their new home, they had taken what they thought they needed. Everything had happened unbelievably fast.

They were moving and were starting a new life, a different one. They were leaving behind a beautiful part of their life—and their hearts, too.

****

Bertrand showed up at the farm a few days before their departure to take Rex. Meanwhile, the dog was basking in the sun, lain on his belly, yawning from time to time. He was shown to Bertrand, who liked the dog.

Bertrand was about six feet tall, with a big paunch, broad shoulders, A thick neck and wide jaws, thick lips, but small eyes looking all the times through his eyelashes, and above them, thick and bushy eyebrows.

"That's the dog, isn't it? Interesting!" he asked, pushing his chin forward.

"Yes, this is our best dog. He replies to the name 'Rex.'"

"No matter what name he answers to, I need a dog. I can't leave my goods unattended in the market anymore. Every day I notice goods missing."

Michael, who was standing a little further away, approached and asked,

"How do you want to take him?"

"I have a leash in the car."

"Sir, this dog has never been on a leash. I think it's right for him to start by getting used to it."

"The dog is a dog. He has to obey his master, no matter what, eh?" the Frenchman answered sharply.

Surprised and shocked, Michael swayed from one foot to the other.

"Michael!" Emily stepped in: "Take the leash and go and put it on, bring him downhill, and get him in the gentlemen's car.

She had felt Michael's concern, deeply upset, and Bertrand's unease as well, but there was no time to find a better owner for Rex.

Reluctantly, Michael took the leash from Bertrand and climbed the hill. As he was getting closer, Rex stepped toward him, cheerfully wagging his tail. Kneeling beside him, Michael hugged the dog, and scratched him behind the ears as he usually did when he brought food and took care of all the dogs. He was the master for Rex, and Rex loved him like only dogs are able to do.

Michael kept Rex close to him, and then began to whisper the remembered beautiful moments spent together. "You've been such a good dog for us, Rex!"

He pressed his head against Rex's neck, closed his eyes and remained there for a few moments. "I hope you will have a good life, Rex! Good luck, boy!"

And with that, he put the leash around Rex's neck. Rex looked up at the boy with a quizzical look, and both set off for the farm house. The dog walked nicely next to him. Michael didn't look at the dog again.

It was too painful; that was their moment, only theirs, and he didn't want Bertrand to notice. Tears were running down his cheeks, and he wiped them on his sleeve, then blinked fast, trying to stop the flow.

Once down the hill, Michael handed over the leash. "Here's the dog, sir! Rex, say 'hello' to your new master!"

"Reach out sir, to give your scent"

He also kneeled next to the dog. Bertrand held out his hand, and Michael, in turn, stroked Rex's mane.

"Come on Rex, take the gentleman's mark!" he urged the dog.

Shy, the dog smelled a little, then turned his head to Michael. Puzzled, he didn't know what was going on and what he was being asked to do.

"And now, what?" Bertrand asked.

"Sir, have you never had a dog?"

"To tell you the truth, not really; actually, I didn't have any, ever."

"Ah, well, then let me get him in the car, if you'll allow me."

"Oh, sure! Really please! Yes ... Thank you!"

Bertrand turned on his heels and hurried to his car and opened the second row of track doors. Michael climbed into the back seat and called Rex, who jumped happily beside him. Michael quickly got out of the car on the other side, and slammed the door behind him.

"Now you can leave, sir!"

"Oh, mercy! Thank you very much, Michael! Goodbye, Emily!"

Soon the truck disappeared into a cloud of dust, and they were left alone.

He had slammed the door in from of his faithful friend. Slammed the door, suddenly changing the path of Rex's life. Emily felt Michael's painful emotions and hugged him. He fell apart and sobbed. Emily started crying, too. It was not only Rex ... there were so many things ... memories, feelings they were leaving behind. From now on, they would cry for them.

****

After about two days, the priest appeared again in Tommy's ward. Stepping lightly, obviously worried, he approached Tommy's bed.

"Hello son, how are you? How are you feeling?" Without waiting for his answer, he went on, "I heard what happened. God, what a mess! Literally besieged by charity organizations and the media. Honestly, Tommy, this time they went too far. You are a patient under treatment. They shouldn't have rushed you like that. I hope you're better. The doctor told me you were starting to recover. Is it true?"

"Yes, thank you, Father. It was ... a cold shower. But now, it's over."

"I'm glad," said the priest, patting him lightly on the shoulder. Then he sat down in the chair by the window.

"Hey, Father, what would you like to talk about today?" ventured Tommy.

"I don't know yet. As I told you before, it's up to you. See, Tommy, the doctors are treating you for physical and mental trauma. I am here to soothe the pains of your soul. What we will talk about depends on you and what you want to know. You need to embrace spiritual food with all your soul. It cannot be imposed."

"You are right, Father! I like the idea!" Tommy said, obviously interested, rising to his feet and adjusting his pillow. "So, what did you say? Spiritual food?"

"Yes, son. I am trying to help you in this way. That's why I'm here. Let me give you an example: The jeweler can distinguish a genuine gemstone from a fake one. If you are looking to buy a diamond and if you are not helped by an expert in the field, you risk spending a lot of money on a piece of glass. In a way, the priest is like that jeweler—he can help you avoid big mistakes that can affect your spiritual life."

"So, you are like a jeweler, father!"

"Please forgive me. Maybe I have not chosen the best example."

"Don't apologize; I got the message and I understand what you mean. I found the comparison very suggestive."

"You know, faith cannot be viewed as unmovable. It should be associated with the effort to understand and draw closer to God sincerely and continuously.

"A human being who considers him or herself an atheist might be sometimes closer to God due to the love he or she shows to others. Other people believe in God with their minds and state it, but their actions are devoid of altruism and love. God judges us all first by our deeds and less by our words. God's grace is ours, given to the extent we are open to Him."

"Father, I have no words to express how this talk makes me feel! Please tell me more about God. How is He perceived?"

"Tommy, let me use an analogy. Water vapor is invisible. At low temperature, it turns into water. At an even lower temperature, it turns into ice. While water vapor does not have a definable shape, ice can take many forms.

"God is also invisible behind His creations, even if His energy moves everything in the entire Universe.

"The divine consciousness encompasses everything—the macrocosm and the microcosm. God is aware of every thought or feeling we have, as He is of the motion of the suns, planets and the galaxies in infinite space."

Tommy exclaimed, almost jumping out of bed, eyes shining and hair and beard in disarray, "You never cease to amaze me, Father! I fought on the ice, then in the war with bombs and mines, and never had time to think about all these things."

"It's normal, son; you don't have to blame yourself for that. You know, in our so-called consumer society, we are dragged into activities and running after material goals, and seldom do we think or have the time to enjoy life. The modern man is so agitated and busy, that he doesn't live his life, as the Dalai Lama rightly says."

"Yes Father, I see what you mean and I also see that you use many examples and quotes by people outside of the Orthodox faith. How does that reconcile with the Church theories?"

"Tommy, I'm trying to be open in my opinions, based on what I read, learn and live. This is the reason for my frequent controversies with my brothers in our Church. Of course, during the services, I keep the canons of the Church and do not digress from them. You see, I believe that different religions represent only different ways of approaching God. I do not believe that any of them possess the supremacy of truth regarding closeness to Him."

"This is a wonderful thought. My word, I like the way you think!" said Tommy excitedly. "And then, what about prayers to God?"

"God does not answer your prayers the way you expect. But if you are totally sincere with Him, then you will receive more than you expected. 'Faith is the substance of things hoped for, the evidence of things not seen', as Saint Paul said. Faith must be constantly nourished by inner experience—in the way you take care of a flower, nourishing it every day. The great miracles of faith were possible only for those who perceived the Divine as a single reality.

"In fact, the purpose of religion is to inspire people to communicate with God. Look, here's an example of the perceptions of God: Let's say that an engineer visits Rome. When he comes back from his trip, he will tell you about the architecture, buildings, boulevards, public transportation, and other technical elements of the city. However, when a politician returns from a trip to the same city, he will describe the political and administrative structure of the city. In this same way, no description will give you the whole understanding of the city. Likewise, no definition will ever succeed in fully expressing God."

"Father, I have to admit that I have ignored that all my life."

Just then, the nurse entered with a tray on which were several syringes and vials.

"Excuse me for the interruption, but it's time for Tommy's treatment. If you like, I could leave the tray here and come back in five minutes. No more please. We can't delay the treatment." Without waiting for comment, the nurse left the room.

"Yes, what I was saying, Father? Ah, yes, that I was ignorant. Now I know for sure.

"Father, in my treatment and in the process of recovery that my doctors are conducting with me, there are also some meetings with a psychologist and a psychiatrist."

"What do you want to say about that, Tommy?"

"I say that, strangely, I feel completely different. I mean, I feel much better after talking to you than after the sessions with those doctors."

"You see, Tommy, those doctors work with you, firstly, to understand your emotional and psychological condition, and help you to overcome so many traumas you went through. They help you to be able to face the difficulties of daily life. I am just trying to help you to come closer to God."

"Well, yes, but I like talking to you more than talking to them."

Thoughtful, looking down, the priest said, "You know, Tommy? I think you are on the right track. We will talk more next time." The nurse had appeared, and the priest stood up and parted, blessing him as usual.

Thoughtful, yet absent to whatever was going on around him, Tommy abandoned his body to the care of the nurse. Something had happened in his mind and consciousness, but he was still working hard to understand it.

****

Tied to one of the wooden legs of the vegetable stand, Rex stood with his head facing the world around him, with a fearful, anxious look. He had never seen so many people in one place. The noise and odors were overwhelming. His nose was working to distinguish through so many smells, which were constantly changing. People were coming and going, standing for a while in front of him, like cattle that never stopped coming.

Just a few moments before, Bertrand had hit him with a club because he had barked at a group of people who had come too close to the stand. With head down between his paws, he had endured the blows. When it stopped, he pulled back, whimpering slowly, until the stretched leash didn't let him go farther. It was hard for Rex—not so much for the pain, but he didn't understand. He had never been hit because he barked at anything. It was his nature and duty. And now, he was disoriented and frustrated at the same time. The world he knew had disappeared, and the rules of this new one were unclear for him.

The first beating he had received that day, about an hour before, was because he had tried to bite a teenager's hand. There were three noisy boys who had stopped in front of the stand, squirming and squatting back and forth on their skateboards.

One of the boys had come very close and tried to touch Rex's head from above. The sleeve of his jacket was immediately grabbed by a pair of white fangs. Rex received the deserved correction from Bertrand: a club to his back.

"Don't be afraid, boys! I know how to teach him. I am giving him a lesson!" he said, smiling, proud of himself. He didn't want to lose money or clients, or to get a bad reputation for having a vicious dog.

It was already the third day since Rex had his new master. He had a collar around his neck, and the leash was short enough not to let him move too much at his will. He was kept near the shelves with vegetables, and because Bertrand wetted the vegetables from time to time to keep them looking fresh, the cement was always full of water, and no matter how much Rex tried to find a dry warm place, it was in vain.

Time was dragging on. During the night, he had a longer leash, sliding on a wire, to let him run from one side of the stand to another. That's all he could move—a few yards back and forth. The goods on the stand were covered during the night with some canvas and plastic sacks. He could lean on one of the bags of goods behind the stand; that was better than the wet cement during the day.

The food Rex was given was bad, except once in a while, when Bertrand was in a good mood. After closing the grocery, Bertrand often went to a pub. His mind was clouded when he returned, and he had no thought to feed the dog.

But that's not what bothered Rex the most.

He was always thirsty, terribly thirsty. He was trying to drink water from the small holes in the cement, or water running down from the wet vegetables. But that weird master, would hit him with a club when he tried to drink water from the wet vegetables or concrete.

"Off you go, rascal!" were the only words for him from the man on these occasions, but never water. Not water, nor kind words. The freedom, peace, and quiet days spent at the Hendersons' farm had come to an end. Pain and suffering had taken their place. Rex didn't understand where it had all gone. Nothing was the same as before. Everything and everyone had disappeared: Michael, Emily, his brothers and sisters, his mother, by whose side he had always felt so protected. He missed the fields, the hills where they all used to run, free and unrestrained by anyone or anything. And Michael, the one who would pet him while bringing him food. He, the dog named Rex, had vanished. He was now a different Rex, destined to endure unnatural and outdated hardships, unfit for a dog raised on a farm. Those beautiful times had faded away, lost to nothingness. The present was cruel and painful, even for a dog.

****

Emily and her family spent more than a month looking for a house to fit their needs and vision. The large spaces from the farm still affected their ability to choose. They visited many houses until they found something closer to their expectations. What they finally decided upon was a two-storey house. The upstairs had four bedrooms and a bathroom. On the ground floor was a substantial living room, a big dining room and parlor, opening onto a large deck. From the deck, two flower beds adorned the back yard, and a narrow path lead to a brook.

Not far away from the residential area, a train station provided easy transportation, and a few shops were nearby, with commercial potential. One shop in particular caught Emily's eye; the front lounge had been an Irish pub and had many facilities. Emily thought immediately that the space could be used as a store. It had everything necessary: electricity, gas, water, sinks, and storage. There was also another kitchen that could be turned into something else, such as a warehouse for imported goods.

"Mom, I like it here! We will renovate the deck and help you start up the store and everything" said Michael enthusiastically.

"Don't forget what you have promised, Michael. You have to go to tutoring, so that next year you'll be able to continue school."

"No worries mom. I can do it all!"

The two sisters were delighted with the new home. They were going to live there, but each would have their own room, and they no longer had to look for rental units.

"Yes," Emily mused aloud, "we are together again, reunited; at least I was able to do after Bill left us."

Time moved quickly. The purchase of the store was arranged within two weeks and all the approvals were received after another week, so the business was ready to start. Renovations were completed by the next month, so Emily ordered goods from the local farmers and stocked the store. The girls went to school, Michael went to tutoring and helped Emily in the store in the afternoons.

In the fall days that followed, they would spend their evenings on the deck. Sometimes they recounted memories from their life at the farm—Bill, the house, the fields and animals, including Rex.

****

After a few weeks, Tommy recovered very well, and hospital management approved a visit of several people. Among them, some of Tommy's older acquaintances: Donovan, the president of the club where Tommy last played hockey; Travers and Saunders, currently club secretaries; Gerry Thomson, president of the Association of War Veterans; some ladies, including Shelly Tricon, from City Hall; and two journalists from the local press.

Extremely reluctant, Tommy accepted, hoping that he would be able to get rid of the pressure of civil society on him sooner. The hospital director and the Chief Physician were also at the meeting.

Gerry started the meeting. "Sir, as you were probably informed, our association organized a meeting with the main aim do help you. You have been exquisite hockey player—one of the best goalies in the history of the Professional League of hockey, and a hero of our country, wounded several times in the war in Afghanistan and receiving military honours.

"Thus, we all have decided that, after so much hard work and self-sacrifice for the country, you deserve a decent life."

"Yes, sir," Sheryl chimed in. "City Hall wants to help you with a one-bedroom apartment, so that you can live as anyone else, and no longer live on the streets."

"We are going to furnish the apartment from donations," added Travers. "The Club has already started a subscription. We'll have enough in a few days. We would like you to choose your furniture."

Sitting on the edge of his hospital bed, in a robe and slippers, Tommy turned his gaze from one to the other, with total detachment. He wondered what these people wanted. God, what a waste! A furnished apartment!"

And on top of everything, the two ladies and the journalists start scooping for interesting comments.

"What is your opinion, sir, about the donation from City Hall?"

"Thank you, I am delighted," Tommy said, offering the answer they were looking for.

"Did you expect any donation from the Club?"

"I wasn't really prepared for that; I didn't expect it. I am really moved."

"What do you think, Tommy, of not being forgotten by the Club for which you won so many victories?"

"Impressive. Yes. Impressive that they didn't forget me, especially since it's been a while since I defended the club colours."

The dull questions continued on the same theme, with small variations. Tommy was finding it increasingly difficult to concentrate and answer the questions. Finally, the Chief Physician noticed Tommy's condition and stepped in, interrupting the meeting: "Ladies and gentlemen, please! The patient is tired and needs rest. If there any further questions, perhaps we can continue tomorrow."

The dismissal signal being given, the guests rushed toward the door, each trying to get out first.

"And they didn't even say 'goodbye'!" Tommy whispered. He laid on his back, but was unable to relax. After a long while, he pressed the button to call the nurse, who appeared almost immediately.

"What happened, Tommy? Are you okay?"

"I just called to ask you something, please."

"Yes. Sure. Whatever you need."

"Please look for the Priest. See if he is in the Hospital Chapel. If you find out where he is, ask him to come to me if he is willing to."

"Yes, I am sure he's at the Chapel at this hour. I'll send someone to ask him." She left the room.

Waiting for the priest, Tommy slowly lowered himself on his back. A nervous tremor gripped him. Alone, in silence, he curled on one side and began to cry. Fed up and humiliated by the whole discussion with those officials, he felt like a prisoner, trapped without escape. Everything was false, distorted. He knew and felt it. With his eyes closed and fists clenched, he wept in jerky gasps.

"What a screwed-up life!"

****

The priest quickly opened the door and found himself in total darkness. A few more steps and he got used to it and distinguished Tommy lying on his side, on his bed in his sweat-soaked robe and shirt. His pillow was also wet with tears and sweat. Disconcerted, the priest touched Tommy lightly.

"Hey, Tommy, what's going on?"

He did not answer but turned, with difficulty, onto his back.

"Shall I turn on the light?" the priest ventured.

"Yes, please. And, could you ask the nurse for a glass of water, please?"

The priest complied, and soon the nurse appeared, bringing water and a clean pillow, pajamas, and a robe. In all this time, the priest was sitting in his chair, obviously confused and embarrassed, staring aimlessly around him.

"Thank you very much, Kathy! Kathy is your name, right?"

"That's right. Please let me know if you need anything else."

"No, nothing at the moment, thank you very much!"

"Treatment in an hour, please. I am coming for that myself."

"I'll be waiting for you; thank you."

Head up and walking stiffly, with an air of importance and efficiency, the nurse left the room.

As he changed clothes, Tommy commented to the priest, "So stand-offish sometimes, but totally dedicated to her job, this Kathy."

"Yes, indeed, indeed," he confirmed, not very convinced.

Tommy continued talking about the medical staff. "Some of them are polite and pleasant. All of them are honest. But, just tell me Father, come on, tell me, am I crazy; is my mind twisted?"

"But what happened, son, what happened to you?"

"They came again—the officials came again. This time with everything approved and all the papers signed and ready in hand."

"How so? Who are 'they'?"

"The very same people as before. This time with their representatives. And in order for everything to be legal, smooth and with ribbons, the chief doctor and the director of the hospital were also present."

"Okay, okay, but what did these people want?" the priest asked, his face still red and slightly sweaty, after he had come running at Tommy's call.

"What did they want? To show-off! There was also the press, only two this time and no TV, no cameramen."

"And what did they actually say?"

"What'd they say? They wanted to give me a furnished one bedroom, to have a place to live, and the Club and the Association to give me monthly rent so that I could make a living. They also wanted to give me help from the Government, something like social help, or something like that."

"Ooh . . . but that's great, isn't it? To be able to have a house of your own?"

"But I don't want it!" Tommy yelled from the bottom of his lungs and his cry rose to the ceiling and into the corridors.

This took the priest by surprise and he remained stunned, his eyes wide. The nurse appeared immediately.

"Everything okay? Did anything happen?"

"Forgive me, please," Tommy apologised. "I lost control. That's all."

The nurse studied him carefully. "Do you want me to give you a sedative, Tommy?"

"No, no; no need. Thank you, Kathy."

"No more loud shouts; you'll get the whole hospital up."

After Kathy left, Tommy stood in front of the priest and continued, this time without bellowing.

"I do not want it! Did anyone ask me anything? No. Not one of them. What I am? A helpless man? Or a guinea pig to appear on TV?"

Tommy started pacing in circles, looking at the floor.

"Did they ask me? I don't want anything from anyone. And I never asked for alms. As a hockey player, I had my life, and I earned my money. Then after the last accident, I had no more. I enrolled and I had my paycheck. Eventually, I was wounded. When I left the hospital, I made the streets my home. I have never asked anyone for anything. I never did! Do you understand me? Never!"

"Okay, okay Tommy, but these people want the best for you. They want to help you."

"Is that so? Really? They want to help them, Father. Media, advertisements, newspaper articles, television, and City Hall as well. The election is approaching, right? Why did they have to make this cheap show? And why wasn't I asked first?"

"Tommy, I can't say you are wrong, but the intentions of these people are to help you. So, don't be so proud anymore."

"What? No longer be proud?" Tommy stressed the words. "Then, what do I have left, Father, but dignity and pride?"

"Son, take the goodness of the people as coming from God."

"And their bragging, too?"

"Leave those to the Lord. We are not entitled to judge the deeds of others."

"Again, I must recognize, Father, that you have answers to everything. You are like a fish I cannot catch as it slips out of my hands as soon as I am trying to grab it."

"Tommy, the work of the Lord must be seen as a gift, unblemished by the hands of people. Take what is beautiful from those who want good for you. That is sent by God. As for the other side, leave it on the shoulders of those who are doing it and God will judge everyone. You are not the one who has to do it. You just pray to Him and give Him your actions and thoughts. You must be very assiduous in your spiritual practice.

"People say they love their fellow men when actually they only love themselves; they love others to the extent they please them. True love is when—even with a personal sacrifice, you are happy to be able to give happiness to your loved one.

"And one more important thing: live in this world as a guest. Your true home is not here. Consider yourself a guest in this world, in which you have to be responsible as much as you can, taking care of everything God puts in your way at your service. And never forget that they are all His and not yours.

You have to start praying. Only those who really have the desire and make the effort will get closer to God. Imagine someone wants to become a virtuoso violinist. He will practice twelve hours a day; but if he practices only a few minutes per day, he will never be a renowned player."

"So, what do you suggest that I should do? Pray like crazy, twelve hours a day?"

"First and foremost, start praying. Then seek to pray as much as possible and dedicate your actions to Him. Water the seeds of your faith in Him daily. And above all, do not be impatient in your effort to find God. Give yourself to Him wholeheartedly, without impatiently waiting for effects. In time, you will find Him in the peace and tranquility of your soul."

"Yes! As it is written in the book, Father; as in the book."

Tommy sat on the edge of the bed, then stretched out. He was far away, immersed in his thoughts.

An awkward silence filled the room. The priest sensed that it was better to leave.

"You need some rest and peace; maybe it's better if I go for now."

"Thank you, Father. Thank you for coming so fast … and for forgiving my outbursts and tirades."

"Oh, Tommy!" The priest stood up. "We are all wrong. We are all sinners."

"Yes, Father. We are all sinners—maybe too sinful …"

****

That night, in the large hall of the Farmers' Market, it was colder than usual. Piles of sacks, full of vegetables, were stacked in the isles between the stands. During the night, everything was in a terrible disarray. It was not until the morning, after the vendors arrived, that the stands were nicely arranged.

In one of the corners, lying on a sack, Rex was watching. His fur was matted. His ribs pierced his fur, like the keys of a piano. His legs had lengthened, and his muscles had become thinner. His head looked angularly deformed, somehow grotesque, in the style of Hallowe'en masks, and his ears seemed very long, piercing the air like two lightning rods. The beatings, the cold, but especially the lack of water and food, had taken their toll.

It was just before dawn, and there were only a few people in the large hall. Some of the owners had spent the night watching their goods; others had lain on the piles of sacks. One of them stood up and start walking through the stands, eating a smoked pork sausage. He was walking aimlessly, stopping here and there and taking a big bite from the sausage.

Rex's nose sniffed the smell of a long forgotten good meal—the well-fried sausage—but didn't move. With a glassy look, he was watching the man with the piece of sausage. Finally, the man turned his back to Rex and threw the rest of the sausage over his shoulder. At once, Rex jerked to his feet, eyes twinkling, muscles tense and strained like a bow. He tried a few times to reach the piece of sausage that laid there in front of him, not a yard away. Suspended on his tight leash on his hind paws, Rex described in air with his front paws in arcs of a circle in his desperate attempt to reach the pray. Then, he tried something different; he crawled on his belly and pushed with his legs, trying to get his snout closer to the much wished-for piece of meat. The smell seemed to have driven his mind crazy. His paws scratched the cement as he pulled out his nails, trying to break the slip-back.

All his attempts failed. He pulled back and tried to free himself from the leash. Inch by inch, he slid his leash over his head. Once over the ears, he pulled away hard, sliding to one side and then stumbled, and ended up in a quick roll. After the fall, he got up and jumped to grab the little piece of sausage, disappearing among the piles of sacks. Safe, he swallowed it as if it were nothing.

He wandered through the piles of sacks until he found the edge of the canopy that covered the market. Rex crawled under it and was outside, breathing fresh air. Outside it was almost dawn; the dawn of his freedom.

****

The next morning, there was a great stir at the hospital. Tommy was gone; he was nowhere to be found. The morning shift had found only his pajamas and the robe, spread out nicely over the bed, spotlessly clean and orderly. Missing were his clothes, as well as his backpack and his military-issue brass bucket. Totally perplexed, the staff were amazed; Tommy was almost recovered—at the end of his treatment. Everything was going well. Nobody could offer the slightest explanation. He was on such a good track—ready to receive a house and money. He hadn't let them feel in any way that he was unhappy or displeased with something while he was in the hospital. The people had surrounded him with only positive feelings. Yet there had to be a reason for his behaviour. Obviously, they had to alert the hospital security and the police.

Tommy was on the street and he felt free … liberated. At first, the strong air outside had made him dizzy, but not for long.

He knew they would look for him. It was obvious, after so much propaganda in the media. City Hall was also involved in the story, so the police, he expected, would be asked for support. He avoided narrow, isolated streets and high crime areas; they were too full of misery and doubtful people. He was a homeless man, not a delinquent.

He ventured up the river, and made his shelter beside it. During the day, he searched here and there to find something to prepare a meal in the evening at his safe place: a vegetable or two from the farmers market, a piece of meat, a bone, or beef tail from a butcher, a handful of rice from a merciful shopkeeper; it was enough to scrape up a meal.

Wrapped up in his old discoloured coat, he sat by the fire in the evening preparing something to eat. He had learned to cook long ago and was able to make great soups in his brass bucket. In the morning, he used it for tea. He still had a good frying pan, which he had bought at a garage sale.

As soon as he had left the hospital, he cut and dyed his hair and shaved his beard in one of the washrooms of the metro train stations. He was blonde now. At least for a while, he wanted peace and quiet and did not want to risk being recognized by anyone, let alone the police.

It was not his first break out of a hospital; he had done so when he was injured in Afghanistan.

And then, as now, he had felt like he was drowning in that hospital atmosphere. Outside he felt liberated, free to breathe air, fresh air. Free of everything and everyone.

****

A few days passed; he was almost into a routine, until one evening when an unusual guest arrived.

He was sitting by the fire on a box covered with some rags, held together as a chair. He had covered his head and shoulders with an old blanket, found near the market.

An alluring steam was coming out from the brass bucket suspended over the fire. An appetizing smell spread around, as a piece of beef was boiling inside, along with some rice and vegetables from the market. The soup was almost ready. He bent forward, stirred lightly with a wooden spoon, and bowed his head, ready to take a sip. Suddenly, he had the feeling that he was being watched. He looked ahead and froze. Two glassy eyes were piercing him through the semi-darkness. Staring intently, he discerned a furry head, bones almost jutting out through the skin, just a few yards in front of him.

"Hi, hell!" was his first reaction. "Don't you look great?!"

Tommy looked more carefully. The animal looked like a horror painting: eyes two pieces of glass, head, angled, only bones … and body the same, brown fur in great disorder—only tufts of hair, with ribs protruding like keys of a piano. The creature looked like anything but a dog.

"Poor beast!" Tommy stood up.

Head down and snout sweeping the ground, the being pulled back, limping. Only now, Tommy noticed wounds on his body. Without warning, he blurted out, "Oh, God! Who the hell could do such a thing to you?"

Tommy took a few steps further. The dog retreated even more. Seeing this, Tommy hesitated, then he looked around and found a piece of bark. Turning back, he searched with the spoon in the bucket and took out the bone covered with meat and placed it on the piece of bark and laid it on the grass, a few yards in front of the fire. Then he turned around and sat down again. The poor animal, mostly skeleton, moved slowly, crawling towards the bone and staring at Tommy. When he reached close to it, his nose moving frantically, he suddenly jumped and grabbed the bone and ran a little further away. He started gnawing, never losing sight of Tommy.

"Holly God!" Tommy exclaimed, unable to believe his eyes. A little further, on his belly and holding the bone with both front paws, the dog scraped the meat in two gulps, and now was breaking the bone into pieces. Soon there was nothing left of it. After he finished, the dog got a bit closer to the fire and looked up at Tommy. Slowly, Tommy got up again and on another piece of bark he placed another piece of bone with some meat on it. Just as quickly as before, the dog finished it.

A little later, Tommy took a sip from the soup. He swallowed hard, when looking away, he met dog's eyes looking at him. Their eyes met, and there was something so painfully familiar in those eyes, but he didn't know what it was. He couldn't remember where he had seen that look, but he had seen it before. Maybe on the front. It was despair … and a painful cry for help.

The dog yelped slightly. A few tears rolled from Tommy's eyes. He got up in slow movements, not to scare the dog. He searched in his backpack and pulled out a small pot and filled it with soup and, with equally slow movements, placed it a few feet further in front of the fire. That's how he and the unforeseen guest had dinner that evening.

"At least I'm not alone," he muttered as he lay down to sleep.

When he woke up the next morning, the dog was there, watching him. He didn't know why, but Tommy was pleased to see him.

"I like to think we will be friends! What do you think?" he asked the dog.

But it didn't happen too soon. He tried a few times to touch him, but the dog pulled aside, avoiding contact every time. Tommy talked to him every evening. He would share his thoughts, some of them the most hidden, and the dog would look at him and listen attentively.

One morning, after he had rummaged through his backpack and pulled out a piece of smoked bacon, cut a slice, chopped it and threw it in the pan, he was thinking about adding an egg or two when the dog come closer. Tommy left the pan and offered him a piece. This time, the dog didn't pull back, but stretched his body very slowly, shyly, bending his head. Tommy outstretched his hand and touched him under his chin. The animal trembled slightly.

"Enough for now," Tommy whispered. "We have plenty of time for more."

They just looked at each other, but didn't move.

"Listen to me! I'll call you 'Dog' as I don't know what name you had before. What I do know is that they tortured you terribly."

Every day they repeated the ritual of getting closer, but it was about a week or two before Tommy was allowed to caress him with his whole palm. When he hugged him to his chest, Dog hid his nose under Tommy's arm.

Tommy had won a friend. They found each other and, at the same time, Tommy had found himself and his troubled soul. Squeezing Dog to his chest, the priest's words echoed in his ear: "Do not hesitate to do a good deed, helping any living creature, but do it without expecting any reward! God will be with you then."

"So be it," murmured Tommy.

****

They met by sheer chance, Tommy and Two Teeth. It was on the corner of Rose Boulevard and 42nd Street. Tommy turned off the narrow street onto the boulevard, where, just a few yards away, he saw a man—a big fellow—propped up against a wall, his hat lying open on the sidewalk in front of him, hoping for a few coins. Whatever he got, however little, it would help someone like him. Tommy recognized a brother in arms, another of fates forgotten.

One glance told Tommy the man was down bad. Unshaven, with long hair spilling out from under a cap that hadn't seen its original color in years, his eyes were hollow and dark. His face, ashen and sallow, matched the worn, trembling hands barely visible from beneath a tattered, faded red coat. His legs were crossed in front of him, boots on his feet whose soles were tied up with string to keep them from completely falling apart. Every now and then, he'd cough—short and hacking—and raise his head to see what was going on around him. Between two gray lips, a couple of big, crooked teeth shone out.

A tear slipped into the corner of Tommy's eye. He dug deep into his own coat pocket, pulled out a knotted handkerchief, and opened it carefully. He picked out a nickel from the few coins he had, tied the handkerchief back up, and tossed the coin into the man's hat.

The man lifted his head. Their eyes met. They looked each other over, reading the story in each other's faces. The man cracked a small smile, a silent understanding passing between them. No words were needed—just a meeting of eyes. Two poor souls, each in a rough spot, one a bit worse off than the other.

"Where'd you come from, stranger?" the man murmured. "Where do you hang around these days, and where do your feet take you?"

"Here and there, all over. Just roaming. I see you're lookin' a bit 'scraped up,' too."

"Yeah," the man replied. "No big deal. Just winter coming up, and I'm caught without cover."

Tommy crouched beside him on the sidewalk. He set his sack down, pulled out a little pouch of tobacco, rolled a cigarette, and handed it over. The man's shaky hand accepted the offering, and he gave Tommy a wide smile. He held out his hand.

"They call me Two Teeth where I roam."

"Tommy," he replied, clasping the man's hand in a firm, silent understanding, a bond starting to take root between them.

They chatted for a while about this and that—the simple, daily stuff.

As Two Teeth talked, Tommy's eyes drifted down to the man's battered boots again. He wouldn't make it through winter, not a chance, Tommy thought. With a deep breath, he reached into his sack, pulled out a pair of new boots he'd just received from a mission he'd visited that day. Holding them by the laces, he handed them over.

Wide-eyed, Two Teeth took them, and for a moment, they held each other's

gaze—no thanks, no fuss, no need for words. Just something simple, soul-deep.

And so, that was the first time Tommy met Two Teeth.

****

From that day on, the two of them were inseparable. In the evening, Dog would go closer to Tommy, but without bothering him. On these occasions, Tommy noticed the ugly wounds Dog had, especially the one behind his right ear above the shoulder. Dog whimpered whenever Tommy accidently touched him in that area. Tommy decided he had to do something for Dog, but he wasn't sure how he could help his new friend. As a hockey player, he had had all kinds of injuries, and he had also seen a lot more in the war, but not in dogs.

The next day, he snuck into a shower at a public park. He dressed in his most decent clothes and hid his belongings in a grove near the bridge. Of course, Dog was always with him.

Looking smarter now, he and Dog walked together along the boulevard looking for a library. Dog followed him closely, skilfully avoiding people. Eventually, they stopped near a tall, old-fashioned building with a big board on the frontispiece: "The Municipal Library." Tommy directed Dog onto a narrow alley and stopped, lowered and took Dog's head in his hands and whispered to him:

"You, buddy, stay here and wait for me. There are too many people on the streets and around, and I don't want someone to hurt you. Wait for me. Stay," he repeated a few times, but as soon as Tommy took a few steps, Dog followed him.

Again, Tommy said, "Stay here! Wait for me!" Eventually, Tommy held Dog's head in his hands and looked into his eyes, whispering, "You have to wait for me. I will be back!" This time, Dog understood and sat down on his hind legs. Tommy departed, climbed the stairs and disappeared behind the large door of the building. There were a lot of people waiting quietly in lines at different counters.

He stopped for a moment, vaguely confused, and then walked along the desks until he saw one on whose window was written "Information."

"'Good afternoon!"

"Good afternoon, sir! How can I help you?"

"You know, I am looking for a book regarding the treatment of wounds in pets. In fact, for dogs, to be more precise."

"You may try on the fifth floor. But why don't you consult a vet?" asked the woman, with a rather superior posture and slightly defiant.

"No, thank-you. I can't."

He turned around and looked for the elevators. Once he arrived on the fifth floor, he stepped into a small passage that turned right. There were high shelves, reaching the ceiling, and he felt lost, like in a maze.

"Oh, my God!" he whispered. "Where should I begin?"

He walked along one side of the shelves until he hit a dead end, so he turned back and followed a different row. At the end of the aisle, he saw a counter where a woman was working. When he came closer, she raised her head:

"Hello! How can I help you today?"

Tommy remained silent. Time ceased to flow. In front of him, two large, deep blue eyes were watching him. Tommy felt lost on an endless sea. Beautiful arched eyebrows offered some sort of anchor for Tommy. The face, with fine features, white complexion, beautifully protruding cheeks, and a small nose above delicate lips, was watching him with great care.

"Sir?"

Tommy, trying to recover, muttered, "I, ... you know, ... I ... am ... looking for a book."

"Sure. What kind of book, sir?

"A book ... a book about dogs' wounds and their treatment. Could I find something like that here?"

"Well, let's see, yes. We have a few books on this topic and you can find them in subject area seven."

Confused and embarrassed, Tommy was able to murmur, "I don't know if ... I can ... ah, ... find it."

Without knowing why, those big, dark blue eyes burned through him, but he couldn't stop looking into them. The woman in front of him made him feel somehow insecure ... in danger. He felt awkward and couldn't concentrate to give a proper answer.

"The books are arranged according to the different themes, on subjects, and each theme is broken down into alphabetical order by authors' last name. Subject seven is in the middle."

Looking at him, the woman realized that he was helpless and he wouldn't be able to find what he needed.

"Wait a minute, I'll help you, sir. Please, follow me."

She strutted through the shelves and he followed her. Without any hesitation, she found the shelves with the subject requested; there were dozens of books about dogs, and some of them discussed their diseases and appropriate treatments for them.

"I'm leaving you now. I have to go back to my desk; someone might need me."

And she walked away, leaving him alone but leaving behind a delicate scent. He was already tired or dizzy, he was not sure as his mind was unable to react properly.

He tried to read the titles—to concentrate on the meaning of the words. At first, he failed, but then he struggled to make out the gist of them. He kept trying and it went a little better.

"Come on, you idiot!" he admonished himself. "You came here with a purpose!" he continued talking to himself.

Slowly, he began to investigate the books. It took him more than an hour until he found what he thought was useful for Dog's treatment. He took it back to her desk, but she was busy giving some information to another customer. He looked at her, mesmerized, listening to her voice, the pitch and pace of it.

"Did you find anything useful, sir?"

For a few seconds, Tommy didn't realize that she was talking to him. "Ah, yes, thank you for your help. Now, I would like to ask you, how should I proceed so that I can borrow the book?"

"No problem, sir. Go downstairs to the counters, and one of the librarians there will help you. Just give them your library card, and they will process the transaction."

"You know ... I don't have a library card."

"This is your first time here? Well, let's see; it isn't a problem. When you go downstairs to the information desk, give them an identity document and they will issue you a card on the spot and will sign out the book for you as well."

Just thinking about the "sour" lady downstairs, Tommy felt the unpleasant nausea feeling deep in his stomach. He must have made a face, for the woman asked, "Did something happen? Don't you feel well?"

"No, no, Miss! It's just that I ... I can't ... I don't have documents. I live on the streets."

"You're homeless?"

For the first time, Tommy felt humiliated by his status.

"And you do not have documents? How so?"

"It's a long story, Miss."

Suddenly, he felt overwhelmed. Those big, warm eyes and her scent made him dizzy. He swayed from one foot to the other, holding the book with both hands in front of him, close to his chest.

The woman looked at the floor and then looked thoughtfully at him holding the book. "There is another way. Here's how we can do it: take it on my behalf. I trust people who want to read, and I think you have a good reason for wanting this book in particular. Please mind the deadline. I will let my colleague know."

She picked up the phone and talked to someone in a low voice. After a while, she put the receiver on mute and asked him, "Your name, sir?"

"Tommy, Miss."

"Listen Elly, call him Tommy. I am sending him to you now."

Turning to Tommy, "Sir, please go downstairs to counter five. I've informed my colleague and she is waiting for you. The book will be borrowed on my behalf."

"Thank you very much, Miss …?"

"Miss Lillian" she said, smiling.

His throat was dry. He was very disturbed in the presence of the woman. This had never happened to him. He turned and stepped towards the elevators. The dizziness didn't leave him. In the corridor, in front of the elevator, he had to lean against the wall. He rubbed his forehead and cheeks with his hand and thought, "It's just a temporary state of weakness," but, deep in his soul, he knew it was something different.

****

In the following days, using the library book, Tommy treated Dog's wounds. As he had no money for medication, Tommy bent his pride and worked unloading some furniture trucks. He also asked the butcher for some sheep sap, the foundation for an ointment for Dog's treatment. He needed some antibiotics, cotton wool and bandages, and he managed to get everything. To his surprise, Dog accepted everything without any resistance. The hardest part was the injections—two per day for a week.

He wrapped his arms around Dog's neck, and spoke softly into his ear, and then, without hiding, he took one of Dog's legs and gave him the shot. Dog whimpered a bit, like a child, while Tommy was holding him to his chest, whispering into his ear. Dog behaved and obeyed; a true friendship was growing between them, each giving the other trust and love.

A week later, he was on the bank of the river, slightly lower downstream of the bridge, where a few wide, flat stones allowed him to wash his clothes. He did it once a week, using a bar of soap. He dunked the clothes, spread them on the wide stones and soaped them well, rinsed them in the river water, and dried them by laying them in the sun on the stones or hanged on the branch of a tree.

That day, he had just bent down, rinsing a heavier towel, when his left foot slipped on the shiny surface of the stone with soap on it. He lost his balance and fell into water. The current was fast and started to carry him dizzyingly down the river. After a few moments, behind him he heard a splash. Dog had jumped after him and was approaching fast. They were soon swimming shoulder to shoulder. Not far away, he saw a patch of sand. Tommy reached it first and Dog immediately after. They crawled onto the sand, where Dog shook himself hard, spraying water all around.

Later, on the sand, in a low voice, Tommy called the dog to him.

"Hi, Dog. Come here, my samurai!"

The dog came slowly, shaking his fur again. Tommy hugged him to his chest, whispering into his ear as he had often done, "You didn't want to leave me behind, did you? You jumped after me. You didn't want to lose me, did you? You are a hero, my boy!"

Even though he didn't understand, Dog whimpered slowly, wagging his tail.

That incident grew into the sincerest friendship; they were friends forever, Tommy felt. Tommy had learned everything about his dog treatment, so the day came when he returned the library book into the slot at the entrance. The woman with big blue eyes the colour of the sea was back in his mind's eye. He had to see her and thank her. Yes, he had to thank her; actually, he was justifying his desire to see her again.

He went upstairs to the fifth floor. He was walking fast, with long strides. Turning the corner of the corridor he saw her, standing behind her desk.

She recognised him at once, greeting him with her delicate smile and a warm open look in her blue eyes.

"Hello! Tommy greeted her with enthusiasm.

"Hello, sir!"

"Call me Tommy," he dared to add.

"Hello Tommy! How are you? How was the book; was it helpful?"

"Yes, very helpful. Thank you very much! My dog is better now and I came to thank you. I couldn't have done it without you, Miss Lillian.

"You can call me Lilly."

"Thank you, Lilly!"

"Tell me, she continued, "Do you really like to read?"

"Oh, yes, I always liked it, although my profession did not give me enough time to do it."

"May I dare to ask you, what was your profession?"'

"I was a hockey player and then a soldier."

"Do you mean a professional hockey player?"

"Yes, Miss. Please forgive me, but I don't like to talk too much about it."

"I understand, I understand. You said you like to read. What do you like to read?"

"I'm not sure. Maybe some novels ... stories about trappers in the Rocky Mountains and the north ... if there are such books."

"Of course there are. We have many shelves with such stories." She stood up, urging him, "Follow me, please."

He followed her through the bookshelves, docile as a child. The same dizziness had gripped him, just like the last time he was around her. Her scent would make him float. In front of him, she was walking with a rolling gait. "Cat walk," he said to himself.

They reached the looked-for shelves.

"Look, Tommy, here are some of the books you might enjoy. Take your time and search them leisurely. Choose one and come back to my desk and will talk about it."

"Thank you, Miss Lilly," he answered in a quiet voice, lost in his thoughts. His gaze met hers, the gate of her soul, and, for a second time, stopped. He moved his eyes over the woman's hair, flowing in strands on her shoulders, giving her a fragile air.

After she left him alone, he needed considerable time to get back to normal.

"Damn! What's wrong with me?" he rubbed his face several times, took a deep breath and tried to calm down. He spent more than half an hour reading the titles of the books and browsing through most of them, but he was still undecided. He hesitated between several titles and actually wanted to borrow few, not a single book. He headed through the shelves back to her desk where she again greeted him with that smile, making dimples in her checks.

"So, Tommy, did you find what you were looking for?"

"Yes, thank you, Miss. This one especially caught my attention, but I'd love to read a few more."

"There's no hurry, Tommy, one at a time. You have time to read as many books as you want."

Lilly reached her hand for the book, and Tommy's eyes remained glued to it and he felt a painful knot in his neck. Her hand was very white, with long, slightly arched nails, painted in cherry red. The cuff of the blouse was just above her wrist. The same black blouse shaped her body and went around her neck in a wide collar. The dark colour contrasted strikingly with her white, velvety skin. Squeezing tightly over her chest, the blouse waved smoothly, hiding two small breasts.

"Look Tommy, let me tell you what I think," she began. "As last time, you can borrow this book on my name. I've already made the arrangements; you just have to show up at counter three this time.

"In the meantime, I will talk to the head librarian, to introduce you to a program for people with special needs, to be able to issue you a card with a name declared by you on your own responsibility. Thus, you will be able to borrow as many books as you want. Well, what do you say?"

"I have no words to thank you enough, Miss!"

"Lilly. Don't be shy, call me Lilly."

"Yes, Miss Lilly."

"And ... Tommy, I'd like to see you again. To see you around more often."

"Of course. I will definitely come. Have a good day! Thank you!"

"You as well, Tommy. Take care of yourself!"

He didn't realize how he got out. He finished quickly at the counter and rushed into the street through the wide, heavy door. He seemed drunk, a strange dizziness gripped him, while hundreds of nervous impulses tingled his back and arms.

When he turned the corner, Dog was waiting for him. His faithful friend stood up and took a few steps toward him, wagging his tail happily. Tommy knelt beside him and started whispering softly in his ear, "You know, Dog, I was given the privilege to meet a wonderful being. A woman. And what a woman!"

That evening, sitting by the fire, he was trying to follow his routine of having dinner, but, looking at the flickering flames, he saw among them Lilly's face. Later, when he went down to the river to wash his pan, on the shining waves he again saw Lilly's face. He closed his eyes, trying to get rid of that smiling face. In vain. She was there, everywhere. He got back to the fire and told his companion, "Dog, I think 'The Flame' got me!"

****

After a few days, he finished the book and headed off to the city, showed up at the library and went up the elevator. Once outside the elevator, he rushed round the corner and .... Dismay!

A middle-aged woman, with short, white hair and black eyes looked at him. "How can I help you, sir?"

He, astonished, dumbfounded, was stuck there and unable to articulate a word.

"Sir?"

"Oh, no, ... no. Thanks! ", he answered hurriedly, and, turning on his heels, he was out into the street in less than a minute. He took Dog and marched quickly back to his home under the bridge. All the way, many questions flowed in waves, whipping his mind, but he could not find answers.

"What has happened? Why wasn't she there? Did she get sick? Was she fired? Did she move to another location?" Only Dog heard the questions that day and the next. Dog listened to Tommy's questions, his arguments and explanations. He talked a lot, almost continuously, sometimes he shouted and gestured to the river, the trees, the moon ... everything. Eventually, he got tired, and he calmed down. He felt exhausted, especially because he hadn't slept for the past two nights.

In time, a sense of guilt overwhelmed his mind. Why hadn't he asked anything? Why had he left without an answer?

Then, he made a decision and told Dog, "Tomorrow, I'm going again to the library and I'll find out what the hell has happened. We are going together, my trustworthy friend." That being said, he leaned close to the fire and eventually fell asleep.

****

The next morning, he was feeling better. He got up, went to the river, washed himself carefully, and trimmed his beard with a pair of scissors. He bent over the water, and, catching a glimpse of his own face, he started to talk to himself.

"Tommy, you should face the truth: You have a crush on this woman, so do not try to pretend that it's nothing. You are hooked and you have to recognize and accept that. Now, since that has happened, know that you can't do anything to stop it. Go forward like a man."

Falling leaves carried over by the river concealed his reflected face for a moment.

"Yes, like thoughts gliding on the water of life …" he thought. Then, firmly: "You have to go ahead, man, as I am telling you, as you always did."

Suddenly, a bright idea crossed his mind. "I have to do something to win her heart! Because I can't live without her. Don't you see, you madman, that her face doesn't leave you, not even in your sleep? Don't you see, crazy man, that whatever you do, you see her everywhere and you can't stop thinking about her one single moment? So, do as you have always done overcoming any difficulties. Go ahead! You never gave up."

He told himself all these things, looking at his face in the water.

But, deep in his mind and soul, he knew he was somehow wrong. How will he react, when, every time in her presence, he felt lost? The purity, the charm released by that being made him dizzy, unable to utter a word. And the eyes, well, those big eyes, open like the pages of a book, blue and innocent, seemed to come from another world.

"Don't fool yourself, Tommy! You'll do what you can. You know you're missing her! You're lost!" and he slapped the surface of the water. The water-mirror vanished, and so was the reflection in it. It had broken into many little waves, "As our thoughts do," Tommy thought.

"Don't be a child anymore! Go there again and see what's going on. That's all you have to do. Go there first!" Tommy told himself, taking heart.

He turned to Dog, who raised his head to him, whining softly. That was the way he manifested his love and Tommy knew it. He took Dog's head in his hands, looked into his eyes, and whispered softly to him. Eventually, Tommy hugged him and Dog pushed his head under his arm.

"We are going to eat something and then go to the library. We are going together, my dear friend; we are embarking on an adventure that only God knows how it will end."

****

All the way to the library, Tommy had repeated in his mind what he was going to say and how he was going to do it when he saw her again. He confided in Dog, as well. And he did all this unconsciously wanting to cover up a hidden thought, which made him shiver: What if she isn't there?

He refused to think about that possibility. It was not an option. That's why he thought hard about how he would approach the discussion and the attitude he should present.

"I'm telling you, Dog, I need to be more determined. Women don't like hesitant men, and I've known it since I could have the pick of the bunch, when I was playing professional hockey. But I always focused on training, on the game. Women weren't an issue for me. They all cheered me on; they all wanted me. I was someone, and I meant something to them. You know, Dog, women like to have someone famous, so they can prove to themselves that they represent something in this world. And they want to influence the man to do as they wish and please. Because of this plan, they use all their charm.

"But you see, Dog, with this woman, I don't know. She seems to be so different from the others, and so pure! Too innocent for this world. I'll meet her in just a few blocks, Dog. Just a few more blocks."

After patting him and talking to him in a low soft voice, he told Dog, "Now, wait!" and the dog sat down quietly, both paws forward, waiting for his friend and master.

He vaulted up the stairs in front of the library. Once in the lower hall, a crowd blocked access to the elevators. He rushed up the stairs and down the corridor toward her desk. Sweating, he rounded the corner and was shocked to see the same old lady, with short, white hair.

She greeted him kindly with the same pleasant smile, "Hello, sir! Can I help you?"

He was sure that she could hear his heart pounding. After his insane race, seeing that lady in the place was he expected to see Lilly, he was completely dazed, unable to believe that Lilly wasn't there.

The kind lady got up and came around the desk toward him, smiling. Only then did he realize how short she was, and, judging by her wrinkles, she might have been in her late sixties.

"Sir, are you okay? Can I help you with something?"

Tommy was still unable to answer. He continued to feel his heart beating in his throat, and its vibrations rattled in his head, rhythmically, like a drum.

"My name is Mary, sir. How can I help? I think I saw you here a few days ago, didn't I? Am I wrong?"

Calming his breath and trying to compose himself, Tommy replied, "Yes, it's true. I was here a few days ago. You know, I was looking for Lilly.

"Oh! I see. Please come and sit here. You climbed the stairs, didn't you? You look like you've been running."

"Yes, Ma'am. It was very crowded at the elevators and I preferred climbing the stairs."

"Call me Mary. Who do I have the pleasure of talking to?"

"Tommy, dear lady. Tommy." Now, sitting on the chair, he relaxed a bit.

"Very well, Tommy. Lillian is away for a week and I took over, but she will be back on Monday. Looks like she has a family issue, something to do with her grandmother. But maybe I could help you. What is it about?"

"Oh! Thank you very much, but there is no need; there is nothing urgent. So, I'll be back on Monday." Tommy's mind was clear again.

"Very well," said the old woman. "However, could you stay a little longer? Can I offer you a glass of water?" Not waiting for the answer, the woman turned, poured a glass of water from a water bottle, picked up a napkin and kindly offered it to Tommy.

"Here, sir."

"Thank you so much." Tommy emptied the glass in one gulp.

"Better now?" Mary asked.

"O, sure, thank you very much, you've been very kind." Then, with slow movements, he stood up and put the chair back, and headed for the elevators. The woman's lively, sparkling eyes had impressed him. He wished he could talk with her more.

Outside, around the corner, Dog was waiting for him, stepping on his paws, raising his head with a cheerful look and wagging his tail.

"Hello, my dear friend! I didn't find her. She has a few days off. It seems to be something about her grandmother. Let's roam the street, buddy. Maybe we will find something." So, for a while, they wandered on the streets and received a can of beans and a bagel given by a generous baker.

Tommy never begged. If anyone saw him and offered him something, fine; if not, he preferred to starve—but had never happened.

He received most of his food from the restaurants; an enormous amount remained unconsumed, wasted, and thrown away. He knew where to go to find it. He always had a few saucepans with lids in the backpack he carried. He avoided the community and church handouts for the poor; after the events in the hospital, he knew that was where they would look for him.

He and Dog walked on the streets of the city for a while, then took a shortcut towards the river, and then out of the city to the bridge.

Nights were getting colder, and he was burning more wood. Tommy thought that their supply of wood was running out, and walked with Dog to gather brush and some logs. He stored some wood nearby, among some bushes to protect it from moisture. Some other wood he had already cut and kept under the bridge, close to his shelter, as an immediate reserve. He collected deadwood brought to the bank by the river and dried. It was hard to cut, but very good on the fire. He used a small axe taken from a junkyard to cut the wood, but also kept it as a defense weapon.

"So, Dog!" he said. "We have to do a good job. Did you hear? She will be back in three days. That's why I am not so troubled anymore. So, we both know what happened and everything will be fine.

Look, we are going to gather a lot of wood to stock up. Then we will take the copper pot to boil and wash all the clothes. On Monday, I will wear my best clothes, cleaned and ironed. Hey, Dog, did I show you how to I iron my pants between two planks?"

All that afternoon and evening, he muttered alone or talked to Dog, and Dog followed and listened to him with the patience of a devoted friend. It had been quite a while since the two of them had met there, on the river bank, forging this friendship. Now, Dog looked completely different; his wounds had healed, and, now well-fed, his strength had returned, his fur was thick and shiny, and his whole appearance and posture was different, showing pride and confidence.

That evening, by the fire, lying covered with his blanket, Tommy tried to cover Dog, too—it was getting colder—but Dog pulled away.

"You are proud and want to be in control, huh? So, boy, good for you; you are a dog and live as a free animal."

In the silence of the night, only the rippling waves of the river and the crackling of the wood on fire could be heard. Even the cries of the crickets could no longer be heard for several evenings. Their concert had been cancelled until the next year.

****

In the following days, he did a lot of work around his shelter, mostly cleaning his clothes. He had experience from living on streets school and had always led a bachelor's life. He boiled and washed his clothes and put them to dry on arched branches. He was very keen on using natural soap that cleaned the most stubborn stains, and his clothes were made of natural fibres, not synthetic, so they kept him warm and reduced sweat. He had learned to keep himself clean even when he lived on the streets. There were so many people living on the street, and it was a tough life. Not many of them took care of themselves, so they fell ill and died.

As usual, while he was working, he was talking to himself loud enough for his voice to be heard by his companion, Dog.

"Hi Friend. Soon we'll have to find some panels; we need to build a real winter shelter here under the bridge. It's already cold at night and we don't need the trouble of catching a cold."

He spent Sunday night easier than he had thought. He'd had a bath in the river and cleaned himself thoroughly, something that had not happened since he had run away from the hospital.

That night a chilly wind start blowing, sometimes bringing the fire's flames too close to them.

"Well, buddy, we need to make that shelter soon," he said to Dog.

He threw some more wood on the fire, then lay down, adding one more blanket, and fell asleep soon after.

The next morning, he woke up stiff. All his joints were painful and were cracking when he moved. Finally, after a few exercises, he straightened up.

He threw some more wood on the fire, and then he went closer to get warmer.

"Morning, comrade!" he said cheerfully when Dog approached him, wagging his tail cheerfully. Tommy patted him on the head, as he did every morning, and scratched him between the ears. Dog pushed his head under Tommy's arm and stood like that for a while. Finally, Tommy got up and went down to the river to wash. There was a thick fog on the river.

He went back to their shelter and to prepare breakfast. He had set aside some bones and stuffy meat for Dog, collected from restaurants' leftovers. He had two eggs and a cup of good herbal tea. He had learned this from Sofia, a homeless woman. She had taught him what plants to pick, where to look for them, and how to dry and store them. She had been a farmer—such a hard-working woman—but in one way or another she had been buried in debts and lost her entire farm and ended up on the streets. But she was still a clean and tidy woman. Moreover, Sofia was a teetotaller. While making tea and thinking about it, Tommy hoped she had managed to return to a normal life as she had dreamt. As far as he was concerned, he didn't want to get off the streets … at least, for now.

After breakfast, he took a little more care of his appearance, adjusting his beard, hair, washed once more, and put on his best clothes: clean pants and a white shirt, vest, striped jacket with wide lapels. He didn't add a tie; he didn't like them because he felt he had no air to breathe when he wore them. He put on a pair of black shoes, which he only wore on special occasions.

"Dog, we're going to town now. She must have returned by now," he said hopefully. For some reason, he was becoming nervously impatient again. He started talking to himself: Stay still, you idiot! If you keep your wits about you, it will be fine.

Eventually, they started out. As much as he wished he hadn't, his steps were getting faster. A few times he had to stop to catch his breath. On the streets of the city, Dog squeezed past the feet of the passers-by as Tommy hurried past.

Suddenly, Tommy realized he was sweating. "You fool! How are you going to show yourself in front of her that way?' He panicked. Then he found a safe place for Dog and told him to stay there and wait. He entered an office building and found the washrooms. He took off his shirt, washed well, and found some scented tissues with which he wiped himself well.

Back on the street, he saw Dog surrounded by three teenagers. Dog was looking tense.

"Leave the dog alone! He's mine! Do you hear?" he shouted, rushing towards them. The boys ran away and, after assuring himself Dog was fine, they continued on their way. Tommy was trying to keep calm and prepare some meaningful dialogue, but he kept worrying. What will she say? How should he start? Of course, he will thank her for the library card, but then what? Eventually, he gave up and admitted to himself, "I don't have a plan, so I'll play it by ear."

When they reached the library and rounded the corner, Tommy stopped, bent over and took the dog's head in his hands. Looking into his eyes, he pleaded, "Dog, wish me good luck. I am going upstairs in this building. I hope there is a wonderful woman waiting for me, Dog … an angel. I need you to give me strength and confidence, Dog. I cannot fight alone. I know, people call you an animal. Not everyone can understand that you have feelings, and you are so much better than most of them. Your conscience is as clean as the day you were born. You have done nothing wrong, and your only purpose in this world is to give love." Tommy continued, "Dog, please, be with me in that building, with your soul." He pressed his forehead to Dog's, and then Tommy stood up.

"I will be here soon, my friend. Wait for me!" Then Tommy disappeared around the corner.

****

He waited in front of the elevator, and was glad it was not crowded. He would have run up the stairs, but he was struggling to stay calm. The elevator arrived and he walked into it. It was going up too slowly. 'Calm down, you madman! How many times do I have to tell you?' he thought to himself.

Out of the elevator, he walked along the shelves until the rounded the corner. He saw her desk—empty. No one was there.

He made a few steps to her desk, swaying on his legs like a sailor on a pitching ship. He couldn't believe his eyes. He leaned his hand on a corner of the desk. He was overwhelmed by a wave of heat, and sweat started collecting on his brow. Looking ahead, without seeing, he stood petrified, unable to think, staring at the wall in front of him.

"But, who do we have here?" a soft sweet voice asked from behind him.

He turned immediately, recognizing the voice. Appearing from the bookshelves and carrying a pile of books, Lilly was coming towards him, smiling gently.

"Tommy, I'm glad to see you again. My colleague told me that you passed by twice, looking for me. She couldn't tell me why, and she was curious. ... Are you all right, Tommy?" she asked, seeing Tommy there motionless, wide-eyed, sweaty forehead and looking rather lost.

"Have a seat, please! Let me get you a glass of water." She left the books on the table and walked away. Tommy bit his lower lip nervously and reflected, "I made a fool of myself again. I'm an idiot, that's me."

He looked at her again and she seemed to him fragile and delicate. He was wrapped in a state of bliss and dizziness at the same time. That always happened to him around her. He tried to compose himself without much success.

Luckily for him, she took the first step: "Well, did you like the book, Tommy?"

"Thank you, Miss Lillian, I liked it a lot. I read it in a blast."

"But call me Lilly. Haven't we agreed?"

"Okay, Lilly, I read it breathlessly! I wanted to thank you for your help."

"Oh, but don't worry; it's no problem at all. I was really happy to do it. And by the way, isn't it one of my duties here to bring in as many readers as possible? Look, Tommy, I talked to the head librarian and we agreed to make you a library card, under the conditions set out before. Unfortunately, we can't do it today, because he is gone to a meeting, but you can apply. What do you say?"

"Well, yes, of course! I am glad." He cleared his throat. "Yes, that would be great. What can I say?"

"All right then, Tommy."

She turned around and opened one of the drawers, pulled out a few sheets of paper, handed one to him and gave him a pen. "You can start, Tommy. I am here to help you."

"And how do I get started?"

"Where it says, 'I, the undersigned …' put your name here."

Tommy tried to write nicely, as well as possible, following her advice, rather thrilled by her closeness. When he finished, she commented, "You have elegant writing, Tommy. Did you know that?"

"No, I didn't know. No one has ever told me that before."

"You know, Tommy, in the opinion of some experts, the writing aspect, and the form of the letters, tell something about the character and personality of the person."

"Is that so? I didn't know that."

When he finished the application, they had some time to talk. Lilly, placing her elbows on the table, joined her palms, prayer-like, and told him, in her gentle voice, about her work at the library and a bit about her future plans.

Listening and watching her, Tommy thought, "She is wonderful! So pure and delicate!" Looking at her arms, her hands, palms together, he couldn't help but think, "Like a flower! So white and fine!" He would like to kiss them with reverence.

"... and so, we can enlarge the area of this library and increase the number of readers," she was saying.

Tommy tried to get down to earth and catch the meaning of her words. Her delicate perfume had made him dizzy again ... in a state of bliss, completely unable to follow her words.

"Yes, of course," eventually he managed to mutter, almost lost. And her eyes, those big eyes, which always looked at him open as a book.

"Tommy, do you want to get a book now, like last time, or tomorrow, when you have your card?"

The question caught him off guard. He was forced to get down from the high spheres where her voice didn't get to him.

"A ... a, ... I'll ... I'll come tomorrow to get a book. Better tomorrow, Miss Lillian."

"Lilly, I told you!"

"Lilly," he complied. "Actually, I'd like to look at the books, so I can get an idea of the next ones I'd like to read."

"It's not a bad idea. Tomorrow, Tommy, with your new card, you will be able to borrow two books at a time." She continued, "In fact, we can celebrate this event together. If you arrive around nine or ten in the morning, we could finish the formalities, and around eleven I can have a 30-minute break. We will be able to go out to the café across the street to celebrate. Do you know that many writers, artists and other interesting people go there? What do you say?"

Tommy was shocked. Time stood still for him. He was being invited to a coffee, as the guest. He was stunned, especially by the easiness and normality of uttering this invitation. It was so natural.

Strongly moved, he felt one leg begin to tremble slightly, and a feeling of panic gripped him. I better leave now, he thought. And he did.

"Thank you, Lilly. Thank you for the invitation. I will definitely come tomorrow. Now, I am going to look at the books again," and he walked away in a trance.

It seemed to Lilly that something was not quite well with him. She watched him and tried to guess what had happened to him. She thought he looked like a sick man, almost helpless! She would like to help him, but he seemed so sensitive.

Walking along the aisle, with one hand on each shelf, Tommy reached the books he was looking for and sat down on the floor. Did he hear right? Tomorrow at eleven for coffee. God! What a surprise! He wouldn't have thought it could be possible.

After a while, he left, collected Dog, and they wandered the streets for a long time. Tommy continued to wonder. He couldn't believe what had just happened. It couldn't be true … but it was. Now he knew.

He began to think about the next step, but at this point he was totally confused.

Next to him, Dog marched stoically. Usually when thy walked together, Tommy would say something to Dog, express his opinion, or comment on something. Not this time. They marched vigorously, as if running away from something, completely silent. And the dog was following him faithfully, no comments, complaints, and no reproaches. They were friends and whatever the master did, it was perfect for him. After Tommy exhausted himself enough, he looked around and realised that they were on the opposite side of the town, far away from their den under the bridge.

He turned around and picked up speed. He had to get back quickly and get ready for the next day.

When they reached their shelter, it was almost dark and a chilly wind was sweeping the surface of the water and the surrounding trees. However, he decided to have a bath and went down to the river where he usually washed his clothes. The coldness of the water made him tremble, but he didn't give up. It made him feel better. Then, wrapped in a blanket and stepping on the stones, he returned to their fire and talked to his friend.

"You see, Dog, we don't have to make a bad impression tomorrow. Let's be clean and pleasant when we meet her."

Then he prepared his clothes for the next day, had dinner, and drank some tea he had made from plants he had picked. He was drinking tea sitting by the fire, holding the metal cup on which the flames were reflected like in a mirror. "Like the moments of a life. Lights and shadows on the path of a life ... Nonsense! Come on, pull yourself together and stop dreaming," he mused aloud.

It was night and quiet now. Dog, sitting beside Tommy, was staring into the dark. From time to time, he looked up at Tommy, as if approving of his words. He never jumped in his arms. He was proud and dignified, calm and confident. They had their moments of love when he put his snout under Tommy's arm and hid his head there. Tommy would pat his head, scratch his ears and his head behind the ears, and take his head in his hands and they would look into each other's eyes. Only a few moments, but it was enough. These were their moments of secret communication and love.

"So, my dear Dog, tomorrow is an important day. Can you believe? Me, to be invited for a coffee!? Hear?" And every time he asked, he turned his head to the dog, who approved in silence.

"How can I tell her that I have no money? Oh, but wait a minute. I am going to search my secret deposit. She doesn't have to know this part of my life. It would be terrible."

He put down his mug, searched through the clothes bag pulled out a pair of boots and slid out a $100 bill from a space at the top of the heel. There were a few hidden there, just in case. He questioned whether this was a desperate situation, but quickly told himself. "Yes, it is! Her soul is so pure and good. I am telling you, boy, we have to be great tomorrow." Dog looked at him.

That's what he said, as he sat by the fire, with his elbows resting on his knees and a cup of tea in his hand. From time to time, his gaze stopped on the embers before him and his thoughts like those flames and episodes from his life.

And suddenly, he remembered something the priest had said: "God cannot be bribed and his grace cannot be bought. The only thing someone can do is to commend his soul to Him. God is the only reality. He is the only power of existence."

"How strange," Tommy said to Dog, "I don't know what to do now. How can I gain divine grace?"

"Pray, pray with devotion, without expecting anything in reward from Him," he heard, like an echo, the priest's words. The only man in that hospital that I miss is the priest, he thought.

"I will pray to Him. I will pray that her soul will be attracted to me." He thought again. Then he jumped up, almost spilling his tea from the cup held between his palms. "No, I will pray as the priest had said: without prejudice, without asking for anything, without secret thoughts. I will pray to Him with all my soul, offering my soul." Tommy threw a blanket on his shoulders and went down to the river bank, and, under the cold moonlight, he prayed with pathos. On his knees, palms together, looking forward, he prayed to Him. Without thinking, the words were coming—he didn't know from where—with an unknown force.

Dog, hadn't accompanied him. He had remained near the fire, sitting there silently, with dignity, as if wanting to respect Tommy's personal moments.

On the riverbank, in the moonlight, Tommy continued praying......

****

Tommy slept soundly all night, as if his prayers helped his soul to reconcile. He arrived at the library that morning, without haste and relaxed. As usual, he left Dog in the back alley to wait for him. When he parted, he took Dog's head in his hands, and, looking at his friend, Tommy said, "Please pray for me. I need it, my friend." Tommy left and disappeared around the corner.

When he arrived on her floor, he looked for her desk. She was there, and greeted him with her smile.

"Welcome, Tommy!"

"Nice to see you, Lilly!"

"Today is an important day, isn't it, Tommy? You know, the manager wants to meet you personally. Isn't that great? That surprised me, too. Look, take a seat here, please, until I'm done with these lists. Then I'll call him. He asked me to call him when you have arrived, as soon as we are ready to see him."

Docile, Tommy sat down on a chair as Lilly delved deeper into her work. There were not many customers on the floor and Tommy looked around at the bookshelves. As if drawn by a magnetic force, he turned to her.

Eventually, he dared to look at her. He could not hold back his admiration … so delicate and graceful … Like an icon! She seems to be a saint, pure … pure and innocent.

Again, he felt the same blissful state he had always felt when he was around her. Time seemed suspended, hanging above them, stopped or passing through an hourglass. One minute … another one … a page turned over … and again the silence.

Lilly was focused on a pile of lists, and from time to time she looked at him, rewarding with a warm smile and a reassuring gaze.

There are so many things you can read in her eyes if you know the language, he thought. Suddenly, the collar of his shirt became too tight, and he felt his throat swelling. His face and neck reddened. Not knowing what else to do, he clenched his fists in his lap and stared at the floor.

"Forgive me for making you wait."

With a speed of a bullet, Tommy's senses shifted from daydream to alertness.

"You know, these lists are urgent and I have to hand them to the head librarian who is waiting for them. So, now we can go to his office."

She stood up, picked up the pile of documents from her desk and put all of them into a file.

"Are you ready to go, Tommy?"

"Oh, yes, sure!"

He followed her up to the elevator door like a well-trained pet. Her fragrance disturbed him, almost dazzled, and in elevator he could really feel his legs ready to buckle under him. He had to hold the bars. He knew he looked lost, embarrassed and stupefied, like a hospice patient. Eventually, they reached the librarian's office.

"Hello, sir!" Tommy greeted him.

He was a short, plump man with round cheeks, dressed in a dark suit. Baldness had conquered almost all of his head, and a pair of wire-framed glasses hung on his nose; a "bookworm," Tommy thought.

The man looked sincere very kind, and seemed pleased to meet him.

"Hello, sir ..." Tommy ventured.

"Schmidt. Gordon Schmidt."

The librarian greeted him, offering his hand, while Lilly politely remained behind, holding the file.

"You know, my dear Tommy," the librarian said in a familiar tone, "I am very impressed by the fact that you want to read, especially considering your living conditions. I would call it an 'impressive attitude.' I would like to share this with others, and I'd like to invite many others, who have better opportunities to follow a path of training and culture, reading our books. Maybe we could arrange a conference with the public, or some kind of exhibitions in schools, here in the city. Well, what do you think?"

"Sir ... well, yes, but, if possible, I would like to avoid any publicity."

"Okay, okay. But can I mention you in my future presentations? With your consent, of course."

"Of course, sir, but no name, please."

"Well then, I understand. I understand."

Suddenly, the librarian was in a hurry.

"Here's your library card," and he pulled Tommy's ID card out of one of his desk drawers and handed it to him.

"Thank you very much, sir!"

Coming closer to him, and tapping Tommy's shoulder, he led him toward the door and said, "You don't have to thank me; I am glad to have you among our library members."

When they reached the door, he noticed Lilly and clapped his hands and exclaimed, as if he hadn't seen her for a long time, "Oh, hi, Lillian! What are you bringing me there? What are those papers?"

In the next few minutes, Tommy became history for the librarian. And he, perplexed, walked out of the office and leaned against the wall and waited for Lilly.

After a while she arrived and immediately reproached him, "Well, Tommy, it looks like you messed up his plans. He wanted to make some exhibitions with you to make an example from you."

"But did he ask me if I wanted to?" Tommy replied, sounding like a child. But the next moment he regretted saying it.

"But, don't be angry, darling. The man is only doing his job. He wants to promote the library and does not waste any opportunity. But, in his enthusiasm, he forgot about asking you and jumped a bit too far."

Tommy shivered. Did she just call him "darling"? He became more cautious.

"Look, Tommy," she continued, "I am going upstairs to get my coat. Please wait for me down in the entrance hall. We are going to celebrate, aren't we? And one more thing: please accept that everything is on me today. Good?"

"Lilly, don't ... it's not possible. I can't—"

"I know, I know. But please, don't say no. It's my pleasure. Another time you will pay. Good?"

And she left him in front of the elevators. He remained there, more confused than before. Had she said such a thing? It will be another time?

Once again, he felt the need for support and leaned his back against the wall.

"Be calm, relax and be careful, you foolish man! Calm down, don't be a child!" he mumbled aloud. Looking at the ceiling, he took a deep breath, and tried to feel like himself again.

Not much later, he heard her voice. "So, let's go, Tommy!"

He came back to reality. She was dressed in a light tan coat with a wide belt and a stylish hat with wide brims, which left her curls to surround her face and flow gentle on her shoulders.

Tommy was mesmerized, unable to do anything else but follow her. Out on the street, it was the usual hustle and bustle. The café was just a short walk away.

Tommy opened the door for her and they walked inside. The atmosphere was stylish yet friendly. The walls had been beautifully decorated with glass ornaments imitating palm branches. Along the walls were lined booths, with leather upholstered benches and solid wood tables, beautifully lacquered. Large, wide windows let in plenty of light. A waiter escorted them to a secluded booth at the back. That worked great for Tommy; he wanted to be away from the eyes of the world ... only the two of them.

As they snaked their way to the table, they looked around the room. A motley world—many young people, especially students, perhaps a few journalists—most of them were intellectuals; it was obvious from the snippets of conversation, posture and attire. There was not the usual uproar common for such a crowded place; a pleasant murmur caressed the ears of those inside, making the atmosphere more familiar.

They sat opposite one another. Tommy tried to compose himself. "Head up!" he admonished himself.

So, here she was in front of him, flipping through the menu the server had brought for them. Her long fingers, with arched nails beautifully painted in a dark cherry red, attracted his eyes.

He tried to concentrate on the menu, but again he looked at her. He admired her delicate wrists, fragile breasts, the hair around her pale face, soft eyes, her perfume ... everything, radiated the air of a holy virgin.

The server cut the flow of his thoughts.

"Have you decided, or do you need some more time?"

"What do you say, Tommy, are we ready to order? I am ready."

"Of course, yes."

"For me, two muffins, a glass of water, a medium coffee, no sugar. Just a little milk."

"And for you, sir?"

"The same," he said quickly, just to get rid of her.

The server disappeared, leaving them alone again.

They put the menus aside. Placing her elbows on the table and joining her hands with fingers clenched, she asked, smiling, "Well, how are your readings going?"

"Well, thank you."

"You just know that's not what I want to hear. Can you tell me something about yourself?"

"I don't have much to tell, Lilly."

"Were you really a professional hockey player? Where did you play?"

"Oh, at a few clubs. You know, I started as a kid, playing on ice in the winter, with my brother and other kids in the neighbourhood."

"Do you have a brother?"

"He passed away. He's been gone for a long time." He answered with hesitation and a trembling voice.

Slowly, Lilly's hands parted and she lowered them, one palm gently resting on his hand like a leaf.

"I am so sorry, Tommy," she said, giving him a sympathetic look. Her words sounded sincere and understanding.

"You know, I am a single child. I wanted a brother or a sister so much!

"You, see? It looks like we are both alone."

There was a silence between them, and a shiver ran down his back while a wave of heat flooded his whole body. His collar seemed too tight and he felt suffocated. He wanted to open his shirt's neck button, but he didn't dare. Her palm over his was burning him.

"And how did you become a professional player?"

"Oh, you know, after my brother left, I made a promise: to play as he would have played. To play for him, I honour his memory. My brother was a brilliant player, Lilly. Really gifted, and fast. He was much better than me. Then, if it wasn't for that stupid accident, maybe we'd have played outside."

"What do you mean 'outside'? And what kind of accident? Can you tell me?"

"I was a forward. After the accident, I played as a goalie."

"But what accident did you have?"

"I was hit by a truck. Since then, I've had a shorter arm; something happened with my bones."

"Okay, okay, but that couldn't be fixed? Didn't you have surgery and physiotherapy?

"Well, you see … I didn't tell anyone, and I didn't accept help from anyone. I didn't want my parents to know, either, and the bones welded there by themselves, in a very strange way. When radiologists finally looked at the X rays, they asked me how it happened. But the weird way the bones fused helped me a lot, then, especially to defend the shots from players trying to roof the puck."

"What's that?"

"It's about defending the shots that rise from the ice up to the crossbar height. On the stick side, it's deflected off the thick pad of the blocker. On the other side, it's caught in the glove and then rolled down. The way my arm healed made it easier for me to catch and hold the puck in the hollow of the glove."

"So, you were different from the other goalies?"

"It seems so. And then the newspapers wrote all kinds of things, many of them foolish, about my short, crooked arm."

He stopped. The waiter arrived with muffins and coffee and arranged everything on the table. "If you need anything else, please let me know. Enjoy!" She turned and left.

"Come on, please tell me, what did the newspapers write?"

"Absurdities of all kinds. That I was tortured in a circus on ice when they taught me to skate and made me perform dangerous numbers; that my father beat me and made me defend the goal as a child, and they didn't feed me if I failed; … and many others. Stupidities. I've always hated the media. They only go after the sensational."

"But Tommy, not all the press is like that. At least, that's my opinion."

"Maybe. But they were ruthless with me. They dissected me like an animal in a zoo pathology lab."

"Ha, ha!" She couldn't help herself. "You are so imaginative in your speech. But they also wrote better things about you. For years you kept the headlines of the top sports comments. You know, ever since you told me you were a hockey player, I've been looking for something written about you. Not much, but it looks like you've been a great player, a very gifted and dedicated one."

Lilly bit into her muffin and contemplated her next question.

"Tell me, did you really defend a shot on goal with your face?"

"Oh, yeah, but it cost me a lot: my front teeth and broken nose, and lots of stitches. You can still see the scars. Just look here! The teeth I have now were implanted while I was in the army."

"What did you do in the army?"

"Well, I volunteered for Afghanistan."

"Really? What prompted you to go there? What did you do?"

"It's more complicated. There's lots to say … and it's hard to explain."

The muffins and coffee were finished.

"Look, Tommy, it's well after lunch now, and I have to go back to work. I have lots to do, but … I'd like to meet you again. Your life seems to have been a real novel, full of adventures. What do you say?"

Tommy wondered whether he had heard properly, or was he derailed, like a train off the railroad tracks.

"Well, Tommy, could we meet tomorrow?"

"No, I can't. I'm busy."

"But why are you busy? What are you doing?"

"I'm giving autographs at the river bank!"

They both burst out laughing. Her laughter was like all that defined her: pure and open; the dimples in her cheeks; her eyes sparkling with the joy of the moment; and a charming sincerity.

"Well then. How about tomorrow at the same time? It's my half-hour break. If I don't show up, look for me inside, as it will mean that something important has happened."

They got up, he obviously marked by the last turn of their talk.

Once on the street, he accompanied her across the street to the library entrance. In front of the stairs, they parted.

"Goodbye, Tommy! See you tomorrow!"

"Goodbye, Lilly! Until tomorrow!"

He strived to walk normally until he turned the corner, but then he jumped a few times and exclaimed, "Dear God! Dear God!"

A few steps away he met Dog, who was waiting patiently, and happily waging his tail. Tommy leaned toward him and clasped dog's head in his hands, exclaiming, "You must have prayed for me, Dog. You did it well."

He pressed his head to Dog's head, holding him tight for a few moments, in a state of affection and unconditional love.

Calmer now, they started their way back to the bridge, walking together, looking from time to time at each other, like two brothers, two souls ...

****

In the evening, he rinsed the last pile of clothes, squeezing and arranging them on the rocks a few yards below the bridge. There was the laundry and the bathroom; he liked order, and put the pants with pants, shirts with shirts, and everything else in order. Returning home, he had decided to clean and go through all his things—that's why he had started the big washing job.

The weather was getting colder and colder. He had learned to hang his clothes on sticks to dry by the fire. When he was in "emergency" situations—when he was in a dire need of certain clothes, he used a crudely constructed wooden rack to dry his clothes.

When he finished, he started for the bridge where he had his den. There he placed all the clean clothes in one of the crates, and sat down on an overturned one.

He added more woods on the fire. He brought his hands closer to the fire to get warmer. Next to him was Dog, who kept him company, sitting quietly and looking at his master from time to time, as if trying to guess what mood he was in.

"Dog, boy", said Tommy, "we'll have to prepare our shelter for winter. Here under the bridge, it's started to get a bit cold, especially at night. Soon, we won't be able to stay overnight without a big fire. But, do you remember the panels from the construction site I hid further up the bridge? Well, I think it's time to put them to work. We are going to build a real castle!"

He put on another blanket. Then he made himself a tea, as Tsuna, an Indigenous woman, had shown him. She had taught him what herbs are good, what for, and where to look for them. She was sick when he had met her. He wondered whether she might still be alive. Life is fickle, and a lot can happen.

"Yes, Dog, boy. Listen to me. We'll make a roof, even if we have just the bridge above. We will leave only one hole, enough for the smoke to come out, and the roof will be sliding to let the hole be as large as I wish, or to close it if we are not at home. Do you hear me? That's what we're going to do!"

Not long after, a cold breath of wind rose and it began to rain lightly. It was as he had foreseen, after the pain in his bones that he had felt a few hours before. His bones ... broken and glued together so many times! How many times he had been hurt! He couldn't even remember ....

Suddenly, it was raining harder. He added some more logs on the fire and prepared another cup of tea. He looked at the flames, and thought of the next day. Still, he could hardly believe it: he will meet her again—a second date. And that proposed by her. God! It cannot be true!

But it was.

"Well, boy, if we are still lucky, then let's be careful and prepare thoroughly. I'm going to take the new raincoat, that damn umbrella and a pair of good shoes. Yes. Those brown ones, Dog. You don't know, but when I got out of one of those shelters, I got them from one of the donors there, an old man with white hair. I remember him. I was shocked, wondering when I would wear such an elegant pair of shoes. Yes, the time has come. But I will wear my rubber boots and one of my overcoats until we get to the street. I will change my clothes there, and you will guard my bag of clothes, like a reliable friend. What do you say?"

He stroked Dog's head, and Dog raised and lowered his head with pleasure under his master's hand, as if sealing the duty he was given.

****

He had tried all night to warm up, and failed. Now with a backpack, he was marching through the streets of the city, overdressed in his coat, with rubber boots on his feet, and followed by Dog. Chills were running down his spine, while a stubborn cough had seized him. "God, God, please, not now. I just have to meet her!"

After half an hour it was clear to him; he was sick. He tried to remain calm and think clearly. He had been through so much, so he knew he had to hold on tight. Being sick was nothing, really. His shirt clung to his back as trickles of sweat ran down. He was tried to encourage himself; he had clothes to change into in the backpack.

A bit later, he and Dog reached some garbage bins where he could hide behind and dress in his nice dry clothes. He tried to ignore the fever and the pains that had started. He walked to the café entrance and waited for her. As the minutes went by, he peered too often at the clock hanging above the entrance to the library.

What was going on? It was getting late! He decided to stay a few more minutes. But what had she said? If she's late, he has to look for her inside. No, he thought, I'll wait here a little longer.

The rain was easing up a bit, but a cold wind was sweeping the streets and was pushing the passersby to head towards their homes. It was getting colder.

He didn't recognize her immediately. It wasn't until she took a few steps crossing the street that he noticed her. She was dressed in a wide-collared, navy trench coat and a black hat.

"Hello, you hockey player. How are you? I'm happy to see you!"

"Hello Lilly. I'm fine, thank you."

They walked quickly to the café. "Let's go inside! The weather is not very nice, to say the least!"

Inside, the atmosphere was pleasant, with couples whispering across booths. A server greeted them and invited them to take a seat at a table in a cozy corner.

Tommy tried to browse the menu, but he felt his eyes burning, and chose something at random.

Lilly was deeply concentrating on the menu in front of her. He looked at her hair, flowing around her cheeks, and heard "coral curls, strings of pearls!" echoing in his head. It must be the fever, he thought.

She finished looking at the menu and looked up at him, smiling. A few moments later, her look changed; her eyes were worried and darkened, like the weather outside.

"Tommy, are you okay? You look like you have a fever or something."

"I am well … no worries … just a slight weakness …"

His words were flowing softly, without conviction.

"You can't stay like this, Tommy! Did you take any medication? Has any doctor seen you? You have to take care of yourself!"

"Lilly dear, I don't take any medication. When I get back, I'll make some herbal tea, using a recipe I learned from Tsuna, and I am going to snuggle by the fire."

"By the fire, huh? And where is that? Under the bridge, where you can have a hot bath, right?"

Stretching her hands across the table, she wrapped her palms around his.

"Oh my God! You're burning up!"

She didn't finish her thoughts. Tommy felt dizzy. He leaned back against the bench seat.

"I'll be fine Lilly, no worries," he said in a low voice. "I've been through more difficult situations than this."

"You need soup, and some pills to get over your fever. You need to take care of yourself."

"Leave it, Lilly, there is no need. You don't need to do anything for me."

"What do you think? I can't leave you like that darling. Here's what we'll do: we get out of here; you wait for main the big downstairs hall of the library. I have a lot of days off and today is not a problem. Any colleague can cover me. The head librarian is gone and I don't need special approval. So, you are waiting for me downstairs. Do you understand? Please!"

"Lilly, I can't come with you. I'm not alone. I'm with a friend.'"

"A friend? What friend, Tommy?"

"A dog. My friend is a dog. Homeless too, like me. We have been walking around together for some time."

"Wow, I see. It's so touching. A dog! Two friends!"

"Yes, we're two good friends. I call him 'Dog' and now he is waiting for me around the corner from the library."

"So ... 'Dog'? What kind of name is that? Couldn't you think of another one?"

"Dog, a dog wandering like me. If I had lived a normal life before, maybe I would have called him 'Man.'"

"Anyway, let's take your friend. We are going to a doctor, an acquaintance of mine. He is a family doctor. You need to be seen and treated."

"No, Lillian! Believe me, you don't have to do this for me. I know how to take care of myself. I'll be fine. You'll see."

"Tommy, please! There is no room for discussion. If you want to please me, come with me to that doctor to be seen."

"But no, you don't have to, and I don't need a doctor!"

"Pleeeease!"

He was in no condition to resist, so he finally nodded. They did not talk much longer, he with his eyes lit and red with fever, and she obviously in a hurry to pay the bill and leave. She looked really worried.

They went into the library, and he waited for her in the lobby, while she went to her office. When she came back, despite his state, he couldn't help but admire her.

"All right, I am free now! Where is your friend?"

"Almost here, immediately!"

They left and rounded the corner. As if he had known that important people would come, Dog greeted them standing and wagging his tail cheerfully.

"But he's a beautiful dog, your friend! What wonderful fur, and his eyes are marvelous!"

"You should have seen him when we found each other; skin and bones only, and full of wounds and scars. Didn't I tell you?"

"Yes, I remember. You were looking for a book on treating wounds in canines. I understand now. And then I told you to see a veterinarian. So, he is the 'friend'. May I touch him? Will he bite me?"

"Of course you can pat him. You are with me. It's amazing how much animals understand people. Unfortunately, the other way around seems to be very hard. We don't understand them, or we don't always want to understand."

Meanwhile, Lilly ran her fingers through Dog's hair who was sitting calmly and looked quite pleased with the touch. She crouched beside him and ran her fingers through his fur, and gave him a hug.

She stood up and looked at Tommy's eyes. "Let's go Tommy! We have to hurry. You are not well at all."

"Look, Lilly, I—"

"No, without 'Look.' Come, please! You promised me!"

Again, he had no chance to argue and followed her.

The three of them set off, Lilly on his right side. Dog followed them.

"It's not far, you'll see," she said. She turned onto several winding streets, obviously shortcuts she knew.

Meanwhile, Tommy's blood began throbbing in his head and his footsteps became unsteady. He tried to hold on tight. Soon they arrived in front of an old building, quite large, with several levels, obviously inhabited by wealthy people. They stopped at one of the entrances. On its door, a brass plate with the name: "M.D. – McCarthy – Family Doctor.

Tommy knew he had to leave Dog outside on the street, as he did when he went to the library.

There were a few patients in the waiting room, and Tommy was feeling worse with every passing second. He felt his head pulsing, the fever was making him dizzy, and he felt a stabbing pain under his right shoulder blade. Meanwhile, Lilly had talked to a nurse and gave her a little information regarding Tommy's condition.

Tommy was biting his lips unconsciously, as he had done so many times on the ice rink when he was writhing in pain after a collision or a fight. It seemed a century when the doctor came out to invite him into his office. The doctor looked at his eyes, checked his throat.

"Do you have pain?"

Tommy nodded.

"Where? In your back? Show me. Here? And there? Lower?"

The doctor turned to the nurse. "Please take him to the consulting room; we have to check him thoroughly, and tell Lilly that it will take a while."

After half an hour he came out to the waiting room, helped by the nurse and the doctor. Lilly came quickly and talked to the doctor in low voice, almost whispering.

"This man has a serious case of pneumonia. If I understand him correctly, he lives outside, under a bridge. He can't be left there."

"Of course. That won't be a problem. He will live in a heated room. And, Doctor, please send the bill to me."

"Well, no, I can't do that. I know you want to help this man. I want to help him too," said the doctor, smiling.

"You are very kind. Thank you. I won't forget that!"

"Don't worry Lilly. Glad to help when I can."

Lilly took Tommy, supporting him like a child. He was unable to protest and had no idea where he was going.

She lived in a four-storey building, in a small apartment on the first floor. Dog had waited outside for a long time, but when they got outside, on the way to her home, he followed them quietly, constantly watching at them at every step. Pets were not allowed in her building, but she promised Tommy she would take care of Dog and find a solution to keep him somewhere close by and inside.

They climbed a few stairs and were inside. Tommy was not aware of anything, and a few moments after laying down on a bed, he lost consciousness.

****

He felt a hand holding his head, another hand giving him a sip of something like tea. He tried to open his eyes, but the eyelids seemed too heavy. He felt as if his whole body had been beaten. All his muscles ached, but it was especially a back pain, under the shoulder blade, which exhausted him.

He swallowed a few sips, then his head was on the pillow again, and he fell back into nothingness ...

He opened his eyes, trying to figure out where he was. He didn't know how long it was since he could remember something. He saw a sponge soaked in warm water on his body. Another time, a cup of creamy liquid, a thermometer in the corner of his mouth.

"For God's sake, where am I? What happened here?"

He remembered being with Lilly at a doctor's office. Then she had taken him to her house. But where was Dog? She had said something to him about Dog, but he could not remember what.

Sitting at the edge of the bed, feet dangling off the floor, he looked at the lighted window.

He was trying to collect his thoughts, to remember. Something it was changed for the better. Yes, the back pain was gone. It was as if he had received some shots ... He remembered; a woman had prepared them, and she had also given him some pills to swallow.

He looked around the room, slowly got to his feet, and, with small steps, went to the window. He looked at the building across the street, then down, closer to the building. Nothing. No sign of Dog. Had he taken shelter in an entrance, or found a place somewhere around?

With the same small steps, he went around the room. He opened a door and found a bathroom. He turned on the light. Everything was crystal clean and had the pleasant smell of soap.

Another door opened onto a corridor, probably to the exit. Back in his room, he opened another door: a few bedsheets, nicely placed on the shelves. The compartment without shelves was empty. 'Where will the rest of my clothes be?' he thought. He couldn't think any further. A door opened and he heard footsteps. He turned and it was Lilly, cheerful, with her usual smile and the same grace in her movements.

"Oh, hello. How are you feeling? I see you're up."

"I don't know, Lilly; I only woke up a little while ago, and I'm still confused. I don't remember much. I don't know what day it is or how long I've been sick."

"Oh, you've been sick for a whole week. And the doctor came by a few times to see you. A cousin of mine took care of you. She's a nurse, and she agreed to help me in her available time. She seems to have done a very good job."

"Lilly, you shouldn't have done this. I don't know what to say and what I can do to thank you."

"What? Did I hear right? Should I have left you with pneumonia on the streets or under the bridge? Never. I don't think anyone would have had the heart to do it. Anyway, not me."

"What can I tell you? Thank you is too little, but I can't find anything else to say at the moment."

"How can I not take care of you? Aren't you the 'privileged reader' of our library? she added jokingly.

"Lilly, forgive me for asking, but my friend, Dog ... where is he? Is he doing, okay?"

"Of course. He is well taken care of. Nothing bad happened to him. He's downstairs. He got used to living in the doorway. You know, he's made lots of allies. The doorman agreed to feed him with what I bring him. And he told me that he feels safer down there with Dog nearby. He can easily drive away uninvited overnight guests. Dog is like the new employee of the building. You know, yesterday, the doorman confessed that, during the night, when it rains, he would let Dog into the hall. Dog is housebroken and very obedient. As long as there is no complaint from anyone, everything will go well."

"I have no words, Lilly!"

Overwhelmed by emotions, he got closer, took her hands in his, and with tears at the corners of his eyes, he kissed them.

Slightly surprised, and with a shadow of a smile in her eyes, she said, "But, my dear, the sickness has made you too emotional. You have to know, that it is a pleasure for me to take care of you both."

"Lilly, now that I feel better, I wouldn't want you to worry about Dog and me, and I think we should—"

"Whaaat? But there is no room for argument, do you hear? You have just risen from the bed after a week of illness that gave us emotion. They gave you lots of shots and medication. Even the doctor was worried. He was talking about the necessity to hospitalize you because of some problem with your heart.

"Well, now you are recovering and will stay here with me. And with Dog. Both of you. I sleep in the other room, whose door, like this goes to the hall. And get out of your mind any thoughts that you are a nuisance. Do you understand, dear Tommy?"

Dumbfounded by her torrent of words, he gave up and just nodded.

"Well, then," she continued, "I've just arrived and I have to change my clothes. Then, I'll go to the kitchen to make some chicken soup with vegetables. Until then, you lie down until Ketty, the nurse, comes to give you your treatment. But first, come on, dare you 'gladiator', go to bed."

Left alone, he walked around the room with small steps, lingering longer in front of the window, hoping to see Dog. But he didn't see him.

He felt so tired, and lay down on the bed. After all, why not? he thought. "I'm tired, so tired …"

****

Days went by, and Tommy's recovery was going well. Ketty came to treat him daily and helped him like a real prof, and Tommy was grateful for that.

But Lilly was another story. Tommy continued to be disturbed and unable to control his emotions in her presence. He felt overwhelmed, as if transported into another dimension and could not compose himself. He couldn't think coherently at all when they were alone. Now, seeing her in her own environment, she seemed to him so delicate and beautiful.

The situation went like that for a while, until the treatment and injections ended and Katy stopped visiting. They parted very friendly and Lilly thanked her for her care and devotion. Now that Tommy was completely recovered, he could take care of himself.

The first time Tommy left Lilly's apartment; he went to the entrance hall to see Dog. Bart, the doorman, let Dog sit with his master to reunite after the long week, discreetly pretending to have some work to do outside.

Tommy still felt like he was floating in another universe whenever he and Lilly spent time together, yet he felt awkward and lost, unable to control his thoughts.

A week after he had recovered, he suddenly decided to put an end to this difficult situation and leave. He spent the next day planning in his mind how and what to say to her.

The next evening, he was sitting on the bed and looking at the floor. He started to explain the reasons why he had to leave and how he was he going to do it. She was standing and listening to him, and, as he was uttering the words, her eyes were getting larger in surprise and disappointment.

Then she sighed and, frowning, sat down beside him. With her left hand she caressed his head, her fingers drawing through his strands of hair. Then she let her palm lower on his forehead, and further on his cheek, where she touched his scar. And he, completely lost now, felt that he would give in. As if moved by an unknown force, he placed his hand on her shoulder, and eye to eye they felt the same burning desire. Lilly felt her body drifted by electric currents.

Her fingers went on, leaving the scar and touching his lips. One next to the other, their bodies bent slowly toward each other. Lost now, too, Lilly felt chills all over her body and heat run through her belly.

Slowly, their faces were closer and closer. Then unleashing, they blended into a kiss, each embracing the other's head in his palms, they became one in an amalgam of joy and ecstasy.

"I do not want you to leave!" she mumbled. "Don't leave. I won't let you ... go ..."

"No. No ... I'm not leaving," he muttered between kisses.

After a while, they collapsed on the bed, and with that, in nothingness ...

****

Time was passing, weeks, and all this time, for both of them, days ran too quickly. Time flew like a thought, especially when they were together. They were like two children, or as if they have returned to their childhood years. They looked for each other, wanting to be together as much as possible. Lilly had her library job and spent most of her time there, but for him it was more complicated. In fact, he was not alone. He always had Dog for company. They sometimes marched together on the streets or through parks.

Years spent alone had taught him to wisely manage everything and he had acquired many skills—he could repair or make almost anything. So, he spent the first half of the day tidying up the apartment, repairing one thing or another. He fixed some pieces of furniture and, after he varnished them, they looked brand new.

"And I wanted to give them to charity!" she commented enthusiastically. Actually, these were rare pieces, made of carved solid wood, rare to find in those times. They also had emotional value for her, as they had belonged to her grandmother.

In the evening, they would see each other again. He usually waited for her outside, on the steps in front of the library building. Then, they ran holding hands, on the boulevard, until they got lost on one of the side streets. It was less crowded there. From time to time, there was a passerby. Once they felt alone, they kissed insatiably.

However, for him, the time he was alone seemed too long. And no matter how hard he tried to focus on something else, his thoughts would fly to her.

Seeking to occupy his time with something—anything, really—one day, to Bart's delight, he climbed the building, disassembled, cleaned and repaired and reattached all the shingles that had started to leak or were badly joined.

When he finished, Bart, smiling radiantly, shook Tommy's hand warmly, and held it until he finished all the words of thanks and gratitude.

One day, while he was waiting for her, he remembered that evening when she gave herself to him for the first time, He hadn't remembered last time when he had undressed a woman. Her bra confused him, but she helped him when she realized it.

Between kisses, eventually they both managed to undress, and to hide under the duvet. Her smell, the scent of her skin, drove him crazy. Gently he touched her breasts, then kissed them one by one, and then continued lower, covering her white belly with kisses. With her eyes closed, her fingers in his hair, undulating rhythmically, Lilly unleashed herself wildly.

Yes, he remembered. They made love many times that night and then many other nights until morning.

And since then, any day they could be together seemed like a celebration. On weekends, they wandered through parks, searching all the corners, as if they were looking for a hidden treasure. They just wanted to be the two of them, looking for something. In fact, they were looking for themselves.

In the evening, they would go to a café or to the cinema. But most of the time, they were together, far from the world, just the two of them.

And the weeks passed.

"Hi, my samurai! How are you today? Still bored due to lack of activity?"

"Not really, my dear. I can't wait to see you." It was one of those day when he had waited for her to finish work and come home.

"Okay, okay, now you see me! She joked and turned onto an alley. They made a few steps, then Lilly stopped and turned to him and said:

"You know, Tommy" she began running her fingers through her curls, "I thought maybe … it would be better for you to look for a job … Please, something …"

For Tommy, it was an alarm signal. His whole being went on alert, announcing that he was facing an imminent, deadly danger. He felt shivers down his spine, as if his flesh being was being darted by an electric shock. He remained silent.

His frozen expression and clenched jaw must have surprised Lilly; she had never seen him like that. He was standing in front of her, motionless, like a sphinx. She looked at him, puzzled and worried. Then a slight smile formed in the corner of her lips, accompanied by a questioning look, encouraging an answer. "What's wrong with you? What's going on? What did I say?"

Time passed. They were flooded in silence.

Eventually, almost imperceptibly, Tommy moved a little and slowly he relaxed. With the appearance of a confused person, and swaying on his feet, he began to murmur something. At first, he couldn't articulate a word, but the words finally started to come.

"You see, Lilly … I … it's been a long time since … a long time since I … actually … you know … I've never worked a regular schedule. I was just a hockey player and a soldier."

The worried expression on Lilly's face changed to a relaxed, happy smile. She turned to him, stood up on her tiptoes and kissed him lightly on the lips. Now, she was radiating a newly discovered optimism, and with wide eyes and a warm forgiving look, she said, "It's nothing, my dear, don't worry. Everything has a beginning. You are a fighter. I am sure you'll succeed." And then she added, "You know, I trust you"

Hearing this, Tommy was confused. His whole being told him that he was stepping into a trap, but, on the other hand, he was happy to have her confidence. And yet, something was alarming. He didn't know what to say, and without thinking too much, he decided to postpone the discussion for another time.

"You make me feel special when you say you trust me, Lilly."

She pressed her head to his chest and he kissed her locks. He continued, "You can be sure I'll try, my dear."

"I'm sure you will! Weren't you the 'samurai' on the ice and then a 'tiger in the desert'? Actually, how did the two reconcile: the 'ice' and the 'desert'?"

"Which two?"

"Ice and desert."

"Well, I don't know. It's been a long time since I enlisted. I did it because I wanted to disappear. The whole press didn't understand why I lived on the street and the club didn't help me. They put pressure on them too. So, I disappeared. I enlisted, and in six months I was gobbling sand a few miles from Kandahar."

"You swallowed, not 'gobbling,' darling,"

"Forgive me," he said.

You see, I am helping you 'lose' some words in your vocabulary. We could start from here. I'll bring you some books. Then you can decide what field you would like to choose and where you will like to work."

"But I don't know anything. I haven't done anything but hockey and soldiering."

"Maybe you could be a sports journalist. With your experience and knowledge ..."

"Please don't mix me in their pot, Lilly. I don't want to run like them all day, sniffing the fresh blood of wonderful being."

"Okay, okay. But not everyone is like that."

"Yes, everyone, because they are all servants to those who pay them, and write what they are asked to, what is sensational, distorting the truth." His voice was trembling. "Newspapers must be sold. And the journalists don't shy away from anything; well, maybe apart from a few independents."

"You see, darling; there are good people among them."

"Yes, there are a few. But to succeed there you need to have a name, relationships, and lot of money, so that you can publish your articles as an independent journalist. Even those are sometimes forced to make some compromises. It's a jungle, Lilly, with many vines and poisonous weeds."

"Very well, Tommy. You will not be a sports journalist. You have enough time to think about something else."

They started walking again, holding hands.

"Lilly," he said in a low uncertain voice, "I am trying to think; however, nothing comes to my mind about what I could do. I do not have any qualifications. I've learned everything by myself."

"Leave these worries for later, darling. We'll talk more and see what we have to do."

They walked in silence. His thoughts flew away as soon as she had uttered—with a slightly imperative voice—the words "to do." 'Where else had he heard them with a similar pitch? Where?'

Oh, yes, now he remembered. They had called him 'Long Lip' because his lower lip was thick and protruding, giving him the air of permanent gloominess. Angry and always in a bad mood, he was mostly upset with all those under his control, as Company Commander of the Arizona Training Centre. And Tommy had come under his command. Long Lip had a real predilection for using the expression "to do" extensively. After Tommy left the training centre for Afghanistan, he didn't hear anything about him for a while. He was in some missions and when he came back to base, they received new recruits, a few who had also done their internship in the same unit in Arizona. He finally heard the story: Long Lip had strained the nerves of too many recruits, and a Mexican named Rodriguez presented himself in front of the Commander and planted in his hand a grenade with its pin removed. Witnesses said that it was the first time anyone had seen him with a frightened, lipless look. And although the Mexican had been court-martialled, not a few were happy that the brave commander after that unfortunate event had changed the way he gave orders.

Some even swore that the man, out of fear, had let go, because the smell around him was so strong.

'Yes ... 'Long Lip" was the one who used to say "you have to do"'!

'Come on, he told himself, you've became too sensitive. She just wants the best for you'.

Waking up from his thoughts, he realized that they were close to home. Dog was expecting them, as usual, in front of the building, cheerfully wagging his tail. He didn't run towards them, just waited for them near the steps of the entrance. They both bent down, caressing him and giving him well-deserved goodies after such a long wait. In the meantime, Bart's smiling face appeared and greeted them.

****

Other days passed pretty much the same. Something between them remained unsaid. Meanwhile, following Lilly's insistence, Tommy started to take the necessary steps to get his identity documents. Because he didn't want to be recognized, he wanted to change his name at the same time. On this last subject, Lilly had a different opinion, but in the end, she gave in.

"Why do you want to change your name? It takes a lot of time and money."

"If all the journalists and cameramen find me, what I will do? Enough! I will hide myself under another name, and that's it. I will be free."

"As you say then, Tommy. But it will be difficult for you. You have to sign legal documents that end up in the public domain. You know that, don't you?"

"Believe me, I am doing anything, Lilly, anything to get rid of those jackals from the media. Anything, and no matter how much time and resources it takes."

"Dear Tommy, I see you are very determined."

"Of course, I am!" he said, walking in circles around the room, staring at the floor with his hands deep in his pockets. "Anyone would want to get rid of those scumbags. Anyone!"

"I see you're so furious. Did they upset you so much? Maybe it isn't worth it."

"How do I not deserve it? After they sucked my blood and destroyed my nerves like vampires, even when I was in the hospital."

"I know that. You told me you had some problems with the press. But really? In the hospital? It's not possible!"

"How? Of course—just like that!" He snapped his fingers. Unconsciously, he had raised his voice. "They camped in the waiting room where I was hospitalized. Like locusts. With camcorders and everything. A lot of parasites. I couldn't even breathe. They looked at me and examined me like a monkey at the zoo. I had taken refuge in my bed and they passed the power cords over me—over my bed. Do you hear?"

"But I know they had guts! And hospital management did not intervene? Did they have nothing to say?"

"Yes! Blah-blah-blah!"

"They are also scared of the power media has. They couldn't stop them easily. These people, you know, if you knock them out of the door, they enter through the windows. Moreover, they can invent some "dedicated" things for you, to remain speechless. They can crucify you for life, if you only dare to say something about them!"

"Tommy, I believe you. But now, calm down. It's not worth getting mad about that."

He turned his back so that she wouldn't read his astonishment. 'Lord, what I am doing?' he wondered. 'God, she doesn't understand anything at all! I've never submitted to anyone! Never! But what should I do? She didn't live in the conditions and environment I lived with the eyes of the public, the club, and the press on her. The peace and quiet of the library gave her this peace of mind. She is not to blame. Take it easy, man! Take it easy'.

He turned to face her. "I got a little heated, Lilly. Sorry! I've calmed down. Let me think ... what are we doing tonight?"

"Okay. What would you say if we went to a movie?"

"Perfect. Let's go to a movie."

But deep in his soul, he was not in the mood for a movie. It was as if the old, scarred wound had reopened, and from it flowed the doubts and uncertainties that made his nights endless.

"Well, how was it?" asked Lilly as soon as Tommy opened the door and rushed inside.

"Damn it! This is the second hearing. They flooded me for an hour with their questions and I had to fill out some forms again with my data. When will all this end? When will it end?"

He went to the bathroom and continued to comment while he was undressing. He had started the name change procedures a few weeks earlier, and the hearings had just started.

"My dear, I warned you that it wouldn't be easy. These hearings are happening only because you refuse to publicly publish your change of name. You knew that and you insisted on doing it. Do you want to quit now?"

"What? Give up? I never give up! Can you hear me? I am not going to let those media vampires get their hands on me!"

"Well, I'm glad to hear that. Although, since the hearings began, it seems you have lost your peace and tranquility."

"But how can I be calm? They rummage through my past and don't leave a stone unturned. Ever since I was born. Do you know what they told me today?"

"What else did they tell you?"

"They want to receive information regarding me from the FBI. Can you believe that? FBI, right there, not anywhere else."

"Okay, but maybe it's probably standard security procedure when someone wants to hide the fact that he wants to change his name. They want to know that you're not hiding from the law."

"Oh, okay, I understand that they might want to get in touch with the army. But I don't care what the FBI thinks of me."

"I don't know what to say."

It had been some time since she started helping him, guiding him through the process of changing his name. They even hired a lawyer, and he recommended Tommy visit a psychiatrist, who would act as a witness in the name-changing process. Tommy was lucky; Jimmy, the doctor who had treated him when he was sick with pneumonia and the Lilly's close friend, introduced him to the psychiatrist. According to the lawyer, the psychiatrist's opinion was decisive for the court decision.

"Maybe they want to be sure there is no hidden reason for you to change your name. I think so darling. This is what I think."

Now in a housecoat, Tommy sat down beside her at the edge of the bed. He held a hand on his forehead, leaning on one elbow. She peered at him curiously, trying to understand what was really bothering him.

In the time that had passed, tactfully and carefully, she had begun to educate him, from a slight brushing of his manners to taming the wild. She engaged herself in the task with the tenacity typical of women, considering it her duty to guide and transform him. She brought him books on manners, but Tommy thought that it was totally useless. Lilly was serious about trying to shape him to be a better man, as Tommy seemed too wild or too abrupt.

He had been a loner, used to doing what he wanted and when he wanted, not asking for permission and not accepting anything from anyone.

For her, this time was unique. From the first moment she had seen him, she was attracted to him and ended up loving him. She loved the manly energy he spread around him. His strong neck, the scar on his cheek, his wide brow, completed the portrait of the strong, daring man that had captivated her.

It was true, however, that sometimes his icy gaze, his piercing eyes, confused and scared her. He seemed to fear feeling something unknown—feelings that were difficult to control; there was something fierce … heathen … coming from deep within him.

In the few months that had passed since they had lived together, her life had changed radically. Now she had 'her man', she had someone to return to when she came home. Tommy became her object of study, and, unwittingly, she had turned him into her 'pet'.

Sitting on the bed, too, Tommy calmed down from the tirades against the 'system' as he was prone to say, and lulled Lilly closer to him, and kissed her forehead, her eyes, her delicate nose, and played his fingers in her curls. Then he gently touched her lips and, looking longing at each other, among the kisses, one by one they get rid of their clothes. He kissed her in the hollow of her neck, behind her ears, and grabbed an earlobe between his teeth and bit it playfully.

Lilly was charged by the same high electric heat she had felt so many times since they were together. They fell back onto the bed and made love many times, caressing each other with passion, as if their time would end soon. She felt a song passing through her whole being, a harmony of colors and trills, all intertwined in an amalgam of feelings and sensations, all descending from far away, from somewhere in a cosmic land.

****

They were there, on the mountain, some crouched among the rocks and others stretched out from the bushes that grew here and there.

They had identified the target and kept close eyes on it for more than two hours. Nothing was moving among the village houses made of stone and covered with piles of branches. The village looked dead. Looking through binoculars, the air vibrated with images—mirages.

They were waiting for the order to attack. Tommy adjusted his binoculars once more, peering down at the valley where the village was settled. Nothing. No movement. An hour before, they had seen some children on one of the dusty streets, if the spaces between houses of that hamlet could be called that. Then, nothing.

Sweat was dripping down his face, his neck, his back. On the side of the access road to the village, nothing moved. Near him were three comrades. Tommy was hidden in a hole behind some rocks. They communicated using only hand signals. Time was running out. Crushed by the scorching temperature, they were trying to dole their water. They didn't know how long the wait or their mission might last.

Eventually, the order arrived. They started moving through the ditches on both sides of the road. Gerry, a tall, heavyset fellow, was in front of Tommy.

At the first house they did not linger long. They hit the door, storming inside. No one. They went on. House by house, they searched almost the entire village. There were a few houses left. Tommy and Gerry ran to the next house—small, crumpled, ready to fall. Tommy kicked in the door, slamming it against the wall, and immediately were met with gunfire. Tommy plunged onto his stomach and opened fire.

Then silence. Still on his stomach, he scanned the room, trying to see through the heavy smoke and light dim. A few yards further, near the wall, a twisted body. The submachine gun and the cap laid aside on the floor. He was wearing a white robe, now stained with blood. Further on, along the wall, more bodies: two women and ... God! Three children!

He rummaged through the other rooms, then turned to Gerry, who was still face down. He turned him. Gerry had no face... his face was gone ... just an irregular mess of broken bones and blood.

He felt sick and vomited in a corner. When he was done, he turned and lifted Gerry to take him back to the base. Gerry was heavy. Tommy was carrying him on his shoulder, in a 'torn in two' position, with the legs dangling in front of him. He kept climbing up the hill. On his back, he felt a sticky liquid dripping. Gerry's blood.

He was out of breath, but he needed to keep going. "I'm not going to leave you here, Gerry. I'd be better to shoot myself. You deserve an honorable funeral!" he said aloud, as though Gerry could hear him. Getting around with difficulty, he finally squeezed his way between two rock faces. He collapsed with Gerry in the arms of his comrades, who had covered his retreat all that time. Tommy was bruised, sweat was running down ... tears, and blood all over. He closed his eyes, trying to calm down. Poor Gerry! What a death! And damn that fanatical bastard! He had opened fire with his two wives and three children near him!

He struggled to recover, closing his eyes and trying to calm his breathing. He looked around at his comrades; Clark, Levy, Norton and Craig were there. Nobody uttered a word. They tried to avoid each other's gaze. There was nothing to say. Nothing at all. Everything was stupid. War, stupid war. No more words.

He woke up suddenly. He tried to collect himself; his shirt was wet and he was breathing hard, as if he had no air; another nightmare.

Beside him, Lilly was sleeping peacefully. With eyes closed, hands under his head, he tried to calm down. From somewhere, the priest's words came back to him.

"We are not just flesh and bones, not even when we die. To think that after death we are reduced to a bag of flesh and bones is a great mistake. Our bodies are the bearers of our consciousness during life. Consciousness detaches itself from the body. Consciousness and the soul are parts of another Universe, the Universe of the Lord, who governs everything, in this world as well as in the others we do not know. This is why it is good to give the body only a little—what it needs, and to concentrate on the soul, on the consciousness, which we should nourish abundantly with our virtues and sacrifices to God."

Oh, if only there was such a father! If only He were so, Tommy thought in the dark.

The silence of the night was surrounding his thoughts. The silence ... What did the priest say about silence?

As if brought by the swish of a magic wand, the words resounded in his ears: "My peace is a song about my consciousness. My peace is a sphere that extends everywhere. My peace is a like a wild fire, with huge flames of pride of my existence. My silence, like the ether, penetrates everywhere; into the black holes and the chaos of the infinite, carrying with it the songs of the Earth."

Yes, the silence. It was as if he now missed the rippling of the river waters and the rustle of the leaves in the wind.

But what else had the priest said in his long lectures? "Always pray deeply until darkness turns to fire and light, showing His presence, the Almighty God. Oh, you Spirit, immortal and almighty! Put aside the weight of indifference and unforgiveness from my mind. Let me sip the blessed nectar of your presence!"

The priest's words and thoughts unfolded before his closed eyes. These thoughts appeared now to him in a new light, as if time had unlocked his mind, bringing him understanding and contemplation.

"Oh, you perfume of all hearts and flowers, my mind trembles with the trembling of life and reminds me to keep away from my mistakes, Lord!"

The priest's parables kept wandering through Tommy's mind. They were coming, one by one, singing in his ears, like a stream of wisdom and a prayer to God.

"I have been everywhere and hidden in small places. Now, I have gone out, opening the gates of human limitation and traveling everywhere, so that I can feel Your Consciousness and Omnipresence again, great God. I will follow the pastor's steps towards faith and devotion to you, steps that will lead me to You and to Your Divinity, Christ our God."

In the dark, Tommy thought that he, in turn, had followed some unknown steps, which had led him out of nowhere, towards her, towards the light.

"By lighting the light of a smile, despair and grief will disappear. I will keep my soul in the light of the smile, leaving behind me the dark times. When I wake up, I will lift from my heart the torch of my soul and my happiness."

"Today I will seek the vitality of God in the rays of the sun. In His light, my whole being will admire the gift of life to You, Lord. These cells of my body are made of light by You, Lord. They are like Your Spirit, immortal, perfect in Your work, the gift of life."

How many other uplifting thoughts the priest had not revealed while he was in hospital. He was missing him. Just like he was missing many other things from his past.

He looked at the window. It seemed that dawn was shyly coming. Another day, and for him, God's servant, Tommy, another sleepless night had passed. Like many others. The power of life entrapped in time.

****

Lilly had arrived home and had a shower. Now dressed in a bathrobe, she was in the bedroom, with a towel wrapped around her head and was polishing her nails. Suddenly Tommy stormed in.

Surprised, Lilly raised her head, widening her eyes with a questioning look. "Well? "

"Well, they put me off again, damn it! To next week. So, what stopped them from giving the solution today? Did they have hemorrhoids?"

"Tommy, I beg you, please don't talk like that anymore. It defines you in a bad way when you use these words. I have asked you so many times!"

Tommy, angry as a bull in an arena, was walking around the room.

"What else can I say about some mentally impaired people?"

His last appearance at the hearing should have taken place and his name change should have been finally approved. But the decision, for reasons unknown to him, had been postponed.

"Okay Tommy, but as I understood it, you were not the only one in this case, and the decision had to be presented to a group. It wasn't like that?"

"Well, that's why, my dear, they've made fun of many people and they don't care about them ... about anybody at all. There were also a few old men and women, ridiculously dressed, some barely dragging their feet on the floor of the Court."

"But, Tommy, it's quite possible that the postponement of the decision was made because one of the causes was missing something, or something was wrong. Isn't that possible?"

"Of course, they put us in a herd, like cattle when they are taken to the slaughterhouse! Very convenient procedure, isn't it? They sit down and decide the lives of several people at once!"

"But there can also be some administrative causes, maybe some paperwork, like missing evidence. It might be possible."

"Anything is possible with these careless people of gross indifference. To tell you plainly, I would strangle them all!"

"Tommy, please, I've just asked you! Stop talking like that."

Rising to her feet, she came closer to him. Looking at her, Tommy lowered his hands and shoulders, simulating unconditional surrender. How could he refuse her? Now they were so close to each other. He chained her with his hands, then lifted her up, spinning with her in his arms, and deeply looking in her eyes.

"What are you doing? You are scaring me. You see, I am dizzy! You know I get dizzy, don't you?"

"I won't let you down! I will keep you like that for a lifetime!"

"Please! Pleeeease! Let me down."

Finally, he placed her feet gently on the floor.

"I know, you are strong, sir," she exclaimed and many kisses followed.

"Lilly, that's nothing. I used to lift weights of 50 pounds with each hand, while I went three laps around the rink on my knees.

"Are you saying that I put you to exercise, to effort?"

"Yes, that's exactly what I mean. I'll show you my physical condition," and he kissed her neck, and then took her again in his arms and rolled over on the bed. Like a storm, Tommy took off her clothes, unable to wait anymore, and they made love with rushing fire until the evening, as the moments of joy and ecstasy were never enough for them.

Late in the evening, they realized they were hungry and decided to go out.

It was an evening, like many other, when they loved and lived together, each sharing their body, love and life. A dream in another dream ....

****

A few weeks later, Tommy eventually received the official documents with his new name.

"All right, my dear Lilly," he greeted her when she returned from work. "It's over; officially I am John Kerry, so my trace will be lost!"

"Well Tommy, since this is over, you could start looking for a job, or something to do."

"Sorry! John now, not Tommy anymore," he corrected her.

"For me, you are and remain Tommy, as I met you."

"Listen, I should have asked to change the dog's name too."

"At least for a moment, be serious, Tommy. Have you thought about what you would like to do? Do you remember what we both talked about? Well? Did you think about it?"

It became very clear for him that she was not going to give up. He had to find a job, or something to do. Unwillingly, he felt again that he was trapped and in imminent danger. He didn't quite understand what the danger was, but it was there.

"Well, what do you say?" Lilly insisted.

"Yeah, you see ... I thought ... I keep thinking ..."

"And?"

"You know, I still can't say what I'd like to do. Apart from hockey and the military stuff, I don't know how to do anything."

"But, you had so much time to think and decide, darling. It just can't be that you don't know."

"I've squeezed my brain with those official idiots, changing my name, damn it!"

"I just told you that before I did, I told you it wouldn't be easy at all. You knew what to expect, didn't you?"

"And that excuses the stupid officials?"

"Tommy, stop blaming others, stop blaming them. You have some important steps to take."

"What do you want me to do? What do you want from me?" he snapped.

Lilly froze. Shocked by the pitch of his voice, she remained stone-still. A minute later, she began to tremble, put her hands to her face and began to cry.

Tommy, in turn, was just as shocked. "Why are you crying? What have I done? Please don't cry, Lilly," he tried. "Please don't cry. I didn't want to, you know, I didn't want to ..."

He tried to hug her, but she was stiff, with both her hands bent and her face hidden in her palms. Trembling slightly, she cried.

Tommy felt lost and didn't know what to do. He wasn't used to this kind of reaction. He tried to calm her down gently, but the more he tried, the worse it was.

Lilly began to cry harder and detached herself from his arms, collapsed face down on the bed, hiding her head in her palms. She cried like that for a long time, while he, stroking her hair, tried to calm her down and reconcile.

He felt helpless. For him, it was a new experience. He was not used to such a reaction. Before he met Lilly, he had had only one-night stands with young women who were not interested in long-term relationships, and he didn't know what to do.

Days passed. Tommy searched about professions and jobs here and there. So did Lilly, eager to see him settled in a permanent job. In fact, she had been completely involved from the beginning. She wanted to refine him, and to that end, since they lived together, she worked hard to teach him—from vocabulary, to clothes and shoes, to manners—. Sometimes, when they ate at a restaurant and she saw him looking confused, she helped him, correcting him as delicately as possible.

"Tommy, dear, lower your elbows when you use the cutlery. You are ready to take off like an eagle."

"Please don't hold the glass so tightly; it's not a hockey stick."

And he received all these remarks submissively. But where was he supposed to have learned all these things? He had lived only among men. At the hockey club, everyone behaved in the same, crude way; everyone behaved as he pleased and there was no concern for gentlemanly behavior.

As for the army, it was even worse.

War conditions ... food rations ... using a bayonet for serving food seemed the most natural gesture.

"From the bayonet to the silver fork!" He joked once, trying laugh on the matter and to get some understanding.

In those moments, looking into her eyes, snippets of memory passed through his mind, sending him back under the burning sunlight of the desert ...

Poor Kelly!

They had been on a combing mission for six days over that part of the desert. Four sectors were cleaned for landmines, 701, 702,

703 and 704. They were ready to enter into the fifth sector, 705, an area of open land, where they expected to find some mines buried in the most frequented roads. During the short break before starting, they sat on the ground, sheltered in the shadow of the vehicles, each consuming their own food ration.

He was sitting down next to Kelly, a tough Irishman. Kelly had just taken the bayonet off his belt to adjust the laces of his boots. When he finished, he wiped it off on the hem of his pants, and then soaked it carelessly in his bowl of porridge.

And now, here, especially in her presence, he had to eat "nicely", with his elbows glued to the left and right sides of his body, using his left hand for the fork and the right for the knife! So, "from the bayonet to the fork!" He reflected again looking at her face.

Lilly was troubled by those empty glances, those eyes that looked through her, telling her that he was there and yet wasn't. He was somewhere far away and he was looking far away from her and her world.

With her feminine intuition, she suspected that those moments would awaken his memories, things that happened in other places and times. She would have liked to know more, but for some reason she was afraid to ask him. She seldom found out anything when she caught him remembering some past event. She knew he had suffered, but she had no real idea what he had gone through.

****

Dog's life had also changed, along with his master's, since he moved to the city. He followed his master on those streets, patiently waiting for him wherever he asked him.

When Lilly took his master to her place, he would follow him with the same loyalty and love. But Dog didn't like the city. He had bad memories, feelings about places and people. Here he had endured so many beatings, blows, pain and famine.

There had been days when some sellers were having fun, throwing rotten potatoes making him the target. For him, every well-aimed hit meant pain and humiliation. He became afraid of humans. The hardest part of his life with the seller was the lack of water. The days spent on the farm were a fading dream.

When he met Tommy, he was at the end of his rope.

Once he found this man, he started a new life. Gradually, he started to trust him and received from his hand the first pieces of real food—not garbage—that he had tasted in a long time. He endured all the treatment Tommy gave him and felt something he had never felt before: relaxed. Tommy had done so many things that pleased Dog, but the most pleasant were the evenings when, after dinner, they sat by the fire and spent long hours in silence looking at the flames.

Moreover, when Tommy sat on the crate in front of the fire, he looked at him and slapped his leg, and Dog understood the message and jumped beside him, pushing and hiding his head in Tommy's lap, eventually sighing with pleasure.

Dog didn't like the city and its hustle and bustle. While he was waiting for Tommy on streets, several times he had been bullied by crowds of bored children who threw stones and sticks to him to see him react. He ran out of their way, retreating further, but not far. He stopped, and after a while he made his way back to the same place to wait for Tommy, to the amusement of the kids.

"Look at the stupid; it's coming back" one of them shouted.

"Take it, don't let it, and chase it!"

And the scene repeated several times, until they got bored and left.

This blind devotion to his master was specific for his breed. His affection was boundless. The master had taken his head in his hand, looked into his eyes and asked him to wait for him. And he had taken this as a command and was ready to die there waiting for him. This was the law, running through the blood of so many generations.

They had so many ways to show their affection: walking on the streets, they looked at each other, Tommy patted him and scratched him between his ears. And Dog would grab his hand in his mouth, pressing lightly with his fangs, gently, only he could feel. Though this act, Dog poured feelings inherited from past generations that had served their masters with faith and self-sacrifice for those who offered them food, protection and shelter.

A whole chain of generations was behind him. Since the canine species was domesticated, it had looked at this kind of master for support and offered faith and love.

****

One afternoon, Tommy was lying on the bed, looking out the window at the blue sky. He had had a long walk with Dog, searching the streets and their "old shelter" under the bridge. Looking at everything carefully, Tommy tried to ignore his emotions. He couldn't. "God, what a life! Free and clean. No convenience, no compromises."

It seemed that Dog felt the same as he searched the area carefully, walking around, smelling everything, rediscovering the old abandoned things, wagging his tail and looking from time to time at Tommy with a questioning gaze.

A cold shiver went down Tommy's back. The old crates. Clothes, some rags and tools, all laid untouched as he had left them. Down at the river, where he used to wash his clothes, everything was the same.

On the way back, Tommy had walked deep in thought, sometimes stopping. Dog raised his head, as if asking, "Now, what?" Tommy, with his head down, urged him bluntly, "Let's move! Let's go!"

Now, alone in the room, he let himself dream. He was carried back to the time when he was talking to the priest and was listening to his reflections on life. He missed those meetings. A sort of bond was created between them, maybe because the priest never tried to impose anything on him. He just visited, told him stories, talked to himself a while, and then disappeared discreetly.

Those moments were like a balm to his torn soul. Now he missed them.

"The Lord is with me and defends me. I will drive away the mourning of my search, leaving me guided by the light of His lessons, which makes me avoid the secrets, mistakes and sins of the world," as he used to say. "Teach me Lord, with care and mercy, to have the courage of life and not of doubts and fear of it!" And, "I am defended by my consciousness. I set fire on my past and I am interested in what is happening today."

"Yes," Tommy thought. "I, in turn, set fire to my past so as not to be discovered. What did I do? And who I am running away from? Fear? Fear of what, of who? Where do I want to go? Where are you going, Tommy? Poor you! You are not even Tommy. You are John Kerry now. You are not you anymore."

****

"Hi, Tommy. Today I found an opportunity. I have to tell you about it."

"Hi, dear. What is it? Are you coming with something new?"

"Yes. It's something I was thinking about and I am sure you can do it to find a profession and get a job."

"All right, I told you: I decided to be a welder. In a few weeks, I am starting courses at the Technological Institute to be a highly qualified welder."

"Yes, I know. But something else has come up in the meantime and it's quite attractive.

Tommy shivered. "Now, what have you prepared for me?"

"Just listen to me. You know the town has a chain of libraries and bookstores. The movement of books from one location to another is done by our dedicated services. Well, the person in charge is moving out of town and the job is vacant. Tommy, I've already talked to the manager and he is more than happy to help you. In fact, the job is yours, and in two weeks you can start work. There is a young man who will be your assistant; you will work from the same vehicle. But, of course, you will make the decisions. What do you say? Isn't that great?"

As he listened to her, he felt hurt and his mind darkened. She had spoken ... She had decided for him. He felt like he was ready to burst, but he told himself to remain calm, but he lost control. "Yes. But did you ask me, woman?" he scowled.

Surprised, Lilly froze. She was shocked by his brutal tone and words.

"Lilly, I decided I was going to be a welder ... a man's job. And now, you are coming with this ... You spoke on my behalf and didn't ask me."

"It was something totally unexpected, a unique opportunity, and a decision had to be made immediately."

"And it couldn't wait until tomorrow? It couldn't wait until you asked me first?"

"I don't know. I didn't think you wouldn't like it. I hoped you would like it, and enjoy this better opportunity. I thought you'd be pleasantly surprised."

"Pleasantly surprised!" he repeated. "Let me be happy!" He was walking fast in circles and gesturing with his hands. "Yes, sure, I should be glad! Who I am to give my opinion?"

"Come on, Tommy. It's just a better job than welding; other people, books, culture, connected, clean. And you will be employed by City Hall, with all the benefits and advantages from the position."

"My dear Lilly, my dear, and dear, but that's not the point."

"Then what, if a better job is not the point, what is?"

"I want to make decisions about myself. What I think doesn't matter at all? Was it the end of the world to wait for another day—just a day—and ask me first?"

"I don't know. You see, I never thought you wouldn't be happy."

"I am saying it again: this is not the case. I am the one who decides where I will work, when I will work, and who I will work with. Don't you think that's how it should be?"

Throughout the argument, he had a high, aggressive pitch, which made Lilly feel uncomfortable, even scared. This was not the way she was used to talking with people. In college, and then at work in the library, everyone talked calmly and nicely, extremely polite, lower voice, not to disturb others, and all these defined her way of communication. And now she was shocked.

She couldn't help it and start crying, just like she had a few days ago, when they had some kind of argument on the same theme. The same nervous crying as last time, and he, as last time, gave in. He did not want to see her crying anymore and did not want her to be angry with him.

But deep down, Tommy felt he was wronged, and, like other times, he postponed the situation until later, not knowing when, but, sometime after, he had time to think of all of these things.

****

Tommy parked the car under the wide garage cover, jumped out, and picked up his raincoat and the bag with food. Then he locked the car and left. There was the Municipality garage. His job was to collect orders from each library and take them, according to customer requests, from one site to another. There were also orders from libraries to some bookstores, and he was supposed to go there and to pick them up, too.

During work, he seldom met Lilly. She was too busy at the Central Library, where the schedule was very tight. At the beginning, everything had been new to him. In time, he became used to it and learned some shortcuts along the routes, in order to save some time when he was in a hurry.

He had easily passed the probation period, as it was a piece of cake compared with what he did when he was being trained in the army. Not surprisingly, it had been difficult for him to get used to his new name, John Kerry. It had happened to him several times when his helper, Danny, called him and he didn't answer. Over time, he learned to be more careful and tried to adjust his ears to "John" or "Kerry" so not to miss any call.

They had different work hours, so they usually met at home, rather late in the evening. Lilly usually arrived first. He was only late once, and that was when a colleague asked him to take over his shift.

Tommy opened the door, entering like a storm, and hugged Lilly and kissed her on the forehead.

"Hello, my Cleopatra! The workman is hellishly hungry, and wants to know what you have prepared for him."

"Oh Tommy, can't you speak nicer and not swear?" she replied, rather annoyed.

"Just because I mentioned Hell?"

"Yes. You shouldn't talk like that," but she stood up on her tiptoes and kissed him on a cheek.

"Well, my dear, the Devil is real who puts his tail everywhere and most of the time makes our life a nightmare."

He went to the bedroom, changed his clothes, and come back dressed in a housecoat.

The food was ready, and Lilly had laid the table, ready to fill the plates. Taking advantage of the fact that her hands were busy, Tommy slipped behind her and leaned on her to kiss her.

"I don't know what's got into you; don't you see I have the pot in my hands; you might get burned!"

"Well, that's because I want to take advantage as you are now a prisoner ... my prisoner!" teased Tommy.

Then he sat down and sniffed the food.

"What do we have today?

"Chicken soup, darling."

"I like that. Didn't you wake me up with a soup like this when I was so sick?"

"Yes, darling, and I would do it again and again, especially if you would be more careful when you speak and more attentive with your manners."

"But I am a mannered man, my dear. If you don't believe me, ask Dog. He'll tell you a lot of good things about me."

"Please stop joking! I am serious."

Meanwhile, she sat down at the table and sipped the soup quietly. Then, getting up to pick up the plates, said:

"Tommy, we should go out more, now that you have a job. It would be nice to go out, to meet people—friends. Look, I have colleagues, classmates and a few other friends I would love to see. It would be fun to meet with them and enjoy their company. What do you think?"

As a few times before, a bell rang out "danger" in Tommy's mind. His senses told him that, again, it was not something for him. For most of his life, he had been a loner. He didn't like groups, gatherings of people, talking without a purpose. Excluding the hockey team and his comrades when he was in the army, he had been everywhere alone. And now he was expected to meet her friends. Some friends, who knows what kind of people, where from. But, as before, he gave in, wanting to be with her and please her.

"As you say, Lilly, if that makes you happier!"

"It's not just about me, my dear. You also have to go out into the world, to meet others, to talk to other people. You are working for the library and bookstores now; you are an intellectual, aren't you?"

"Of course, my dear. I often go out with Dog and he recognizes my intellectual value!"

"Please don't make fun of that!"

"Well, well, as you say."

Turning the spoon around the bowl, Tommy thought about the "intellectuals" …and the journalists who followed them, scooping for sensational stories. Beasts, not humans. No feelings. No remorse.

He thought nostalgically of their long walks, he and Dog, along the river, and their life before … clean and calm … no parties or 'intellectual' conversations.

In winter, it was harder, but not impossible, to live. Everything was beautiful with Dog. Only the two of them, confidently relying on each other.

"Well, are you 'far away' again? Come back again and tell me if it's not a great idea for us to go out and enjoy people and the world."

"As you say, Lilly. If you believe it's a good idea, then whatever you say."

"Dear Tommy, I was interested in your opinion about this. It's probably a lot different from mine, right?"

"I've always done as you liked, Lilly. You know that. Does it matter what I thought, or what I think?"

"You don't really approve of my ideas and opinions, even if you follow them. Do you?"

"Does it matter to you? Isn't it enough that I always do as you wish?"

"Yes, it's true. And the way I tell you is always good. Isn't that right, love?" she asked, accompanying her words with a meaningful smile.

Silent, with his eyes on his food, Tommy reflected. Yes, she loved him, and she had saved his life.

He had been reluctant to follow her advice and directions she had given. He was used to following orders without question, both as a hockey player and a soldier, so he had listened to her, more and more, resignedly, despite his feelings. Deep in his soul, he was not convinced that he had done well.

"Yes, maybe you are right. That's how it is," he answered with a soft voice.

Later in the evening, in bed, after they made love, she on one side, embracing him with her arms, he looking at the ceiling in the darkness above. Two heads on the pillow, two blended bodies, lost among the sheets, melt into each other by the sublime and ecstasy of self-giving. Chained together, they rested in their nest of pleasures.

Tommy's gaze scanned the darkness above, to the ceiling, hoping to find an answer. Something. He waited, believed and hoped, but nothing showed him the way.

****

Soon, Lilly started to introduce Tommy to a few of her friends, then, as time passed, others followed. Some of them were former high school friends, others she met in university, and two others were good friends and colleagues from the library.

The first opportunity to present Tommy to her friends came when Maggie, a former classmate, invited them to her birthday party. The party was organized outside, in a garden. The warm, late spring weather was inviting to all guests, scattered everywhere in the backyard on camping chairs, as well as a few tables full of tasty appetizers and snacks. In a corner, Maggie's husband, Craig, was bent over the barbeque, acting as the chef. With eyes filled with smoke, he was watching the sausages and steaks sizzling, turning them, and helping himself to some beer. To the delight of all the guests, jokes, food and beer flowed unhindered.

Such a party was nothing new to Tommy. When he was playing hockey, they sometimes had these kinds of parties, and then during the army when they were sent to the base for recovery. Those were rather different, but no matter what or where, he was not a fan. Now he agreed to come because she had asked him to.

He was a bit lost in the middle of all those people who knew one other. At one point, he was found and grabbed by Lilly, who had lost him in the crowd.

"Honey, come meet Hilda and her boyfriend, Jerry. They are both very nice and we are very good friends. I want you to meet them. You know, Hilda works for us at the library."

"Hi, Hilda, Jerry! Let me introduce my friend, John, about whom I've told you before."

"Wow, he's the Robinson Crusoe? But he is gorgeous, my dear! You are lucky!" joked Hilda, eyeing him up and down. Jerry, on the other hand, was restrained.

They both wore shorts, as did most of the guests. Tommy felt insulted and clenched his teeth, barely controlling an outburst.

Sensing the danger, Lilly pulled him aside, whispering, "They're not bad people; you'll see and in time you will get used to them."

"Oh, yes, I'll get used to it. Get used to being looked at like a gorilla taken from the jungle and put in a cage at a zoo!" he replied. Turning, he headed for the exit gate.

Lilly ran after him, grabbed his shoulder, and begged him, "Please, please, don't leave! Don't do this to me! Please! If you love me, don't do it!"

As if touched by an electric current, Tommy turned around, and, like so many other times, gave in. And so, he met not only Hilda and Jerry, but also Bill and his lovely wife, Clara, and Frank, Amy, Tim and Jessie, and many others.

On their way home, Lilly started. "Tommy, please understand, it's not my fault. Or theirs."

"So, what did that animal want from me?"

"Tommy, please! You didn't have to give him so much importance. Frank was a little tipsy."

"Tipsy? He was drunk like a skunk. He could barely stand. And he was looking at me as if he were the elephant and I was the mouse! What can I say? Very kind and polite."

Now they were close to home and their steps slowed.

"You have to know, that actually I liked the fact that you didn't fight back; and everyone else appreciated that."

"Don't say that! Didn't you see how they all laughed? They were full of beer."

"Believe me, I know them. Everyone admired you for your control and diplomacy."

"Control and diplomacy? Let a jerk mock me and I should stay still and say nothing? This has never happened before?"

"But, Tommy dear, that's exactly what your strength is. The man was intoxicated."

"Drunk, you mean."

"Well, if that's what you want to call him!"

"And the others? Why did they behave like sheep?"

"Please, look; people were in a good mood and everyone wanted to have a good time."

They were now already in front of the building and Dog was there, happily wagging his tail. That put a smile on Tommy's face.

****

In the following weeks, Lilly continued to arrange meetings with friends, some of whom had been at Maggie's party.

"Please, my dear!" she was begging him, "let's socialize more; let's go out with friends and acquaintances. Let's enjoy life a little more."

Tommy was stoical, enduring all the gatherings, and saw in them her attempts to introduce him to her friends, but also transform him, and teach him good manners.

On a Saturday afternoon, they went to the beautiful Royal Park to meet Christine and her friend, George. They walked together on the beautiful paths of the park, through the vigorous old trees. At the end of the trail, they discovered a beautiful lake with a spectacular island in the middle. Surrounding the lake's cobbled pathways, guarded by chestnut trees, were a smattering of benches, inviting the passers-by to relax. There were also a few arched bridges, connecting the lakeshore with the island. Pedal boats and recreational boats were gliding on the water. Lilly's friend suddenly asked, "What do you say about a boat ride?"

"Why not? What do you think, boys? Are you ready to row a boat and offer two young ladies a pleasant afternoon?"

"Okay, I really like the idea," said George. What do you say, John?"

Tommy just nodded.

They went to hire a boat, and a young man showed them to the wharf and invited them to choose a boat.

"Not that one. The green one," Tommy decided, and the man complied.

"What's wrong with that boat? Lilly asked, but Tommy didn't answer and she didn't persist. She assumed that Tommy must have received so much training that he knew more than any one of them, even though he had been in the army and not the navy.

"What do you say, George. Can you row?" she asked.

"I'm not an expert, but I can try."

"Then let John. He sure knows."

Tommy helped the women get into the rowboat. When they were all seated, he grabbed the oars and deftly steered the boat from the dock.

Christine could not stop admiring the view and said enthusiastically, "But it's wonderful! Darling, look at the view! What a great idea I had."

Tommy was secretly enjoying the effort and rowing faster and faster. The moves were precise and efficient; he was working like a perfect engine, doing everything automatically. The sunlight reflected off the water, hurting his eyes and thoughts.

Poor Benny! Remembered. The waves took him far back in time.

It had been an observation mission along the coast. Apparently, it was nothing special or eventful. They had to land, march inland and search some settlements for hypothetical enemy forces, which hadn't been seen in the area yet. So, once they reached the shore, they quickly disembarked and off-loaded their equipment. Finding shelter around some rocks, they hid the amphibious boat and threw a camouflage net over it. Everyone picked up his own gear, grouped up, and set off, led by Hank. Hank found a path and they sneaked behind him, through the vegetation available near the shore. They walked fast in silence, taking short breaks. Hank gave them hand signs to stop, sit and wait. Then, after checking the compass, they started again.

They reached at an open field and Hank raised his arm, clenched his fist, and lowered it a few times, signaling crouch down and wait. They stopped. Hank left and went out into the field. Soon they could no longer see him, and started waiting. The minutes passed and it was so damn hard to wait. Much of the time spent in the army was waiting. They wait to be transported, wait to receive orders, wait to get into the shower, and so many other times.

Hank came back and they started walking again, moving carefully, stopping at Hanks command and restarting. Although it was early morning, it was getting hot. After one hour of continuous walking, they encountered the first settlement; actually, the hamlet was made of only a few huts, scattered among some bushes in an almost bare field.

Hank ordered them to split up and approach from opposite directions, with the mission to carefully search everything in their path. Hiding where they could, they searched the little village thoroughly with their binoculars, but didn't see anything suspicious.

They started walking again. The next area to be combed was a fifteen-kilometer strip of land about two kilometers from the shore. The teams were advancing slowly and it was almost afternoon. Wet with sweat, they were close to the last group of huts and they didn't have any more water.

Hank signaled for Tommy approach him. "You stay put and guard the equipment. It's late now and we should move faster. We are taking only a few loads and light weapons. The rest stays in place here under your care. Understood?"

"Clear, Lieutenant."

Then Hank grouped the others and started for the last target. They had to split into several groups because the shelters were scattered around. Tommy was watching carefully everything that was going on, with his weapon ready. He peered into the distance to the first houses and beyond, trying to see something, but the bushes and trees barred his sight. Sweat was running down his face, his back was wet too, but he was stubbornly watching what was happening there.

Suddenly, a dry sound split the silence. His heart skipped a beat. He checked his weapon and the two grenades in his vest.

That was not a war weapon, he thought. It can't be. Too weak, short and breathless, he thought.

The next minutes dragged into a painful wait. After the shot, he was only ears, trying to catch any unusual sound around him. He knew it couldn't have been one of them. What had he heard?

After some time, an eternity for Tommy, he saw, above the bushes, the comrades' helmets, moving towards him, in two parallel rows, close to each other. Why two rows and why so close to each other. When they got close enough, it became clear. They were carrying an improvised stretcher. He felt a painful knot in his throat; the one lying in the stretcher was Benny, who was gasping heavily, gnashing his teeth.

He looked questioningly at Hank.

"Stupid!" Hank said. "A kid came out of his house to pee in the weeds. He saw Benny's back and ran into the house, grabbed a gun and unloaded into Benny's back. The bullet broke his right shoulder blade and through his lung. The kid was alone in that house. We retreated and then fell behind him. Nick killed him with his knife and we buried him immediately in the sand so he wouldn't be found soon. We need time to retire. Let's get out of here fast."

Meanwhile, Benny had been seated and was supported by two soldiers. He was spitting blood and his lips were covered by a red foam.

They set off on their way back. They aimed straight for the shore and then along it to the place where they had left the boat.

"Damn, be careful!" Hank exclaimed. "Now, only speed matters. Benny needs medical help as soon as possible."

Once on the boat, they had to cross the waters to the corvette that was waiting for them at the horizon before nightfall. They were exposed a lot, and there was nowhere to hide. Towards the evening, they reached the target. They marched to the waterline, so that their tracks would disappear with the tide.

Rig went out to greet them. They quickly loaded everything into the boat and moved away from the shore, paddling with two pairs of oars, changing shifts at Hank's command. All who were to row, had done it until they were exhaustion. They would have time to rest afterwards.

Tommy did the same when it was his turn. He rowed in a brisk rhythm and looked at Benny, who didn't look good. Closed eyes, mouth slightly open and his head moving from one side to the other, a bad prognosis.

Tommy didn't feel his arms and palms anymore, but he was repeating to himself, like a mantra, the words his hockey coach told him during their grueling training sessions while he was playing in the NHL: "No pain. There is no pain. You don't feel any pain; it doesn't exist for you."

The sun descended on the horizon and sent rays at the level of water that reflected painfully into his eyes. With narrowed eyes, he struggled to keep up. Someone whispered that the corvette was in sight and Tommy sped up, as if he was the one running out of time......

"But slower, darling! We are not in a competition and more than that, you started spraying us!"

Lilly's voice brought him back to the real world, out of his painful memories.

"You did it like a pro in a competition for life," George exclaimed admiringly. "I know you are great; tell me please, have you done some canoeing?"

"He did so many other things" Lilly added with a hint.

Tommy slowed down his pace and looked away from the glistering water, and then invited George to row and showed him how to do it. Guided by Tommy's advice, he caught on easily and did a great job.

Pulling ashore at the girls' proposal, they huddled on the terrace of a nice restaurant, "The Pearl."

As they arrived home late that evening, smiling and with twinkling eyes, Lilly exclaimed, "It was a successful evening, wasn't it, darling?"

Tommy refrained from saying anything, but, damn it, he didn't agree. When she wrapped her arms around his neck, he forgot everything.

****

Time passed the same way: work, and weekends with small parties or gatherings with Lilly's friends.

Danny turned out to be a very good and helpful man, especially when he taught Tommy a lot of details about their duties and how to avoid any customer complaints. Both were hard working and organized. The weight of the books was not a problem for them, neither to arrange them in order of delivery to save some time to rest after each delivery. All in all, they formed a very good team and complement each other at work.

At the end of his shift one afternoon, after Tommy got out of the delivery car and locked it, he changed his way home, turning onto a narrow and quiet street, following a longer path. He needed to be alone, to think, to put his thoughts in some sort of order. The echo of his footsteps reverberated to the walls of the buildings bordering the street.

With head bowed, his gaze on the pavement, he walked thoughtfully, meditating on many aspects of his new life. Work. The weekend, with many parties, or going in groups to the cinema, often after to restaurants. Many get-togethers with Lilly's friends. Although he met a lot of people, he felt alone, different from them, as if he came from another world. He did not share their opinions or beliefs. He agreed with them only to avoid a longer discussion and arguments. He was not like them and could never be.

During this time, walking thoughtfully and looking for answers as from far afar, the words of the priest resounded in his ears: "Teach your mind to rejoice with good and noble thoughts. Carry joy in your soul and the candle of love in your heart! If you keep your eyes closed, you cannot see the Son of Joy embracing your senses of happiness. Open the door of your soul and remove all the non-essentials. Take refuge in the ecstasy and magnitude of Him, and there in the wisdom and His eternity!"

"Snatch yourself from the dangerous nets of materialistic cramming. Approach God's spirits, merge with it, following Him in all His greatness. Feel like your whole life could shine only as a creation of the Lord."

Those words meant something to him. And he, in his daily routine, with weekends carefully planned by Lilly, felt the lack of something fundamentally true, deep, and significant. He was struggling to find that something. He didn't know what it could be.

Lost in thought, he didn't know when he arrived in front of the building. At the entrance, Dog was waiting and at that moment he realized what he was deeply missing: the quiet and peaceful life he had before he met Lilly.

Leaning down, he clasped Dog's head in his hands, scratching the roots of his ears and then patting his back. From Tommy's eyes, tears came off falling onto his good friend's fur.

"Oh, God!" he murmured.

****

"Honey, I told you to take the brown shirt today. I left it on the chair especially for you, so you would wear it today." That's how she greeted him when he got home that day.

"Lilly, the brown one is too thick and is too tight around the neck. It's strangling me."

"Well, I understand, but did you wear a wrinkled one? How could you go like that?"

"My dear, spending time in the cold for a long time in the past made me avoid thick clothes."

"Well, that's not the point; that's not an excuse to wear a crumpled shirt."

"Dear Lilly, do we really have nothing better to talk about now but shirts?"

"Honey, we could talk about many more things. For example, why haven't you cleaned your shoes for two days?"

"For God's sake, what's the matter with you now? I wiped them with a cloth. What's wrong? I work. There's a lot of dust and they get dirty in no time. What should I do?"

"Be more careful, love! Be more careful with your attire, and not only—"

"Shall I wear a bowtie?" he smirked.

"Do you think I'm kidding, Tommy? Do you think I am struggling in vain to make you change some things in your clothing and behavior? I want you to look good—more elegant, in manners, and in overall conduct."

"And who I am to be like? Like Bill, Frank, or George? Is that how you want me to be?"

"Well ... yes. Why not?"

"The, my dear, don't be angry, I am not going down so low that I get like them."

"And why not, please?"

"Because your friends are hypocrites, mean people, not genuine, and sort of morally fallen."

"And you think you are much better!" In the same second, however, she wanted to withdraw her words.

Tommy gave her the same metallic look, his eyes piercing her like two drills, a look that frightened her, once again.

Without a word, Tommy left the room.

A few days later, while they were having dinner, he asked her, "What would it be like if I take Dog with me, to have him in the car?"

"Are you crazy? You want to be called 'the man with the dog'? And they won't spare me either. It is now known that we are together. All my friends know that."

"So what? Do we have to take their opinion into account? Who are they, or who do you think they are?"

"But we can't live without them. We can't live without friends."

"Lilly, you mean you can't live without those creatures. Don't speak on my behalf, please!"

"I understand Tommy that you don't like some of them, but not all of them are useless."

"I don't say they are fools. In this world, they are important people. But for me, they are ... nobodies."

"So, for you, all of them are the same: useless?"

"Yes. Just like that!"

"And who would you like to live with?" she challenged.

"With you and Dog."

"But I can't live this way, not going out with others, not seeing anyone ... It's not possible."

"Why?"

"But, how are you going to live like this? We need each other to live."

"I don't!" he answered sharply.

The argument continued for a while, until, tired and lacking the desire to continue the argument, they decided to find their own way to stop. She sank into an armchair with a book, and he went downstairs to take Dog for an evening walk.

"Hey, Dog, my good friend, how much can a man endure in this world?" he asked the dog.

****

Lilly became more and more determined to impose a certain behavior and a certain kind of life. He was her achievement and she could not admit defeat; she had to change him to make him better.

As for Tommy, he was torn between his conscience and his love.

She was dear to him—her whole being ... those big eyes ... her perfume—everything was charming him and make him dizzy every time. And every time, love won. She was stronger and he gave up.

However, lately, he noticed something changed in her behavior. She had become more attentive when she talked to him, more thoughtful. Not wanting to bother her, he pretended not to notice.

One rainy Sunday, they were having their coffee in the kitchen; he was sitting on a chair and she was standing next to the coffee machine. Tommy was looking out the window, watching the raindrops falling on the window. His thoughts were with Dog. He was sure he found shelter somewhere, or Bart had left him inside, not to be out in the rain. This Bart was a good soul.

With her back to him, Lilly was moving her hand on the edge of the coffee machine. Finally, she broke the silence.

"You know, Tommy, I'd like to tell you something ... and I don't know how to do it."

"Don't worry. Shoot."

"You know, I feel I, we can't stay like this anymore ... And please, don't get mad about what I'm going to tell you."

Tommy's eyes widened questioningly.

"Look, it's ... I've been asked by a lot of people about you, about our relationship, about us ... Tommy, we've been living together for almost a year and we are not married. Honestly, I would like to know what your intentions are, regarding the two of us ..."

Tommy felt his chest trembling. But he didn't want to start a new quarrel. Anyway, not now. Feeling his heart pounding like a sledgehammer, he stared into his cup of coffee and managed to say, "But you ... what do you want?"

"Well, I... I want to get married. I've wanted it for a long time. If you were more attentive to some details, attire and manners, it wouldn't be any problem and we could have a very sweet life together."

With eyes fixed on his cup of coffee, his shoulders down, Tommy replied, "Then, as you wish. As you say, my dear!"

Lilly's eyes brightened. Turning around, she grabbed him by the shoulders and kissed him on the cheek.

Stunned, Tommy was unable to say a word; there was nothing for him to say.

In a state of exaltation and euphoria, in the following days, Lilly unleashed herself and introduced Tommy to everyone: relatives he hadn't known, friends he hadn't met yet. To these and many other acquaintances, Lilly shared the great news, unrestrained. Taken by the hand and presented to everyone made Tommy feel ashamed. However, seeing her so happy and full of enthusiasm, he followed her silently in all these visits and parties.

"Honey," she would say, "do you realize, it's like we've just met. We will be husband and wife and all our friends and acquaintances will envy us!"

Tommy felt a knot in his throat. He was a monkey, exposed at the zoo. No difference, just that one is kept in a cage. Both are paraded around and presented as obedient things.

Every day, it was something new.

"Listen Tommy, isn't it fantastic? The head librarian knows a tailor who makes suits for brides and grooms, specializing in London fashion! You are scheduled for next week. My appointment is the day before. Don't worry; I'll give you all the details and the address, too. It's not too far."

"Lilly, but what special costume should it be? One from the rack isn't good enough? And after the wedding, where could I possibly wear it?"

"This is out of the question, Tommy! You can't show up in a regular suit!"

Another day, she told him, "Look, I need to tell you: the wedding will be at the Cathedral and there will be over a hundred people; a quick count gives us one hundred fifty. But we'll know for sure when we have made the guest list and sent the invitations. So, you have to understand that you need to wear tuxedo and you will look like a movie star! Isn't that great? I am so happy!"

Tommy felt his stomach shrink, and his head was being hit by a pneumatic hammer. Her words and ideas hurt him, and he felt defenseless. Over 150 people! ... a Cathedral ... invitations. "Who the Hell needs invitations? It's like selling tickets to the Zoo! God, what am I doing?" Tommy thought.

But to her, he replied, "As you say, my dear, as you say!"

"So, as I say, my soon-to-be-husband, and it will always be fine as I say, won't it?"

Then, just a few days later, she announced, "Listen darling, Calypso is rented for the next two months! This is so regrettable, as I had so many hopes regarding the venue."

"Hold on, Lilly. What are you talking about? What Calypso is rented?"

"Ah, honey, did I forget to tell you? Of course, the place where we are going to hold the reception after the religious wedding at the church. Anyway, because we cannot wait for two months, Uncle Bill and I have thought of something else."

"Just a moment. What party? Why do we need a party?"

"That's the best part, darling! Everyone does that. That's the tradition! And there will be a lot of friends who will bring us presents!"

"I don't need their presents! I don't need anything from anyone!"

"But you can't be serious, darling. These are my relatives and my friends! And yours! We can't ignore them."

"They certain aren't mine."

"If you love me, then you would accept everyone, for my sake. Please!"

Tommy paused. It was no use arguing against her. "Okay, as you say. I see that everything is arranged in advance. So, what does it matter what I think?"

"But we have to follow the traditions and expectations of our friends."

"Traditions, expectations! In my opinion, if after the wedding only the two of us went to a restaurant to celebrate the moment and were happy, it would be enough."

"We cannot change that; we have to have a reception. That's when everyone celebrates our marriage. Otherwise, we insult our friends and embarrass ourselves."

"I don't care! Why do I care?"

"No, darling, you should care. I was starting to tell you about my Uncle Bill. You know him, don't you?"

"No, I don't know him."

"I just told you about him. My mother's brother. We pondered over the issue together and we had a great idea!"

"I would have been shocked if it hadn't come to you!"

"It's not the time to have fun about this! Do you know that beautiful restaurant, the Emerald, on the shore of the lake with a large terrace? It's on outskirts of town, but we can provide the transportation either by shuttle bus, or by taxi. It would be wonderful! Just imagine, the terrace, the view of the lake and the surrounding trees! A paradise!"

"And this will be in the afternoon, won't it?"

"Yes. And we could have photos taken there, with the lake in the background. That was Uncle Bill's idea. So convenient!"

"Sure, it's perfect. And all the guest should be soaked in alcohol, drunk as devils"

"Don't talk like that. I have asked you so many times to speak nicely and avoid insults. And I don't understand why you think they would be drunk."

"Because my dear, they need to be anesthetized against mosquitoes. It will be full of mosquitoes there."

"Mosquitoes? What mosquitoes? Why?"

"I am telling you. I've lived in such places. In the forest, near the water. That's where they like to frolic."

"I was there once and there were no mosquitoes."

"And what time were you there?"

"I remember exactly; at the end of spring, towards summer."

"Well, a perfect time, when the nights are still cold and they haven't exploded yet. But a little later, around this time, it's their season. They gather in swarms and they take shelter among the branches of the trees, glued to the leaves. Your guests must be in a state of drunkenness, so that they won't feel too bad."

"Please don't talk like that; they are your guests too. They are coming to celebrate with us."

"Well, you know better!"

And so, despite all the arguments, in the following days he went to the tailor with Lilly and chose the tuxedo. English. Of course, she chose it for him.

They went to the photographer, as well, to print the invitations. Everywhere, she had been the one to speak, to choose, to make decisions, down to the last detail.

All the while, inside, Tommy felt like he was boiling. He felt like he couldn't stand it anymore, and eventually he closed himself off.

"What will happen in the future? What kind of life is this? How far? Until when?" he asked himself aloud.

But he didn't have the answers. It wasn't there yet.

****

He woke up suddenly in the middle of the night. Next to him, Lilly was sleeping. He groped in the dark for the clock. It was too early, so he returned his head to the pillow. But sleep was gone and a state of panic, danger and insecurity overwhelmed him. Anxiety and fear had taken over him. He felt betrayed, as if his conscience was wounded. He was feeling trapped in a maze and lost.

He sat on the edge of the bed, covering his face with his palms. "God, what am I doing? Where am I going, Lord, Where?"

But now, from the darkness and silence of the night, sounded the words of the priest:

"You alone are responsible for yourself. No one else can be held accountable for your actions when the final judgement comes. Fix your mind on the rays of the moon. Don't go looking for happiness in expensive clothes, grand villas, appetizing dinners and soft, luxurious sofas. All these will drag you into a race, and you will be kept there, thinking it is your destiny.

Free your mind from connection with the demands of your body. Look for eternal peace. Do not use any excuse to accept limitations. Remove your consciousness from the connections with your body and its pleasures. Push your consciousness to go beyond the body, guiding it to the mind, heart and soul.

Feel fully the Lord's creation!"

With his hand on his forehead, he murmured: "God! Father, how right you were! "

He got up slowly and moved to the window and looked out. He stood there looking out his window, staring at the ground … at the entrance to the building.

Their eyes met. His friend stood there, dignified. He has always been devoted, never asking, never demanding, without conditions or prejudices. With his ears raised, his eyes glistering in the darkness of the night, Dog was waiting.

Tommy kept looking at his friend.

"Of you, faithful one, some might say about you that you are just a dog. But, for me, you are a higher being, above many people!"

In the dark, a flash of understanding ran through his being. He looked up and murmured: "How come I didn't think? Why didn't I know?"

In a few minutes, he was down on the street. One last look toward the bedroom, as if to say goodbye, and here he was on the street, near Dog. On his knees now, he took Dog's head and pulled it closer to him:

"You, my good faithful friend. You, who have been waiting for me every time, who are devoted to me without asking nothing, expecting nothing, let's go together, away from the temptations of this world."

They set off. In the sky, a big, bright, full moon, lit their way. Their shadows projected on it. Two shadows on the moon, two destinies destined to live together.

Shadows on the moon….

The End